never told you to love me

affinity series
book one

Brittney C. Nobles

Nicoyce Publishing LLC

Never Told You to Love Me

Brittney C. Nobles

Book design by Brittney C. Nobles
Edited by: Cassidy A. Lee Press
Cover image: Depositphotos.com, musefoto
Interior images: Adobe Stock

ISBN: 979-8-9862603-5-8 (paperback)
ISBN 979-8-9862603-3-4 (ebook)

a word from the author

This has been a long journey for me with branding and rebranding, publishing then pulling several books from publication. I'm still here and still creating. This year has been all about learning for me.

Thank you for sticking it out with me and for reading my stories. I'm excited for this novel and novels to come. I appreciate all readers, new and day ones.

To my family and friends, thank you for listening to me rant about these characters for almost a year.

To my husband for allowing me time to create and my children for asking me over and over was I done writing.

Special thank you to my sister in law for being a honest beta.

Enjoy the read!

Thank you,
Brittney C. Nobles

chapter
one

Malani

"I swear if you don't tell him how you feel, I will tell him myself." My best friend, Harmony, called out from the guest bedroom of my apartment.

My fingers weren't off the end button on my cell phone before she all but hollered the comment. I checked my phone to make sure I'd indeed ended the call with my male best friend, Nolan, who called with a peace offering of food.

"It's not the right time," I stood against the door frame, watching her bury her face into her own phone. She was still dressed in last night's sequin cocktail dress. We'd partied hard and up until that first phone call from Nolan at six a.m. I was still in last night's clothes.

"I see what you're doing, stalling. That nigga just rescued you from…"

"All right, I get it." I cut her off before she took another step in Nolan's and my complicated friendship. Although, it's complicated for me—not him. "But it wasn't no rescue shit. It was more of a," my eyes lifted to the paint blotches in the ceiling. I tried to think of the perfect word to describe what he did last night. I snapped my fingers, "it was a scolding."

Harmony fell out with laughter holding her stomach like it was the funniest thing she'd heard in a century.

"It's not that damn funny, Harmony."

"Admit it, you liked that shit."

I smiled inwardly because I did in fact like it, downright loved it. After all, it was him. If any other man snatched me out of a party, we would've had unsavory words. But him—that shit turned me on.

I sat on the bed that Harmony has occupied since she'd broken up with her cheating ass boyfriend a month ago, with my head lowered to the neon socks on my feet I said the words I've been saying to her since I told her about my true feelings towards Nolan, "he doesn't like me like that."

"How would you know if you've never asked him?"

"I just do. Now get your ass up so we can eat breakfast. I'm starving."

Harmony groaned, "can we order in? I'm tired."

"No, we can't," I said as she tossed the covers over her head, "they're waiting for us."

"Who?" She asked underneath the cover.

"Nolan and Ezeke."

"Ezekiel? Eww. Hell no, I'm staying right here, but you can bring me something back."

Taking a fist full of the thick comforter, I snatched it from over her, "you're coming whether you want to or not. Now, get dressed. I'll be downstairs waiting."

Harmony huffed and puffed as she tossed her legs over the bed. "Yeah, let me get my shit on because I have something to tell Nolan anyway."

All it took was one look for her to recede. Harmony has been my friend since freshman year in college. We were dormmates. I was home sick, and she was a ball of fire that ignited me to drop my woes and enjoy the experience. But I'll be damned if she causes issues in my friendship with Nolan, especially with a secret I've only disclosed to her and Ezeke.

"WHERE ARE you going looking like that?" Nolan called out from the driver's seat of his truck. His eyes slowly wandered over my body.

My breath hitched when his eyes landed on mine. Even the scowl on his face made my juices flow. I couldn't help but love him, so I no longer tried to fight it.

Looking over my attire, what I chose was perfect for the cold wintery weather. It had to be the skinny jeans with black thigh-high boots he didn't like because the bomber coat was purchased by him two Christmases ago.

"What's wrong with what I have on?" I spun around, giving him the full view of my fit. I looked damned good. Makeup was on point, and hair, bone straight courtesy of the expensive curling iron I treated myself to last week. He was hating hard as hell. "Ezeke, do you have a problem with my outfit?" I looked for solace in my other male best friend.

Ezeke exited the passenger seat, arms stretched wide inviting me in. Embracing him, he whispered, "Nolan is still trippin' about last night. You look good, baby girl." When we separated, he spoke loudly, "those tight ass pants gotta go." He winked at me before sliding into the back seat.

"I'm fine sitting in the back with Harmony." I zipped the bomber jacket as the wind blew around me.

"Take the front seat. I got Harms." Ezeke said, wearing a mischievous grin.

Turning back to my scowling best friend, "do you really want me to change?" I would in a heartbeat if he commanded it.

Nolan cranked his truck, kissing his teeth in the process. "Lani, I'm hungry as fuck, and you said ya'll were ready. What's up with it?"

"I'll check on Harmony," I said, tight-lipped. I wanted to curse him out, but my mama always told me to never bite the hand that feeds me. "Harmony?" I called out when I reentered my apartment. She was still in bed, and still in the dress. I was on the verge of losing my patience with my best friends, minus Ezeke. I immediately pulled her into my arms as soon as my eyes landed on her beautiful brown face full of tears. I didn't ask any questions because the only person who could make her cry like this was her current situation, she called a boyfriend, an ex, or whatever. I could only imagine what he said to ruin her day that quickly. I don't know why she still answered his phone calls. My phone buzzed in my jacket, "Nolan, you can leave." I barked into the phone, not even looking at the caller id.

"What's wrong now, Lani?" The annoyance in his tone caused my own annoyance to emerge.

"Harmony's having a moment."

Since last night, he's been in this don't give a fuck mood, and I'm sick of it. So, I hung up on him. I don't want to be surrounded by that energy. He could leave, and I'll pick up food for me and Harmony, no big deal.

I rubbed Harmony's back giving her the room to release all of her pent-up emotions. It doesn't matter how I feel about the situation, I'm always here to support a friend.

The scent of him swarmed around me. I glanced at Nolan when he entered the room, silently begging him to be nice. Tucking his phone in his pocket, he towered over us as he lifted her chin with his long fingers. Nolan grimaced when he saw her tears, "I know you aren't crying over that bitch ass nigga." I rolled my eyes because he was not helping the cause whatsoever.

He shrugged his shoulders then effortlessly pulled her into his arms, wrapping his heavy arms around her body. I wanted that to be me, and I didn't care how selfish that sounded. I hung my head while he held Harmony as she cried.

"Everything good in here?" Ezeke asked. I brushed past him, heading into my room to change. "Are we going to eat or what?" He asked after me.

Snatching clothes from my closet helped me release my anger and jealousy. I sat on the floor in my closet staring up at the clothes hoping a Nolan-approved outfit would fall into my lap.

Nolan came into the closet, joining me on the floor. "Harmony's ready, are you?" His sandalwood scent permeated my nostrils like it was meant to hypnotize me. "My bad about last night." His tone was different, softer than how he'd spoken to me minutes ago.

"It's fine."

He draped his arm over my shoulder, pulling me close to him, "it's not. I embarrassed you last night, and that wasn't cool, Lani." He kissed my forehead with his soft lips. I imagined the day his lips kissed every inch of my body. "I wanted to take you to breakfast to apologize for my actions."

I lifted his pants leg playing with the hairs on his legs, a habit I developed as a teenager. It was therapeutic, tugging softly at the little soft hairs. Nolan stopped flinching years ago because he was just as used to it as I was.

"I'm ready."

"A'ight, help me up." I stood, helping him from the floor with both hands. He pulled me into him for a hug. He rubbed the top of my head, messing up my hair, "let's go, best friend."

With my back to him, I rolled my eyes. I've grown to hate him calling me that, although I am. It still stung when it came from his lips. The four of us exited the apartment enroute to the best food New Bern had to offer.

chapter
two

Nolan

Nicoyce's Lounge was too fucking busy for a Sunday. Do people not go to church anymore? I was not expecting this, but this food is unmatched in New Bern, possibly North Carolina. We were finally seated after waiting in the long line for forty-five minutes. Harmony griped and groaned the entire time, Ezeke chain-smoked, and Lani was unusually quiet, but shit, it was her and Harmony's fault we were late anyway. I should've ordered via the app and took the shit to Lani's spot. That way we would've had peace and quiet while watching her favorite shows. She's standoffish right now, moving when I get close to her, ignoring me when I ask her a direct question.

I went beast mode on her at the party last night, so I don't blame her for still being pissed. I gave all of them 'the talk' before we went to the engagement party for one of my student's parents. Rule number one: don't have more than two drinks. Rule number two: we arrive together, we leave together. Most importantly, rule number three: do not show your ass in front of these people. I was lucky enough to receive an invitation, and my friends were not going to fuck up my image because it'll only make me look like I'm an incompetent teacher. Lani got drunk as fuck, shots after shots like she was drinking water or some shit. Sloppy ain't my thing, and I stay away from anything that could unleash my trauma. I was engaged in a good conversation with a baddie when I heard hooting and hollering from the ballroom. I'm a man who enjoys a good show. I wanted to see what entertainment the couple hired for their night. To my surprise, Lani was standing on a table with one arm still in the strap of the tight ass dress and the other hanging out, exposing her strapless black silk bra. I didn't know I'd snatched her down until we were outside, and she was pinned against my truck. Ezeke pulled at my shirt like I was going to harm her. Lani's my best fucking friend; I would never hurt her, and I will never let her go out bad like that, especially in front of a room of niggas she didn't know from a can of paint.

I PUSHED LANI'S LONG, black hair off her shoulder, "what's on your mind?" She shook her head, indicating nothing, but I knew her better than anyone. I playfully bit the exposed part of her neck hoping it would loosen her up to talk, but nothing, only a smile that lasted two seconds. I'd learned a long time ago not to push her if she didn't want to discuss it. "Do you work tomorrow?" She shook her head again, not meeting my eyes, pretending to look at the menu like she didn't know what she was ordering. "Check," I referenced chess, our favorite game, letting her know I was ready to listen when she wanted to talk. I'm sure I said something that pissed her off back at her spot. She'd looked good in her fit, too fucking good for breakfast at *The Lounge*. What the fuck was she trying to do—catch a man in this motherfucka? The only nigga she needed was me and sometimes Ezeke.

Breakfast was at the back of my mind as I thought about the upcoming week and how busy I would be. I teach math at Nicoyce Prep particularly to seventh and eighth graders who would rather be anywhere else other than in my class learning about long division. I try to make shit fun, though, and I have to stay on my toes with my kids. They don't mind calling me out on whack shit. I love my job and the kids. I've met many kids during the ten years I've been teaching, but the class I have now are my all-time favorites despite their attention span.

"Sorry for the wait. It's crazy in here. What can I get you guys this morning?" I looked up to find the most beautiful woman I'd seen in a long time staring back at me. The nametag she wore read, 'Willow.' She has to be a new employee because I wouldn't have missed this beauty. *The Lounge* gets my money every week.

"Damn, close your mouth, Nolan." Harmony's loudmouth broke my trance. "I'll have pancakes with a side of eggs. This fool beside me..." She continued.

"Why I gotta be a fool?" Ezeke smiled an annoying smile he reserved for Harmony.

Harmony rolled her eyes, "he'll have waffles sprinkled with powdered sugar and two blueberries. Only two blueberries, anything more than that, he'll have a whole fit." She paused to laugh, "my bestie will have a bowl of grits topped with spinach, egg whites, and one pancake. The guy you had drooling, he'll have the same as my bestie."

"Except," I started.

"Except," Harmony popped her lips. "He wants a waffle instead of the pancake because, for some reason, these fools genderize pancakes and waffles." Willow opened her mouth to speak, but Harmony had all the answers. "Don't ask, and for drinks, three glasses of water because they're healthy like that. I'll have an iced coffee, six pumps of liquid sugar, and a dash of almond milk." Ezeke was the only one to applaud Harmony. It wasn't like she read our minds or some shit, we've been ordering the same shit for years, but I'll let her have that.

"Can I add Bobby's cinnamon roll?" Willow nodded at Lani's request for the manager's special vegan cinnamon roll. Something was definitely wrong with her. Willow collected the menus from the table, and then I watched her walk away.

"Could you be any more disgusting?" Harmony chastised me like I was her child.

"I'm just looking, Harms. Ain't nothing wrong with looking."

"There's looking, then there's gawking, and you, my friend, were gawking at her."

"Why do ya'll always got some shit to say when I look at women? But don't say shit to Ezeke."

"Don't say ya'll because I don't say shit," Lani looked out the window of the restaurant. "I couldn't care less," she mumbled under her breath.

"Lani, what's up? What the fuck is wrong with you?" I was out of patience and seconds away from walking out, leaving all of them right here.

Harmony glared at me, "leave her alone."

"Fuck that. Malani?" My hand gently gripped her thigh under the table.

Lani drew a deep breath, "I'm fine, Nolan, just hungry." She faked a smile at me before turning to Harmony with a look I didn't recognize.

"Can you help me grade papers tonight?" I threw a bone, testing her level of annoyance. She didn't know I knew she hated grading papers, but she was better at math than I was in school. Her help came in handy plenty of nights I was too tired to do it myself.

"Yeah, dinner on you," she bargained. I would happily pay for anything she wanted.

The food hit the spot. After putting food into her system, Lani's mood changed drastically for the better. She's been like this since we were kids. Lani always had to have things her way, and if it didn't go like that, she'd be full of attitude. It didn't help that I encouraged it, but I was brought up to make her happy by any means necessary. Nursing her attitude is my specialty.

Me and Lani sat in my truck while Ezeke and Harmony ran into a grocery store. I don't know what this fragrance was Lani was wearing, but the shit smelled good as fuck. She wore it last night, too.

"Queen?" I addressed her by the nickname I'd given her in junior high.

She glared at me with those big, beautiful doe eyes.

"Don't get fucked up like that again—unless it's just you and me."

"Okay, Dad," she looked away from me, but I grabbed her chin making her face me. Her eyelashes fluttered before her eyes met mine.

I didn't say anything, only rubbed my thumb across her soft cheek, never dropping her gaze. Her skin as smooth as the first time I touched it. Blemish free and full of natural glow. The heat blowing wildly from the vents caused her hair to slowly sway from its impact. Lani's beautiful as fuck, inside and out.

"Promise? I didn't like that shit," I spoke in a whisper.

"I promise, just don't be mad when you have to take care of me."

She laughed, but I didn't.

I pressed my lips to her forehead. "I'll never be mad at that; I got you forever."

chapter
three

Malani

I removed my bomber jacket when my boots crossed the threshold of Nolan's one-bedroom apartment. There was a faint scent I didn't quite recognize traveling through the air. It's probably from his many conquests because he had a problem with keeping his dick in his pants. "Do you have any wine?" I needed it if I had to endure knowing he'd recently had another girl over.

The exact reason why I couldn't be sober last night. I saw him talking to that girl, and it made my blood boil. Getting his attention was the goal, and I got it. After my stunt, he and I left the party.

"No, do you really need some?"

Patting the stack of papers resting on the marble countertop, "if I'm going to help you grade all of these papers, yes."

He blew out a breath, "I'll run to the store. But go ahead and get started."

I did just that when he left, not exactly at first. I wandered around his apartment, looking for any signs a female may have left behind. He hadn't told me he had someone over, and that wasn't like him. Nolan continuously informed me of every female. He didn't know, but it hurt me to hear about girls getting the chance I'd never gotten.

His bedroom was as neat as a catalog, with dark gray plush carpet—steam cleaned weekly, and a perfectly made bed. I ran my hands over the soft navy-blue comforter bringing my fingers to my nostrils and inhaling his scent. I've slept in his bed many times with him, but not in the way I really wanted. Not exhausted from the rounds of love making, only side by side with a touch of me laying my head on his chest.

The purple lipstick on his dresser's mirror caught my attention. Slowly, I walked to the dresser, my heart beating loudly in my ears. A female's lips kissed his mirror with the message that said call me in the heart. Why didn't he wipe it clean? Because he didn't have to Malani, he doesn't have to hide with you because he doesn't see you that way. I rolled my eyes at the mirror then stalked to the bathroom for tissue. I snatched off three squares from the roll and vigorously wiped the message from his mirror.

I didn't used to be this jealous. I used to be able to handle seeing Nolan with another girl, even looked forward to the stories he told so in my daydreams I could insert myself in them later. If he'd stopped looking at me like he does or touching me exactly when I craved his touch—I wouldn't be so far gone.

It was hard, but I minded my own business to focus on the original task. With the quizzes and homework in front of me, I wondered why Nolan was so behind. With winter break approaching, Nolan knew how important it was for the children to have their current grades so they could enjoy their break without any worry. He's an excellent teacher, and every test, quiz, and assignment I've graded received a score of no less than eighty-five.

My best friend is very good at his job. Nolan teaches in ways the children can relate and understand, always trying to find ways to meet them on their level. He puts a lot of thought and process into his lectures, researching the trends and relating math to real life. I love to see him in action. He always invites me to sit in at least once every semester, but sometimes I get to sneak-in even when he doesn't know I'm coming. I admire him and his work. The way his mind works when he's lecturing is sexy to me. Nolan in his element is breathtakingly beautiful.

I was halfway through the stack when Nolan returned, "got lost?"

"Nah, I stopped by *The Lounge* to get food." He slid his coat from his broad shoulders, and my eyes couldn't help but stare. Nolan's thick and really never stepped foot into a gym. He handed me the signature gold bag from *The Lounge*, "I got your favorite," he smirked.

Being friends with him for over twenty-five years, I knew when a smirk crossed his lips, it was some bullshit. The clam container popped open to reveal drunken noodles, *his favorite*.

He handed me a cold glass of wine, our fingers briefly touching, sending chills throughout my body. "Damn, are you done?"

"I'm done with one stack. I don't grade slow like you, which is why you're so backed up. I've told you to lay at least five papers out; checking them like that is much faster."

"That shit only works for you Lani, not me."

He sat close to me on the floor. I occasionally leaned into him or brushed myself up against his body to see if he'd react, but he didn't.

As we graded papers, I sipped on the sweet wine, all while we laughed and chatted about nothing.

Once all the papers were done, he started to cram them into his bag.

"Where are the folders I got you last year?"

He shrugged, "I don't know, probably in my classroom."

"Well, let me put them in your bag because you're wrinkling them, and it's fucking with my anxiety." I took the bag and papers from him, "also," I handed him a piece of paper. "This kid is getting questions wrong on purpose. I can see where he wrote the right answer, then erased it and put the wrong answer."

"Yeah, I see what little man doing. He's got a crush on the tutor assigned to my class. He keeps begging me to let him sit in on the sessions, but his grades have been good, so I told him he didn't need it."

"So, he would rather risk his grade point average for a girl?"

Nolan smiled. He was proud of the kid. "I'm sure it'll be worth it to him in the end."

I swatted at his arm, "don't encourage that. He's too young."

"It's what he wants. Some people could learn from him."

Was that a jab? Does he know? "Whatever, that's stupid."

"He's a kid, they do dumb shit. Don't act like you didn't do dumb shit in middle school. Shit, even high school."

"Boy, bye," I tossed the empty containers into the trash can and helped myself to another glass of wine. "Don't be treating me like your hoes with this Rose´."

"Lani, you're the only one I let drink in here. Plus, I don't buy wine for everybody."

Liquor, wine, weed, and especially pills were his emotional triggers and sometimes I forget his battle. "I'm sorry," I sat at the opposite end of the sofa adjacent from him.

He smiled a smile that's been melting my heart for years. "It's cool." He stretched out laying the leather throw pillow in my lap and placing his head there. "What was bothering you this morning? The shit from last night?" Nolan's eyes were on me, but mine were on the ceiling. Being this close to him was hard for me. We've hung out before, exactly like this—but this was different. I craved him wrapping me in his arms and holding me until I fall asleep. Kissing my forehead mere seconds before I drift off.

Telling him how I really feel, is easier said than done. There's so much trust between us that revealing this two-decade secret would ruin our relationship, I mean friendship.

Closing my eyes, I parted my lips, "I forgive you for last night." Deeply sighing to shake the nerves building in my body, it's time to release this energy. "Truth is Nolan, I love you more than a friend and it's been so hard to tell you. I get jealous when you're affectionate with other women because I don't want you touching anyone but me. I want to be with you." He didn't say anything. The apartment was so silent a pin could fall on a pillow, and we would hear the impact.

Opening my eyes, I looked down at him, and he was asleep.

Wow! The one time I verbally tell him how I feel about him—he falls asleep on me. I've rehearsed in my mind many times. I damn near had an entire script, but all for nothing. I will not stop until he's mine, and I am his. What I will never do is jeopardize any relationship he has or will have with another woman. But the blast of peace I experienced moments ago when I thought I was spilling my guts to him—I want that forever.

chapter
four

Nolan

The pressure from Lani's heavy ass head on my chest woke me from my slumber. The urge to pee in the middle of the night came like clockwork, it never failed. I didn't realize how sleepy I was until I actually laid my ass down. The two glasses of wine Lani had at dinner must've knocked her on her ass, too. When I woke up last night her head was uncomfortably thrown back onto my couch. I handled my business in the bathroom then carried her to my bed.

Waking up with her leg thrown across my waist and head on my chest was a sight until I also realized her calf was resting on my morning wood. She's always been a wild ass sleeper, guess that's something you never grow out of. "Lani?" I gently shook her, easing her leg over.

"Hmmm?" She stirred wiping the moisture from her mouth with the back of her hand.

"I got to get ready for work before I'm late. Are you staying?"

She kept her eyes closed and groaned, "just for a little, I'm tired." She hadn't realized she was all in my personal space and shit.

"Make sure you lock my shit and set my alarm this time." She slowly nodded. I showered and dressed in the most comfortable shit

I could find. I wasn't one of those stuffy ass teachers who dressed in a suit and tie. Hell no. Instead, I dress like my students, in t-shirts with jeans and, of course, the latest sneakers because that's the thing in New Bern. No matter the fit, your shoes must be hot. Nicoyce Prep's newest principal tried to enforce a dress code for faculty, but like I told her and keep telling her, the handbook nor our contracts say anything about a specific dress code. Me and other teachers broke the rule by consistently forcing the newbie to pick her battles. Either retain their dope ass teachers or enforce some bullshit grown ass motherfuckas are not going to follow anyway.

I'm only rebellious when it's a movement I stand behind one hundred percent. The shit they need to focus on is my success rate, not my attire.

"Do you want to have lunch later?" Lani was sitting up in my bed, looking beautiful as ever. If she wasn't my best fucking friend, I would've taken her down a long time ago, but since we've been friends since snotty noses and missing front teeth, I have to shake the thoughts out my mind.

"I'm cool on the lunch. I'll eat the bullshit they serve the students."

"Did you hear anything I said to you last night?" She said fighting through a pout.

I shook my head, "I'm not gonna hold you; I didn't."

"I just told you I'm not mad about the party. I shouldn't have drank so much."

She's damn right—she shouldn't have.

"It's all good, Queen," I kissed her forehead before leaving her in my bed. If I didn't give a fuck about being late, I would've stayed cuddling with my best friend longer.

I hate winter. The gray of the skies and the cold stiffness of the wind is downright depressing. Winter doesn't do it for me. Not to mention, I lost a very important person to me during the winter. Winter was supposed to be a happy time filled with holidays that create happily ever after. For me it was just a countdown until spring.

My students' faces lit up when I handed back the graded papers. I heard a couple of them mumble, "about time," under their breaths. Ungrateful motherfuckas.

Two more weeks until winter break starts and staring at my desk, I had a shit ton of papers to grade. Lani helped me with only a fourth of the stack last night. This season puts me in a mood where I don't want to do anything or have the energy to do it. But I also can't keep relying on my best friend to bail me out, not to mention cuss me out if she saw how much I was backed up. I haven't graded anything in a couple of weeks. My students wanted to know their average and all I could say was, "you're doing good. Keep up the good work," but in actuality some weren't doing their best, some needed tutoring, and some were borderline failing my class but that is my fault for bailing on my responsibilities.

"Mr. Hudson, my mom's been monitoring my grade on the school's website, and she's upset because she says I have missing assignments, but I know I've done the assignments. I try to tell her you just have to grade them; she doesn't believe me. Can you call her, please?" My star student, Justice, requested.

I nodded, letting her know I will call her mother before the end of the school day. I got to get my shit together.

To get ahead, I spent my free period grading papers. Honestly, it was bullshit and not something I wanted to do. So instead, I graded one quiz then I surfed through my social media.

I liked the picture Lani posted from the night of the party, then put heart eyes in the comments. That dress she wore, against me telling her it was too much, fit her like a damn glove. The dress had thin ass straps, and it stopped way above her knees. I couldn't take my eyes off of her then and now, but I needed to.

"Damn!" Grant, an old college acquaintance and fellow history teacher, stood behind me looking all in my motherfucking phone. I locked the screen, shielding it from his prying eyes, "when are you going to put me on to her?"

"Lani?" I was surprised by his request because Lani's not the type of girl he's into. Grant like them tight lipped with legs spread wide open, and that wasn't Lani by any means. She doesn't get down like that.

"Yeah, she's bad. I've been seeing her pictures on your social media, and I've been meaning to ask. I know you're not together because you always put your best friend. Set me up with your best friend."

"Oh man, I don't know, Lani's different."

"How so? Did you smash before she magically became your best friend or what?"

I bore into him letting him know to shut the fuck up. I've been asked this question so many times it shouldn't upset me, but it does. Damn, America acts like males and females can't have a platonic relationship. "Nah man, we're basically brother and sister. We've been friends for a very long time."

Brother and sister was a stretch because I damn sure don't look at my sisters how I look at Lani sometimes.

"Well, link us," he invited himself to take a seat in a desk.

Putting the ungraded papers away because I wasn't going to be able to get shit done with this nigga grilling me. "I'll ask if she's interested. She's been focusing on her surgical nurse career."

"Damn," he held his fist over his mouth. "She's on her shit! Just my type."

Grant's been the same since college, creature of habit. Open legs were his type, and he didn't care how they looked or their career goals. I don't believe his interests changed, but I do know Malani Dawson will not be tangled up in his shit.

"I'll get at her and let you know." Only because I'm not a hating ass nigga, and my Queen can take care of herself.

"'Preciate it," he dapped me.

The principal's voice on the intercom was even more annoying than in person. "Mr. Hudson, please, I would like to see you in my office."

"Be right there, Principal Danders." I hollered back.

"All right man, let me get up out of here. I'll see you later, though. And don't forget to put in a word with shorty."

"I got you."

I was greeted with a fake smile when I pushed the door open to Principal Danders' office. She's only been working at this school for two years and none of the faculty likes her, me included.

"What can I do for you?" I hated being called to the front office for any reason. Earlier on in my career, I expressed to the staff to shoot me an email. Obviously, Principal Danders didn't read the memo thoroughly, but I have no problem reminding her.

"Come on in and take a seat," the deep purple lipstick she wore on her ultra-thin lips did absolutely nothing for her personal appearance. "It's not what you can do for *me*, but more of what you can do for your students."

"My kids are great, what's up?" Looking at my watch, I only had ten more minutes of free period before my next class. I do not have time to sit here and solve riddles with her.

"Mr. Hudson, it's been brought to my attention that your students are missing a lot of grades. In addition, a concerned parent called earlier requesting their child to be placed into another class because they seem to be failing yours." She folded her arms across her chest.

"None of my kids are failing."

"How would you know if there are no grades entered into the system?"

I scrubbed my fingers across my face, "I just know, anything else?"

"Why yes, you have until Friday to enter all grades into the system to update the children's' grades or we will be having a different conversation."

"All right," I tossed over my shoulder as I exited her stuffy office. I couldn't concentrate on shit for the rest of the day, so I made the kids in my last period break off into groups to discuss the current subject and create problems for one another to solve. The four big stacks of papers intimidated me more than Principal Danders. How was I going to finish all that and put it into the system by Friday? There's no way. I had a janitor bring me two big boxes to load up the papers, and like always, I carried my work home with me.

"HEY, stay right here, don't move and don't talk to anybody," my oldest brother, Liam instructed me. We'd just gotten out of school, and he insisted we make this stop again even though it was freezing cold. I clutched my coat tightly around my body and slid my hands into the warming gloves.

"I know," I said annoyed, we came to this apartment without a screen door every day. I knew his rules but for some reason, he explained them to me every single time.

"Where is that twenty dollars Mom gave you this morning? I need it."

"But you said I can use it for candy," I pouted.

"Nolan, what I need is more important than candy. Plus, you don't want rotten teeth, do you?" I made a face, shaking my head as I slid my fingers into the little pocket of my jeans and gave him the money. Watching him disappear into the apartment building without hesitation. While he was gone, I looked around the neighborhood, The Bricks, was not a place for kids like us without adult supervision. Liam was in eleventh grade, so he thought he was grown enough. He convinced me that we needed to go to The Bricks, so he can get trading cards from his friends, but he never showed me the new card. And I was tired of coming here every day, he never let me go in, and it's cold out here.

When he finally came out, Liam grabbed my arm, and we ran home. I completed my homework with help from my sister, Kennedy. Liam was in the only bathroom for a long time, so I knocked on the door profusely because I needed to pee really bad. I twisted the knob opening the door. My brother was laying on the floor, his entire face was blue.

I JUMPED UP, blackness surrounded me. My shirt clung to my skin, and my breath was caught in my chest.

"Are you okay?" Lani's voice soothed me, but I didn't see her. "Nolan, open your eyes," Her small hands cradled my face.

I moved away, "yes, I'm good." Yet I struggled to inhale and exhale a complete breath. She smiled when I met her eyes, "what are you doing here?"

The familiar smell of onions and peppers permeated my nose once I regained my composure.

"I called and asked if you wanted to do dinner tonight, and you said, 'yes.' When I got here, you were asleep."

"How long was I out?" I rubbed my eyes in search of my phone on the couch—checking the time, it was only ten minutes after five.

"I'm not sure," she shrugged, making her way over to the kitchen. My living room was a complete mess, papers scattered everywhere. They must've gotten knocked over when I fell asleep. "No, no, no," Lani said stopping me from gathering them up. "I'm organizing."

"Thanks, but I have to grade all these," then I looked down at one of the papers and saw it was already graded with that cute little smiley face she always does when the students scored a ninety-five or above. "Malani?" I stared at her in amazement. Shaking my head, I asked her, "you graded all of it?" Knowing the answer to my question because both boxes I brought in with me were empty.

"Yes, and I put them into your little grading system, too. You need to change your password. It's been the same for the past two years. I don't know why the system hasn't prompted you to change it. At work, we have to change ours every ninety…"

"You don't know how much I appreciate you right now." Halting the rambling, "you really saved my ass and possibly my job."

Lani always did shit like this unprompted—warming my heart. I couldn't contain my eyes from wandering over her. She's fucking brilliant.

"Why didn't you tell me you were so far behind? We could've knocked all this out yesterday."

My head sank. Embarrassment, shame, and guilt creeping in, I said, "you know how I get around this time."

"I expect you to talk to me. Liam was a brother to me, too, and I miss him. We barely talk about him anymore."

"Yeah, I'm hungry. I'm gonna take a shower. How long before dinner?" If I could leave the past in the past, I would. I wasn't about to get into this conversation today. My mind was muddy with the shit I got to deal with at work. I wanted peace in my home—peace with her.

"Thirty minutes."

That gave me enough time to shower and wash this worry away.

Lani was my safe haven, with her I could unleash all my emotions without being judged. She'd never clowned me for shedding tears in front of her and trust me, it's been a lot of tears. My brother meant a lot to me and losing him at a very young age affected me deeply. I didn't know death before Liam, but that bitch introduced himself with no remorse for me at eight years old.

"Eww, you're all wet!" Lani giggled when I hugged her from behind as she stirred whatever was in the pot. She managed to squirm out of my hold.

"Thank you," I kissed her forehead and didn't miss the deep inhale she took. I lifted the lid to the other pot on the back of the stove. "Damn, Lani you throwing down like this?" I put my hand over my heart, "what did I do to deserve Lani's famous mashed potatoes?"

With a faint smile she said, "actually, I had a taste for them."

"Fuck that, you're using my food though, right."

"Boy please, you know damn well you didn't have anything but the butter I used. When are you going grocery shopping?" Lani turned off the stove, the signal I've been waiting for.

I couldn't wait to dig in. A nigga was starving. I don't care about nothing else she cooks when her mashed potatoes are on the menu. She might as well put the entire pot in front of me.

"Grocery shopping with my ace was scheduled for last Saturday, but you opted to stay in bed. No way I was going alone, so it's your fault I don't have food."

When it comes to homecooked meals, Lani's outranked my mother and she's a close second to my grandmother. Lani's food hits all the right spots; it's just what you need even if you don't know you need it. I'd miss shopping if it meant she'd cook for me every day. I fell into the barstool positioning myself for the feast resting in front of me.

"I picked up a few things that should get you through next Saturday." She said sitting beside me, that fragrance hit me again.

"I have something to tell you." We said at the same time.

She nodded for me to go first. "Someone wants to take you out."

Her brow creased, "someone like who?"

I stuffed my mouth with mashed potatoes, the creamy mixture of butter and sour cream danced on my tastebuds.

We've never interfered in each other's love lives before. She was free to date whomever she wanted, and she never objected to anyone I dated. In high school, niggas used to try to get at her through me, but I shut that shit down quick as hell. They knew not to approach her while she was by my side. Rumors circulated of us dating rather than being friends, but that was kid shit. People stayed assuming.

"Is it you?"

"Why would it be me?"

"Because you play so much."

"Remember Grant from college? He saw a photo of you and asked if you would be willing to go out with him."

"And I hope you told him no," Lani snapped.

"That's for you to say, Queen. I said I'll ask." She stood, walking deeper into the kitchen. She grabbed foil to wrap her unfinished plate. "Are you going somewhere? Lani, we're having a conversation."

This is new territory for us. Like I said, in high school, I didn't have this problem, so I never had to worry about having this conversation with her.

"I forgot. I have to check on Harms. I'll call you later this week." She left pissed, and what the fuck did she mean later in the week?

What the fuck just happened?

She left in such a fucking frenzy her car keys were still on the island. I grabbed them, sliding them into my sweatpants.

"Have you seen my keys?" She asked, looking around when she came back in.

Shaking my head like I wasn't lying my ass off, "nah."

"Nolan, stop playing."

"Come here," I called out to her, grabbing her hands when she was close enough. I sat her into the same stool she occupied before. "If you don't want to meet him then I'll tell him. Nothing is set in stone, just let me know."

"I'll do the date."

"Don't think you have to off the strength of me." I rubbed her knuckles with my thumbs.

She sat quiet looking at me.

"What did you have to tell me?"

A smile spread across her lips, but quickly vanished. "Nothing. I can finish organizing the student's papers before I leave. My keys are probably underneath it all."

"Maybe, but let's finish dinner first." I fed her a spoonful of mashed potatoes. My eyes were drawn to her lips when she pulled the bottom one between her teeth. Tearing my eyes away from her I said, "when are you going to show me how to make this forreal?"

She smirked, "I showed you before, your ass didn't pay attention."

"I did," I defended. "But when I tried on my own, it didn't taste like yours. I want my shit to taste exactly like yours."

"Keep trying, that's how I mastered it when we were in college. Then again, don't. Because if you get it to taste like mine, then you won't need me anymore."

"Not a chance, I'll always need you. 'Specially to clean the dishes," after swatting my arm she joined in on the laughter.

I helped her with organizing the graded papers by the student's name. Each kid damn near had a booklet worth of papers, and I felt ashamed of not doing it sooner. I kept giving out assignments to keep them busy. Once neatly packed in the boxes, I carried them down to my car, so I didn't have to in the morning.

Lani was looking at the photo collage that hung inside my bedroom when I returned. She made it of us when we were in eighth grade.

I stood beside her, "what are you thinking about?"

She pushed out a breath, turning to me with out-stretched arms. I was confused at first, but she only wanted a hug. "Every year around Liam's death, I watch you let this mood overtake you. Let me help you."

I broke the embrace to sit on my bed, "help me how?"

Lani dropped to her knees in front of me cradling my face. "Tell me how you're feeling."

Staring into her eyes momentarily, I contemplated revealing my feelings, but this was Lani. Outside my family, the only person I've trusted with my whole life. She would've left years ago if anything about me freaked her out.

"I'm angry," fell from my lips, and a sense of relief washed over me, cleansing me anew with the omission. "I'm angry he died the way he did. Pissed that he went out like that, and even more pissed that he left me behind to cover for his ass like I always did."

My tears freely fell onto her tiny hands, but she didn't move away. She wiped them.

"I don't think he was thinking when he took you with him, and I don't believe he thought it was going to go the way it did."

I nodded, "I was young and wanted to hang with him. Thing is, I would've walked miles with him. Had I'd known he was getting drugs—I would've told my parents before it got too bad."

"Then, he would've been mad at you."

"It would've been better than losing him forever."

Lani wrapped her arms around my neck, and I pulled her onto the bed beside me.

"Liam made a mistake, but don't beat yourself up over it. He loved you."

I chuckled. I knew it was true, but my pride couldn't accept the fact he put me in a position that caused me to hold a big secret from my parents.

I pulled her car keys from my pocket and handed them to her. She hit me playfully causing me to laugh. "I appreciate you being here for me all the time."

"I'll never not be your support," Lani smiled. I never doubted her.

She spent the night again, passing out during our movie time. She nuzzled so close to me when I laid beside her, wildly tossing her leg over mine. My arms wrapped around her body and my chin rested on the top of her head. Her scent sheathed around us, and I gently caressed the soft, smooth skin of her exposed arm when she stirred. I stopped my action realizing I was too comfortable with touching her.

chapter
five

I was overly excited for today. Dr. Jamel Cooper, a transfer from Miami, aka my boss, was performing liposuction on four patients. I set up the first room just the way he liked. Dr. Cooper didn't like many people in the room—well he only liked me, him, and the patient—while he worked his magic. As his surgical nurse practitioner, I made sure he got what he wanted.

"Everything set?" He asked me over his mug glossed with pictures of his siblings.

We stood in his office drinking coffee like we always did before surgery. When he first came to Nicoyce Med, I could not take my eyes off of him. His caramel complexion, light brown eyes, tall, muscular build, and curly hair had all the girls in the hospital wanting a piece of him and damn if he didn't pass it out.

Professionally, he's the best plastic surgeon in New Bern. Personally, I think he could be a bit more private with his love life, or rather his sex life. He overshares, and I know things about some of these nurses I shouldn't.

"Yes, sir. I had administration put on the classical music you like." I beamed proud of myself because the administration was putting up a fight regarding the surgeon's request.

"Perfect. Let's knock these out so we can go home," he winked at me.

I would be totally okay if I didn't have to witness liposuction for at least a month or two. Even the simple motion of someone sucking drink from a straw sickens me.

"These flowers are beautiful," I gushed at the arrangement of flowers sitting on administrations' counter in a bright pink vase. There were sunflowers and peonies, two combinations that didn't particularly go together but look very well put together by the florist.

"Aren't they beautiful?" Tisha, one of the nurses, exclaimed with enough excitement to fuel the entire department. "They are for you," she smiled sliding them towards me.

"Me?" I searched the bouquet for a card only for Tisha to hand it to me, "if they're for me, why do you have the card?"

Tisha was so fucking nosey it made no damn sense, but she was the only admin I liked since she's the only one that hadn't seen what my counterpart's penis looked like. The other two gave me side eyes and made rude comments because Dr. Cooper fucked them over. It had nothing to do with me but whatever. That's how it is in this hospital. I'd learned to take the good with the bad. I'd rather work and learn under the most skilled surgeon than gain work friends.

"I wanted to see who's sending you such beautiful arrangements. Last we talked, you, ma'am, wasn't seeing anyone." She primped her lips into a smirk.

I snatched the card from her hand, "And I'm still not, these are probably from my best friend. I've been helping him catch up with work, maybe this is just appreciation." I smiled within because this was a first. Nolan never bought me flowers. Maybe candy on Valentine's Day, but never flowers. I don't think he knows how to pick out an arrangement.

The message on the card revealed it wasn't from Nolan, drastically lowering the high that originally consumed me.

The card read, '*I think it's finally time we meet and get to know one another* - Grant'.

"So, do you want to tell me who Grant is?" Tisha quizzed.

I sneered at her, "don't you have work to do?" I picked up the arrangement heading to my office and set them on my desk. I went to social media for Nolan's page to search for Grant. He and Nolan attended college together and have been friends since, but Grant and I never crossed paths. Nolan kept his guy friends to himself, and I didn't care because Nolan's never on his best behavior around his boys.

It didn't take long to find Grant's page. He's cute and all, but he wasn't Nolan. I called Nolan, not caring if he was in class. I needed to give him a piece of my mind about giving this guy my workplace information. That's not cool.

"Hey, what's up?" Nolan's voice making me drip with excitement.

Stay focused, Lani.

I let him have it, skipping verbal pleasantries, "I don't appreciate you telling Grant where I work. I thought last night I told you it was a definite, 'no.' I don't want to be in a relationship with anyone or date—"

"Wait, I didn't tell him anything. I haven't talked to him yet. But what happened?"

I huffed loudly, I wanted him to hear and feel my irritation. "He sent flowers to my fucking job! Beautiful flowers, you can tell him thanks for me, but I don't like feeling like you're pimping me out."

"What the fuck you mean pimping you out?" Nolan raised his voice. "Lani, I didn't give that nigga nothing. So, why the fuck you calling me with this energy?"

"Look, I'm going to leave it like this… I don't want any of your motherfuckin' friends. Don't try to set me up with no fucking body. I'm not pathetic little Malani from high school who can't find her own fucking man." Nolan tried to speak, but I talked over him. "I'm content in my life and my career. I don't need any more added stress. If you can't respect that, maybe we shouldn't be friends." I hung up the phone in tears because I didn't want to take it out on him, but I had to draw the line somewhere.

Nights ago, I poured my heart out to this guy. How could he not see I only wanted him? When he called back, I didn't answer. I turned my phone completely off because I needed time to cool down.

"**WHAT HARM IS** it going to do if you go on one date with this guy?" Harmony chastised me when I told her about the altercation I had with Nolan.

We lay across my bed, her face buried in her phone. I'm surprised she heard a word of what I said.

Shrugging my shoulders, I asked, "have you met him?"

"No, but I've taken the liberty of checking out his social media and baby boy is cute. Lani, I know you want Nolan, but one date would not hurt. He left his number on the card, right?"

I nodded my head because I stared at that number all day long contemplating calling him only to thank him for the flowers and nothing else.

"It may not even go anywhere other than one date but at least you tried. Nolan has no problem going out with other bitches, and you shouldn't restrict yourself from going out with other guys."

I was taking everything she was saying in, but in the back of my mind that logic didn't work for me. I haven't dated in a very long time. I've always wanted Nolan, and I want to be available for him when he finally sees the truth. Then again, maybe she was right. I've been waiting for years, and he hasn't seen me as anything other than a friend. If I go out with Grant, it might trigger something in him.

"I don't know, Harms," I said truthfully.

"Well, I do, and you better call him, or I will call him for you. I'm tired of you moping about Nolan."

"What if Nolan—"

"What if Nolan what?" She rolled her eyes, obviously annoyed with me waffling. "Bitch, you've known Nolan since you were in fucking diapers, he hasn't got the clue yet? It's time for a change. I'm all for Black love and you getting the man of your dreams, but it's time to really reflect on if Nolan is that guy. If he is, like my mom always said, true love comes back. But I'm telling you now

Lani, if he's pushing you to go out with this guy then he's not feeling you romantically."

Everything she was saying was absolutely right to a fault, but she didn't see our interactions when we were alone. How physically, mentally, and emotionally close we are. To the subtle touches he places on the back of my neck that make my hairs stand to attention. The way he grabs my waist, and the way he hugs me. I feel all that even if it's not seen by outsiders.

My eyes fell on Grant's number again. I shook my head, tossing the card across my bed.

Not today.

Tonight, I needed to return the twenty-six calls and countless text messages from Nolan. This push and pull between us was starting to become our norm. I laid in bed with my finger hovering over Nolan's contact number. I didn't know if I should be the one to apologize or just wait for him. But waiting for Nolan can take forever when he thinks he did nothing wrong.

I opted into scrolling on my social media accounts, posting the picture of the bouquet of flowers on one app that would delete it in twenty-four hours.

Then, the unthinkable happened. I dialed Grant's number with unsettled nervousness, but my parents didn't raise me to be rude. The least I could do was call him.

"Hello?" He answered on the first ring, his baritone voice filling my ears.

"Thank you for the flowers." I smacked my hand across my forehead, I should've said 'hey' first.

"Who is this?"

"Does that mean you sent more than one girl flowers today?" I teased, gauging his personality.

His deep laughter breaking the silence, "you are more than welcome, Malani."

It went dry on both ends for a moment as my thoughts wondered to why I was calling this man when the man's voice I wanted to hear—I was ignoring. Harmony's words replayed like a song in my head: *he hasn't got the clue yet; it's time for a change.*

"How was your day?"

"It was good, yours?"

"Horrible, until now."

"What happened?" Fell from my lips before I gave it permission. Maybe because I'm nosey not because I cared because I don't know him like that.

"It's nothing I can't get over. When are you going to let me take you out?"

"Straight to the point, I can appreciate that." It was my turn to giggle.

"Your boy's been keeping you all to himself. I'm curious about you, and I'm not going to beat around the bush. I had to dig deep and research you on my own."

"Research me?" I quizzed. "Anything you needed to know, you could've asked Nolan."

"It's pulling teeth trying to get Nolan to say anything about you, always has been. I got the attention I wanted, so...?"

"Why do you want to take me out?"

"Why are you making it hard? I don't know much about you Malani, but I want to. You're a beautiful girl and from what I'm learning, you're also driven. Two qualities I adore in women."

It's time for a change. "I'll let you take me out but on one condition."

"Name it."

"You have to let me pay for dessert."

He laughed, "I can do that. How is your schedule on Friday?"

"I'm normally out of work at six, but it depends on the surgeon and our schedule."

"Well, can I pick you up at eight?"

"Can I meet you there?" I countered.

"If that makes you comfortable, I'll send you the details tomorrow. Goodnight, Malani."

Grant had me laying in my bed with a big smile on my face. It's been a while since I've had a conversation with a guy that wasn't on a platonic level.

chapter
six

Nolan

I love being able to inspire the young kids of the community I grew up in. The faces of my students give me pure delight when I teach and interact with them. Through all the years of teaching I've never had a child fail my class because I push them to do their best. When they've run out of their best, I let them borrow my best. It's not about my success rate, it's about the kids tapping into their full potential. At the beginning of every school year, I tell the fresh faces if you can pass my class, you can pass any math class. I only get behind on paperwork, but I still teach them everything they need to know.

"Mr. Hudson, can we have a pizza party tomorrow?" Justice suggested because she loved to eat and stay making me spend money.

"Only if you can correlate it to the lesson plan."

"I got it covered Mr. Hudson. As the class' team leader," she started.

"Teacher's pet," another student yelled out, causing Justice to become embarrassed enough to hang her head, while a handful of kids laughed.

"Aye, chill out," I said, giving the young man the evil eye. "Continue Justice because some of us were interested in what you were saying."

"Never mind, it was a dumb idea." She returned to her desk, but I was heated.

"Don't ever shrink down because of the ignorance of others. Boys who treat girls like that will stay boys forever," the room erupted with a bunch of oooh's.

"Imma be a man, Mr. Hudson," Ryan stood up, patting his chest.

"Act like it because disrespecting women isn't a good first step." I looked around the room meeting the eyes of the nine young boys in my class. "My very best friend is a female, some of you have met her. I've never disrespected her or allowed any other man to disrespect her. Black women, hell, all women are our queens and should be treated as such. I feel like I teach history, as many times I have to remind ya'll. In this class, females will be respected, or you'll leave." I crossed my arms over my chest. Eighteen sets of eyes were on Ryan.

"I apologize, Justice," he spoke, loudly. The class erupted with applause like we've just watched a movie. Ryan took it a step forward helping Justice from her seat, so she could convince me to sponsor the pizza party. Although she failed at correlating scatter plots to the pizza party, I agreed but instructed each student to compose a word problem from all we've learned over the first semester.

With the school day coming to an end, I checked my phone to see if Lani called, but she didn't. I must have left hundreds of messages between yesterday, last night, and this morning.

Grant knocked on my classroom door as I was packing my brief-case. "Are we good?" He asked with a smirk I wanted to wipe from his face with my fist.

"Nah, nigga. You overstepped. She thinks I put you up to that shit."

"I talked to her last night. She's good, man."

"What the fuck you mean, she's good?" A grimace rising to my face.

"Malani called me last night. She's okay. I wanted to make sure we're okay because it got pretty heated yesterday."

The fuck was she calling him for?

"Yeah, we're good," I dapped him.

I didn't appreciate Lani spazzing on me yesterday, so that nigga had to see me. It was bad, the gym teacher had to pull me away from him. I got even more pissed when Lani stopped answering my calls because she's really mad at me about some shit I had no control over. I didn't know that nigga was going to go stalker mode and find out where she worked. I was well prepared in letting him know she wasn't interested when I came to work yesterday, only to be bombarded with an angry call during my free period. Ultimately, my issue wasn't with Grant. It was with Lani believing I think so lowly of her. When have I ever given off that impression?

———

WILLOW'S beautiful face drew me directly to her when I walked into *The Lounge*. She smiled, and I gave her a head nod.

"Nolan, over here." Ezeke called out from our usual spot. I slid in the booth, but my eyes were searching the room for her. "Go talk to the girl."

I shook my head, "it's not time yet. I'm letting it marinate."

Ezeke shot me a look of confusion. This wasn't the first time I had to school him on females.

Being best friends with one has its advantages, and it teaches you how to look for signs she's ready to be approached. Of course, all females aren't the same, but I take it slow and steady when I work my magic. "Little Miss. Willow has only been here two, maybe three weeks. The regulars have made their comments and probably gave her their number in hopes she'd call to hook up. The ins and outters have done the same, but when the traffic dies down, that's when I step in. I gotta see if she takes the bait from other niggas before I shoot my shot."

Ezeke nodded, "I guess, my nigga. I'm more direct."

"Yeah, how far has that got you?" I chuckled, "I'm fucking with you. So, what's been up?"

"Nothing, what's up with you and Lani? She called me today telling me something about you and Grant."

"I'm glad she can call other motherfuckas other than the one that's been blowing her shit up." The waitress halted our conversation by coming to take our orders. We ordered Bobby's Thursday night special, black bean burgers with sweet potato fries. "Grant sent flowers to her job, and she thought I was urging him to push up on her."

"That's it? Because Baby girl was mad as fuck. I've never seen her that pissed off before."

"That's all I care to talk about. Lani and I will solve our own issues."

"I got you, bruh. What's up with Grant, though?"

"I don't trust him."

"Since when? That nigga was your right hand in college, and we not too long ago played ball with him."

Leave it to Ezeke to call me out on my shit.

"I hung with that nigga because he knew where the girls were at, that's it. As far as Grant being my right hand, hell nah. Lani's the only one with that title and the position will always be filled by her."

Ezeke made a face like he didn't believe what I just said. "I'm trying to connect the dots, my nigga."

"To what?"

"Why you all of a sudden shading your mans."

"Let me rephrase. I don't trust him with her."

"Because of his past?"

"Especially because of that. If he breaks her heart, I'll have to break his face and I'm not trying to take it that far with a nigga I've been cool with since college."

"Why didn't you shut the shit down when he asked about her?"

"Because I'm not a hating ass nigga."

"But you *are* her best friend though, right?"

I glared at him, "what you getting at?"

"I'm just saying. I wouldn't trust my crackhead ass uncle with my car. I know I couldn't trust him with someone I love." I stared at him, waiting for him to elaborate on the outrageous analogy. "You should've told him she wasn't interested when he first asked about her."

"And that would've made it look like I'm blocking."

"In your words, 'Who gives a fuck what it looks like?' Nigga, you've been saying that about you and Baby girl since I met you. You know her better than anyone, and you know she wasn't going to be feeling his ass. Right?"

I shrugged, "I guess. Fuck me for wanting her to make her own decision."

"It's not about that, and you know it."

"But it is," I countered.

"But it's not. You may have been friends with her longer, but you don't pay attention."

"What the fuck does that mean?"

He shrugged, "Imma have to start charging your ass."

"Fuck outta here! We help each other," I dapped him across the table.

"Did she ever find out you wired her ex's jaw shut for three months?"

"Hell nah, that's between the two of us. Just like with you threatening Harmony's dude. We do what we have to do for our girls." We laughed as our food was delivered to the table by the beautiful Willow. "Thank you," I said dragging my eyes over her body. She filled out that damn waitress uniform too good. Bobby's going to have to change the dress code to keep patrons from thinking something other than food is being served.

She smiled meeting my eyes, "you're welcome." She sashayed away with extra sway in her hips.

"What if I was interested in Baby girl, how would you feel about that?"

I bit the burger and stuffed fries in my mouth before the answer could form into words. I swallowed hard, "I know you'll have her best interest at heart. Grant, not so much."

"Back on Grant, like I said, that's your boy."

"That doesn't mean I want him dating Lani," I admitted. Lani deserves a man, and that man isn't Grant. I thought he'd be suitable for her considering the other motherfuckas she's dated, but thinking about all the shit he did to women in college, I don't want that for Lani. "I thought you wanted Harmony."

Ezeke smiled, "I do. I wanted to see something. I think we're going to have to see how this thing plays out with Lani and Grant. I'll fuck up any nigga behind Harmony and Lani," his eyes told no lies.

"Ain't shit going on with Lani and Grant." I bit the burger again.

"Talk to Lani, dawg," he suggested.

"What do you think I've been trying to do?" Particles of food flew from my mouth.

Lani's acting like a child by talking to everyone else except me. This is the longest we've ever stopped talking to one another. She's mad as fuck, but if she'd answer the fucking phone, I could fix it.

I always fix it.

Willow placed the bill on the table, "when you're ready."

I presented my card, "we're ready now. Can I also order Bobby's cinnamon roll to go?"

"Are you taking that shit to Baby girl? Trying to butter her up into talking to your ass?"

I smiled, "yeah, she can't turn me away with that in my hand."

Willow returned with the heated cinnamon roll and the little book with my card. Opening the book to put my card back into my wallet, I saw where she had left her phone number on the receipt. Smiling inwardly, I left it in the book. Me and Ezeke exited *The Lounge*.

"Hey!" Willow called after me. She rushed over with a scowl, "you forgot something."

"Nah, I got everything." I peered in the gold bag for extra effects.

"I was talking about this," she held up the paper with her number scribbled in pink ink.

I chuckled before telling Ezeke he could leave, and I'll get at him tomorrow.

"I'm sorry, beautiful, but I don't do subtle. If you want me to have your number, hand it to me."

Her eyes dropped to her feet, "sorry, I'm never this forward." Willow stretched the paper out to me, "Call me sometime?"

I took her number this time, leaving *The Lounge* with a huge grin. I knew she would make her way over to me.

I called Lani's phone as I sat in the parking lot of her apartment complex, but it went straight to voicemail. She's taking this shit too far. I used my key to unlock the door, and the living room and kitchen lights were off.

The room where Harmony slept was empty. She must've had to work overnight.

Lani's room door was closed. Letting myself in, I could hear her singing horribly in the shower. I set the bag from *The Lounge* on the bedside table, waiting for her to finish. She exited the bathroom wrapped in a small towel that exposed a quarter of her body.

"Nolan!" Her eyes bugged out with astonishment seeing me in her room, relaxing on her bed. "What are you doing here?" Lani sat on the other side of the bed to apply her usual warm vanilla-scented lotion. I could sense the irritation radiating off of her.

"If you'd answered your phone, you'd know why I'm here."

"I want you to leave." She folded her arms across her chest like that was supposed to make me comply.

I shrugged, "tough shit, I'm not going nowhere."

She stood pulling a nightshirt over her head. "Close your eyes."

"Nah," with one motion, she let the towel drop and completed pulling the shirt down to her thighs.

Of course, Lani never shied away from me, and I've seen her naked more times than I should admit, but shit. My dick was bricking within seconds, so I repositioned myself on her bed.

She continued her nightly routine, floating around the room like I wasn't inches away from her. The silent treatment was on full blast, and I hated that shit.

"I'm sorry, okay? Can we get past this shit?"

Pulling her wavy hair into a high bun, she looked me up and down before continuing to cover her hair with the bonnet. "Admit you told Grant where I worked."

"I didn't tell that motherfucka nothing, Lani. I told him you were a nurse, and I guess he tracked you down."

"You told him too much. Like I told you, I can meet people on my own. I don't care to be set up—I'm not a charity case." She slid into the bed laying with her back towards me.

"I know," was the simple response. I touched Lani's tensed shoulders. Her feelings were valid, and I wouldn't talk her into feeling any different.

"We're going to dinner tomorrow."

"Where are we going?"

"No, me and Grant."

"Lani, he's no…."

"I don't want to hear it. This is what you wanted, so this is what you get. If you're spending the night, turn off the light. I have an early morning."

Defeated, I removed my t-shirt, sliding under the same covers as her and realizing she wasn't wearing panties. I need a release as soon as possible because having a hard dick beside my best friend will have me making a decision that will change both of our lives.

Lani was asleep before me. I was up like a dog in heat, having a texting conversation with Willow. After her nerves subsided, she loosened and opened up about her life. She wanted to video call, but out of respect for Lani, texting is all I could do. Plus, I didn't want to have to explain early on why I'm lying in bed with my best friend. Explaining me and Lani's friendship is phase three, if we make it that far. Another message came through, but Lani shifted.

"Nolan?" She reached out, doubting I was still beside her.

I gripped her hand, pulling her to my bare chest. "You need something, Queen?"

"Just you." Her body relaxed minutes later and rhythmic breathing told me she'd fallen back asleep.

After solidifying a date with Willow, I leaned over to put my phone on the dresser. I continued to hold Lani until her scent put me to sleep.

chapter
seven

Malani

The nerves building in my stomach were enough for me to turn around two times before talking myself into meeting Grant at the park downtown. It was a nagging feeling in my stomach, like I was doing something wrong. Like I was cheating on Nolan. I was getting ahead of myself, thinking this date would blossom into more than a meet and greet from two people who share a mutual friend. I parked my car behind the one he described as his and got out. The wind was not my friend today. It made my hair fly all over my head because it wanted to be disrespectful. I leaned into the window, positioning my unruly curls to their original place. Doing so gave me a little more time to let the nerves pour into the river surrounding the park.

"Hi," He greeted me with a warm smile and beautiful teeth. I underdressed in a thin t-shirt, jeans, and a light jacket. The coolness from the water brushed against my face causing a shiver. "Are you cold?" He immediately removed the leather jacket from his broad shoulders, placing it around me. Chivalrous, I like that. "I thought a nice stroll in the park would be a great icebreaker."

"A little secluded, men take women to parks to murder them." I half-heartedly joked.

We began to walk past the well-lit gazebo, one of the many tourist attractions downtown.

"We can go somewhere else if you'd like."

"This is fine. I haven't been to this park in a long time. It's nice to walk around this time of the year."

"I thought so, too. I'm a history teacher and love learning new things about this quaint town."

"Are you not from here?"

I'm not even going to pretend I know everyone in New Bern because with the area growing so much in the past ten years, transplants are coming from all over the states.

"No, I'm actually from Greensboro."

"What drew you to New Bern?"

"Believe it or not, my job. Nicoyce Prep is one of the most prestigious academies in the state. I got the call to interview right after I graduated, and here I am. What about you?"

"Born and raised. I've thought about other cities within North Carolina, especially for my career, but when the number one plastic surgeon in the United States transferred to my hospital, I fought to work under him."

"Dr. Cooper, yes, I've heard a lot about him."

"He's great. At first, I didn't think he was needed in New Bern, but the scope of what we do is expanded beyond liposuction and BBL's."

He directed us to sit on a nearby bench overlooking dark river water. The lights on the draw bridge illuminated parts of the river. I also stole a glimpse of his handsome features. A well-connected dark beard adorned his face. He wears gold-rimmed glasses that make him look sophisticated.

Nolan was calling my phone, and I should've left it in the car because he's been calling since I left work. Since this was his doing, I want to enjoy this evening with Grant.

"Do you need to answer that?"

"No."

"Someone making sure I'm taking care of you?"

"Probably. I'm sorry," I said powering my phone off.

"How is it we've never met? Nolan's been a good friend for years."

I shrugged, "he has his friends, and I have mine."

"Are there any friends of yours he doesn't know?"

"No."

"It's just odd to me. Being a history buff, I've learned to ask the why's. Let me know if I overstep."

I looked at the cars passing by on the drawbridge, "you'll have to ask Nolan."

With a sigh, he said, "now that the hard part is over, would you like to grab something to eat?"

I nodded as he helped me from the bench. I was comfortable being around him; therefore, I allowed him to drive to the restaurant down the street. Grant's conversation was great, and it wasn't a dull moment between us. As promised, he let me pay for dessert, and we shared the chocolate cake with watery vanilla ice cream.

We ended the night by walking around the park again and talking more.

"You went to school in Greensboro, too?"

"Yep, it was a fun time."

"Literally, miles away from me. Did you ever go to parties?"

"I went to all the parties thrown by my college mates and yours if they didn't conflict."

"Damn, I can't wrap my head around not crossing paths with you."

I shrugged, "maybe we have. But our attention was elsewhere."

Grant shook his head, "no, I would've remembered encountering a beautiful woman like yourself."

That made heat rush to my cheeks. My mouth welcomed a smile, "well, here we are." I removed his jacket from my shoulders, placing it in his hands.

"We should do this again sometime." He held my car door open, and I slid into the driver's side seat.

"Call me," I flirted.

Grant kissed my hand, closing the door and wishing me a good night. His vibe is different from guys I've dealt with before. He's so chill, and our interaction was freakishly natural.

My last relationship was over three years ago with a guy I was only dating to pass the time. I cared deeply about him. We worked because we gave each other space. He was convenient and sweet. The downside was he didn't like Nolan. It was hard to balance between the two. It ended badly because he decided to stick his dick in another girl. Although I wasn't in love, I trusted him. The betrayal left me in pieces that my best friend had to help put back together. That day I swore off any relationship that would distract me from Nolan. I've sat back and watched him date, fuck, and become serious with many girls, but that never swayed me from wanting him to myself. Me and Nolan have an unspoken agreement —we don't get close to the other's partner. We have mutual respect, but I'm not about to be friends with a bitch who has what I want. 'Hey' and 'Bye' are all they get from me. Over the years I hid jealousy very well—hyping myself up knowing, or rather hoping one day it'll be my time.

I skipped up the steps to my apartment. Harmony was in the living room watching some drama-filled reality show when I entered with a massive grin.

She muted the TV giving me her full attention. "Damn, bitch, did ya'll fuck?"

I pursed my lips and flopped down beside her, "who do you think I am, you?" Rolling my eyes playfully, "it was borderline perfect." I swooned in my seat. "Grant's a vibe."

"Where did ya'll go?"

"To the park, then that nasty ass seafood place downtown, then back to the park."

"So, he's not from here." Harmony laughed.

Nobody, and I mean nobody, that's a native from New Bern visits that disgusting restaurant on purpose, but I didn't complain. First thing I did was put Harmony and Ezeke on game when they relocated to New Bern after college. I ate the safe options and still got full.

"I'm glad you had a good time! Are you going to see him again?"

"Maybe. He's really nice, and I guess I enjoyed his company."

"That's good. He got a brother?"

"There you go," I kicked my shoes off, placing them neatly beside the couch.

"I'm just saying. I need to be hooked up, too. I'm ready to mingle after what's his name."

"Yeah, right. You were just crying over his ass a couple of nights ago."

"Okay, damn, maybe I'm not ready. But I think a few deep strokes will get my mind off of him."

"Eww, I'm going to bed on that note." I gave Harmony a hug and then walked toward my room door.

"Nolan's here, by the way." She said casually with her back to me.

I stopped in my tracks. Why didn't she lead with that when I first got in? I hope he didn't hear about my date with Grant, not that I wouldn't tell him. "What?" I whispered.

"He said you weren't answering the phone, and he wanted to wait until you got home."

"Harms, let that be the first statement out of your mouth next time. Goodnight." I scolded—pausing in front of my bedroom door, I inhaled a deep breath before stepping in and closing the door behind me.

Nolan's furrowed brows got my attention. "Where have you been?"

"I had the date with Grant tonight." Why did I sound like I was answering my father?

Nolan looked so fucking sexy, laying on my bed comfortably between my sheets. His black overnight bag was in its usual spot in front of the bedside table—on his side.

"No shit Lani, where did he take you? And why wasn't you answering your phone?"

"We went to eat, and I didn't answer because I was on the date. What is the problem?"

"I expect you to answer when I call."

Fuck, I hated how much I liked his demands. "I think I was in safe hands, after all he is your friend."

I grabbed the nightgown hanging from the back of my closet door before retreating to the bathroom to shower. I used the makeup wipes to wash the light beat from my face. "The date was fun by the way, thanks for asking."

Nolan scoffed, "was he a gentleman?"

"Yes."

"He didn't try to kiss you or any of that shit?"

"No, geez, overprotective much! Besides I don't kiss on the first date."

"Since when? You kissed ugly ass Donnie on the first date."

I started the shower, so it could get hot, "actually he kissed me."

"But you didn't stop it."

"Whatever, I was sixteen."

"Excuses, Queen." He tapped on his phone.

Closing the bathroom door, I stripped off my clothes and stepped into the shower. Immersing under the shower head to drown my thoughts.

The brother side of Nolan was emerging when possessiveness is what I wanted him to show. I want him to be selfish over me. Is wanting him to see me as his girl and not want to share me with anyone else too much to ask? All it takes is for him to admit he's feeling me just a little bit, and it'll be up from there. All I need is a window to climb in, a door to burst through, to a house that stores his feelings for me. But maybe I'm asking for too much. Maybe that will never happen, and I'm only fooling myself.

Then, I take one look at him and fall all over again. I love the way his hair curls against my fingertips and the smoothness of his beard. My hands roamed my wet body as I pictured him in my head and listened to his voice talk about his day at work, the pizza party for his students, and how he finally felt back on track. I pushed my fingers deeper into me, suppressing a moan when his voice was closer. Now, he was talking about his sister, Kennedy, calling to set up a memorial party for Liam. I became completely unhinged when he asked me to come with him.

I came, trembling from the orgasm.

It was no question I was going to be there, but the fact he'd asked is what excited me the most. I stepped from the shower, wide eyed because he was right there with the towel outstretched. "If I didn't know any better, I think you like seeing me naked."

He grinned, "looking at you never hurt nothing. You don't like it? Want me to stop?"

His eyes were trained on mine, the grin was gone from his face. "I—I," I stammered.

"You what?" His voice was low, lusty.

Or am I trippin?

"I—I don't. I don't care if you look," I all but whispered. He had me in a trance, feet cemented in place, heart pounded as loud as a bass drum.

Nolan wrapped the towel around me, partly enclosing it in the front, but he didn't let go. "Do you like me looking at you? Admiring your body?"

What the fuck?

I bit my bottom lip not sure how to respond.

"Queen?"

He was close, I hadn't realized he'd taken a step closer.

I cleared my throat, "Nolan, you can look all you want."

"And I will." His tongue ran over his lips.

I pushed him aside entering my room, "whatever. Are you staying tonight?" He nodded, "I think we're at each other's house now more than ever."

"I don't see a problem with that."

"It says a lot."

"Like what?"

"You're in between girls."

"So?"

"So, you use me to pass the time until another one enters your life."

"When you say it like that, it sounds bad as shit. I like hanging with you."

"Do you?" I put on my nightgown and laid in my bed facing Nolan, who was still standing against the bathroom door.

"Do you want that cinnamon roll I bought you last night?"

"I ate it for breakfast."

Nolan was out of his mind if he thought that cinnamon roll would last twenty-four hours. We watched TV until he fell asleep with his head on my shoulder. I kissed the top of his forehead—lingering there, imagining the day I would kiss his lips.

DR. COOPER CALLED me for an impromptu meeting, which wasn't uncommon for us. We would work our asses off for weeks before we actually had the time to talk about all the procedures we've completed. Dr. Cooper's thorough. We will see the same patients' multiple times a month to ensure they are healing properly because you can tell a patient what they need to clean and compress, but they are so eager to show off their bodies they ignore our recommendations. Dr. Cooper ensures that doesn't happen because his name and reputation is behind the work of art. As his surgical nurse practitioner, I do the job of administration as well. Paperwork and paper trail is my strong suit, and he appreciates it. Well, I think he has for the past three years I've been working under him.

"I won't keep you long. I called this meeting to update and inform you on a few items on our agenda." Dr. Cooper placed a cup of coffee in front of me on my side of his desk. I balanced my notebook on my knee, ready to write down everything that came from his mouth. "In January, we have a conference to attend in Miami, Florida. The hospital from which I previously transferred is hosting. I want you there." I opened my mouth to speak, "no questions. You and I both know you are more than qualified to speak on the panel, but for your first year, I want your ears and eyes open. I want you to make connections in this plastic surgeon world.

I boast about you and your abilities every opportunity I get, and when you're ready for the next step to become a plastic surgeon, I will personally sponsor you as well as continue to teach you everything I know. Malani, you can already do everything I do and more."

I appreciated the accolades, but I love being a SNP. I didn't join this career to actually do the procedures on my own. "Thank you, Dr. Cooper."

"I saw you were having issues with Ms. Johnson."

"Yes, sir, she wasn't taking the antibiotic you prescribed. When I asked her why, she didn't have an answer."

"Put her on the do not return list. I make it very clear to the patients at consultation they must follow every recommendation I give, or they will not be touched by me again."

"Yes, sir," I nodded as I scribbled on the notepad.

"Business aside, what's going on with you?"

Here he goes.

"Just working and ready for the holidays to be over."

"Over? I love the holidays, especially Thanksgiving. Do you have any plans?"

"My parents live in Hawaii, so I'll have dinner at my best friend's family's house like every year."

"When's the last time you've seen your parents?"

"We video chat often. In person, it's been like four years."

"Do you miss them?"

"Of course, I do, but they understand I can't come there as often as I want. My best friend's family is my family."

"You're lucky to have that." He stared at me longingly like he was lost in his own thoughts.

"What are your plans?"

"We celebrate at my grandparents' house. My Grams only allows a handful of people to cook in her kitchen. If you're ever out of plans, you're welcomed with us. I can't promise it won't be a clusterfuck, that's your warning."

"Thank you."

He nodded then switched back into business mode. "We do have two consultations scheduled the morning of Thanksgiving. We should be done before ten if you scheduled it correctly."

I laughed, "I saw your note written in all caps and highlighted. I scheduled exactly how you advised."

"Good because nothing stands in the way of my food."

After the meeting with Dr. Cooper, I met Ezeke for lunch at *The Lounge*. I was craving a cinnamon roll but noticed the peach cobbler was back on the menu and opted for that instead. If they ever got rid of Bobby or transferred him to another location, it would be the end of my run at *The Lounge*. He has done so much for this place, and I was happy when he was finally awarded with creative freedom of the menu. He didn't change anything, like many in charge would have, he only added items to cater to vegans and those who choose a plant-based lifestyle. Bobby's one of the main reasons this place is packed every day of the week.

"The date?" Ezeke jumped right in, I did a double take to make sure I was talking to him instead of Harmony.

I gave him a knowing grin, "it was okay. Should've been you know who, but I'll take free food and good conversation when I can."

"Nolan was tight about that date."

"What did he say?" I asked, genuinely amused.

"The normal, buddy not good enough for you."

"He can realize that, but can't realize he's who I want to be with."

"You know Nolan better than any of us."

"Yeah, but he talks bro talk with you. I only get that when I ask. Has he ever talked about me romantically?" I knew the answer and often doubted it, but the paleness in Ezeke's tawny toned face solidified my horror. "How do I change it? I'm out of options. I tried the make-him- jealous route, failed. When I push away from him, he pulls me back in. I need help." I hadn't noticed the tears on my face until Ezeke took a napkin to wipe them away. Holding this secret from my best friend is overwhelming. Pretending to be buddies when I love him deeper than existence is draining. "Dr. Cooper thinks I should consider becoming a surgeon." I stabbed at the diced peaches.

"Don't switch up. Baby girl, I know how you feel. I've been at Harmony for a minute, but she's not taking the bait."

"But she knows you like her."

"Which is worse. I'm not trippin; she'll come to her senses."

I began to sympathize with him. Would I rather be unknowingly rejected or rejected to my face? Both suck!

"What should I do?"

"With Nolan, you have to be upfront with him. Stop hiding, what's the worst that can happen?"

Rejection is the worst that can happen. A ruined friendship is also the worst that can happen. Broken trust is the worst that can happen. It's layers that come with this secret, and I'm not sure I'm ready to peel them back.

At the end of the day, Nolan is family and I care for him a lot. I don't want to lose him. I nodded my head while listening to Ezeke tell me about his upcoming plans for Thanksgiving. My mind was far away from the table thinking about the many outcomes of telling Nolan how I feel about him. I'm making a goal in my head to tell him before the new year. This time, I will make sure he's awake.

chapter
eight

Nolan

Thanksgiving Day

I COULD NOT WAIT to dig into my mom's baked macaroni and cheese and glazed ham. Lani was driving too slow, considering we were supposed to leave damn near an hour ago, but she had to make sure she was appropriately dressed. My family didn't care what she had on. She could wear a paper bag as long as she's seated at the table. All week my mom kept asking if Lani was joining us, and like every year since her parents moved to Hawaii and her siblings were on the west coast, I said, "yes."

There were more cars than I expected in the driveway when we pulled in. "Who the fuck are all these people?" I asked to no one in particular.

"They are probably here for Liam's balloon release. Kennedy said your parents weren't up for a party but agreed to release balloons in his honor before dinner."

That's exactly why she's my Queen; she pays attention to that type of shit.

Lately, I find myself thinking Liam's not dead, he's just away, but I can't talk to him right now. It's a weird feeling when losing someone you love. At a young age is a double whammy. I've come to terms with his demise, and I'm learning how to grieve the loss of him. My emotions go from angry to sad in seconds. Then, the guilt pokes its head. I didn't understand at eight years old, but over the years, I've learned a few things.

Liam, seventeen at the time of his death, was smart as hell in school. I vaguely remember attending spelling bees where he took home the first-place prize. The trophies are still in a glass cabinet in my parent's house. Liam was a prodigy, but he experienced pressure from teachers and from our parents.

April, my oldest sister, was in college at this time and rarely came home to visit, even now. Kennedy is four years older than me. Back then, our parents allowed her to go to her friend's house after school to study, and our dad picked her up on his way home. Liam's job was to pick me up from school, and we'd walk home. What my eight-year-old mind thought was trading cards actually turned out to be Percocet. He'd been using for months, and nobody knew.

When he died, our parents became so strict we weren't allowed to do anything alone. Lani's family were the only people allowed in our house after Liam's accident. Lani's the only one who knows about Liam's stops in The Bricks. I couldn't imagine how she felt when I often laid my head in her lap and cried about my brother for years; sometimes, it was every year. Twenty-four years later, it's like it just happened yesterday. When I walk into my childhood home, I can still see him lying on the bathroom floor cold as ice.

I got through the balloon release without emotions leaking from my face, but I held onto Lani as she cried. Liam was important to her as well.

My heart was filled with joy having all of my family together. Holidays are my favorite because we all got to be in the same room and crack jokes on one another. April and her husband finally made an appearance. Kennedy with my eleven-year-old nephew, Anison and her husband, Socari. A couple of aunts, uncles, and cousins stayed after the balloon release. Lani was mingling with more people than I cared to talk to. I joined my dad and Uncle Bill outside as they gathered around the fryer containing the turkey.

"Hey, son," my dad greeted me with a warm hug. I swear this man looked the exact same as when I was a kid—he doesn't age. His bald head was covered by a toboggan as he blew in his hands for temporary heat. "Glad you can finally stop by and see your old man."

"I stopped by last week to bring mom money for food, where were you?" I quizzed since he tried to check me.

He scratched his chin, "uh, probably sleep."

"Nah," I laughed at his bullshitting, "I heard you were out playing them numbers. I thought you stopped."

"Son, you can't win if you don't play."

"Exactly what I say," Uncle Bill and my dad bumped fists. "Nephew, that's not little Lani, is it?"

My eyes narrowed, "yeah that's her, why?"

"Hmmp, hmmp, hmmp, hmmp, hmmp," his old ass grabbed his junk. "She filled out nicely."

"Watch yourself, don't be disrespectful Unc. She's beautiful but don't do *that* shit."

"Bill, don't you dare, she's my baby." My dad warned. About his girls, Lani included, he'd go to war with anybody, and I've adopted those same qualities.

"My apologies, I'm toasty right now," he staggered to a nearby chair.

My dad lowered his voice, "everything okay with her?"

"Yeah, she's considering becoming a surgeon. The doctor she works under is encouraging her."

"Oh," his eyebrows shot up.

"What?" I queried.

"They work closely together?"

"Yeah."

"Very close?"

"Dad, don't go there."

He chuckled, "it's been a while since she dated someone."

"She's focused. She doesn't need no one distracting her."

"You know what your problem is, nephew? You think she only need you. That girl got needs." Uncle Bill inserted himself back into the conversation.

I shot my dad a look letting him know I was going to lay hands on dear Uncle Bill.

"Cut it out, Bill." My dad said, sternly. My uncle waved him off. "Plastic surgeon, huh? She's damn near doing that now."

"Yeah, same thing I said."

"Support and take care of her. We're all she's got over here."

"I know dad, and I'm trying. Just had the same conversation with her dad."

"And what did Michael say?"

I pushed my cold hands into my pockets, "same as you. Take care of his baby. I've *been* the one taking care of her." I reminded him. I'm the one who sees her highs and lows. I'm the one who she can let her guard down in front of. I notice after every call with her parents; how her eyes gloss over and she excuses herself to the bathroom. My chest tightens when she runs the water and quietly sobs. I've been holding her down, and I'll never stop.

"Does that mean what I think it means, son?" My dad chuckled.

"C'mon, don't start this year. Might want to check on the turkey." I said walking away, "oh and your brother." Uncle Bill was slumped over the chair, seconds from falling over.

Lani was in the kitchen with an apron helping my mom cook and chopping it up with some of my cousins. She looked up at me from the bowl she was stirring.

"Y'all need help, Ma?" I offered only to be respectful. The money spent was as much as I wanted to contribute to this dinner besides enjoying the food.

"We're almost done. How's the turkey looking out there?"

"I don't know. Dad had it covered." Lani smirked, "what's funny?"

"You're non-cooking behind. I'll go check, Mama Steph."

She stepped towards the back sliding door. I looped my finger into her belt loop, and pulled her into my chest. Placing my lips close to her ear I whispered, "since I've been standing here, Grant has called you three times. I know you feel that shit."

"Nolan, let her go so we can finish," my mom fussed.

"The fuck is he calling you for?" The sweet vanilla smell of her skin mixed with the mango butter in her hair caused my dick to brush the zipper of my jeans.

Lani shrugged. This nigga Grant was starting to become a pain in my ass. Thanksgiving is a day for family. He could've texted Lani if he wanted to wish her a happy Thanksgiving, but don't blow her shit up. It's a respect thing.

"Nolan Hudson," my mom fussed again.

I took Lani's phone from her pocket and slid it into mine, then I released her. I have to contain myself. Lately, I've been acting out the norm, and I couldn't explain it even if I tried.

Thanksgiving in my family has been the same since I could remember. My mom would start cooking and preparing the night before. Then, she'd wake up early in the morning to finish and put food into the oven. My dad has always fried the turkey and dared someone else in the family to cook another turkey without his permission. It's an unspoken law to never bring a turkey to another Black man's house on Thanksgiving. Dad will bless the food then we would go around the table saying what we're thankful for. That's always my favorite part.

I keep mine simple, "I'm thankful for God, good health, family, and great friends."

"I'm thankful for God, family including everyone here, my career and friends," Lani said while squeezing my hand.

When my dad carved the turkey, it was on and popping. The chatter ceased and all you could hear were the clanking of silverware against the decorative plates which held the food. I was so hungry my stomach was touching my back.

After dinner, there's a Hudson tradition of drawing names for Christmas. Lani was drinking eggnog and whiskey with my dad, throwing it back without a care. She reached her limit two cups in, but she kept drinking. On that note, I retreated to my old room. Laying on the stiff bed looking at the ceiling caught me in my own thoughts about life and family.

Lani's phone vibrated in my pocket. Grant again. "What's up?" I answered slightly annoyed he didn't catch the hint to stop calling.

"Oh, what's up Nolan? Is Malani around?"

"Yea, but what's up, man? It's Thanksgiving."

"I know. Happy Thanksgiving by the way. Malani and I are going for drinks later tonight. I was letting her know my day is going as planned, and I can meet her earlier if she is up to it. I've been trying to reach her all day. I feel like I'm going to be stood up." He chuckled and my annoyance reached a new high.

I blew out a breath, "Lani won't make it tonight, but hey, happy Thanksgiving."

"W—wait," he called out. This nigga didn't quit. "Can I ask why?"

"She's getting sauced with my dad, and I'm not about to have her drinking and driving."

"I could always swing by to pick her up."

"Nah," Just like a cornball ass nigga. Ready to take advantage of my gir—my best friend. Hell no.

"Can you have her call me?"

"Sure," I powered her phone off the second I hung up with Grant. I rejoined the party in the living room. Most of the family had cleared out. That good ole eat and leave shit. Lani was now playing Spades with my parents and Kennedy.

"We're about to head out," April announced.

I gave her a long hug because I didn't know when I was going to see her again. It was nice to have her around the family for at least one holiday. All other holidays she spent with her in-laws. I don't blame her. There are too many memories in this house and with us, it's easier to block it all out if you don't come around. "See you, sis. Travel safe. I love you." I dapped her quiet ass husband. He always seemed uncomfortable around us, and they've been married almost ten years. One of my cousins set a glass in front of Lani, "what's that?" I asked her.

"A gingerbread martini, you want one?"

"Nah, and she don't need one either."

She shrugged, "Nolan, she's grown, and she said she wanted one. What's the big deal?"

It wasn't a big deal if Lani knew her limit, which she does not. I monitor her intake because she over drinks then shows her ass. I'm not going to be her dad tonight, though. I watched her consume drink after drink until she could barely keep her head up. Then, I swooped in like I always do. I carried her to the room, laying her down on the bed and covering her. Before I could walk away, she reached to grab my hand. "Lay with me for a minute." Reluctantly, I did. She laid her head on my chest. "I love you." She spoke low, but we were extremely close; I couldn't miss it.

"I love you, too," slid from my mouth with ease.

In relationships, telling women I loved them was a task I had to coach myself into, regardless if I was feeling it or not. With Lani, it always flowed easily. She first told me she loved me when we were about fourteen, years after losing Liam. I didn't know how I felt about saying it to her. Recapping the times she'd been there for me, I spit it out the next time she said it. I still remember the smile she held on her face.

"No, I love you," she slurred.

That sounded different.

When I looked down at her, her eyes pierced into me. She gently grabbed the back of my neck pulling me down towards her and put her lips on mine.

At first, it was soft, delicate pecks that deepened into our tongues tasting each other for the first time ever. The sweet alcohol coated her tongue, and the remnants rushed into my mouth. My heart raced from the unknown as I closed my eyes, instinctively pulling her body into mine. Lani's lips were like a puzzle piece I've been missing for so long I had no idea where it was, but I knew I needed it to complete the whole picture.

This isn't right, though. She's drunk.

As hard as it was, I pulled back from her, touching her forehead with mine. "Lani, you're drunk." I reminded her. She hung her head, but I lifted her chin giving her one final kiss. "If you weren't..." I licked my lips letting my voice trail off because I didn't know what the fuck I was about to say. I was Lani's best friend, and we cannot take it there and leave our over a quarter of a century friendship intact.

chapter
nine

Malani

Nolan's laughter filled my ears like a melodic tune as it drew nearer. "Are you ready to go?" Nolan's voice was low from exhaustion, his eyes met mine causing butterflies to surface in the pit of my stomach. I love the way he looks at me with so much love and admiration. What my brain couldn't comprehend was—was it friendship or something more? It couldn't be something more, right? Was my own mind still playing tricks on me?

"Where are we going?" I asked, curiously. We hadn't made any plans, the only thing I planned tonight was curling up to a good romantic movie and eating a cinnamon roll with coffee.

"Are you coming or not?" Nolan's annoyance surfacing more than it should have.

Looking away from him I paid more attention to my legs swinging on the side of my bed. If he didn't want to tell me where we were going, then I wasn't going.

Nolan kneeled in front of me clasping his hands on my bare thighs. The butterflies and goosebumps I felt when he was far now surfaced on my skin because he was near. His touch causing a river to form mere inches away from his hands. He was still—not saying anything until my eyes met his. "Kennedy is hosting a game night."

I heard his words, but his touch had my attention more, the way he ran his hands up and down my thighs as he spoke.

Damn, I almost lost it.

A sexy smirk curled at the edges of his lips as I tried to come down from this high. The man was only touching my fucking thighs, and I was ready to come completely and utterly undone.

"What should I wear?" I forced out because he licked his lips before standing.

"Whatever you want." He made his way to my closet, and seconds later, after composing myself—I joined him, looking at my wardrobe, trying to find something suitable.

Kennedy is very prim and proper. We used to hang out when I was ten and she was fourteen, but then she was very much interested in boys as I was not. Kennedy was like a big sister to me because my sister, A'Lisa, was grieving over Liam. So, she stayed in her room the majority of the time. I never told Nolan, but since Liam was mature enough to walk Nolan from school, A'Lisa begged my parents to allow her to walk me home. It was our secret. Every day we followed them to The Bricks. Half of the time, getting catcalled by much older men, it was disgusting, and I hated her for dragging me along. Liam's taste for that feeling grew more and more. He would visit that building in The Bricks every day, multiple times a day. I only knew this because he and my sister called themselves talking. She changed when we got the news he was no longer with us.

On days when I went to the Hudson's house after Liam's demise, it was because I was hanging out with Nolan, but sometimes he would fall asleep or had guy friends from the neighborhood over. Missing my sister, I was left going into Kennedy's room to hang with her. She talked a lot about fashion and design and the importance of always looking your best—something she read in a magazine. Back then, I had Kennedy on one shoulder and Nolan on the other. Dress nicely, she would say and hanging out with boys wasn't a good look in her eyes. Nolan often encouraged me to dress how I wanted, making Kennedy mad when I didn't listen to her.

It's all love now, but I still remember her kicking me out of her room because I wore sweatpants and a t-shirt. I choose comfort over fashion, but if it catches my eye—I throw my money at it.

Kennedy lived across the big bridge on the other side of New Bern. When we pulled up to her house in the suburbs, the ten or so cars surrounding her home were a clue Nolan neglected to tell me, this was an all-out party, probably with some of New Bern's high saditty lawyers and doctors out to play for the night. I cursed myself for not asking more questions. Nolan could rub elbows with anyone, me—on the other hand, not so much.

He parked the car, but I didn't move. He waited about two minutes before opening the door and pulling me from the seat. "What's up?" His knowing smirk made it hard to be angry with him now.

I wanted to tell him to take me home because five to ten people were okay, but an entire house full—no way. Even with a crowd of her friends walking about the open space of her foyer, Kennedy's home was beautiful inside and out.

Paintings adorned the walls, along with new pieces I hadn't seen. Kennedy's an artist of many sorts, a finger painter. It still surprises me someone of her caliber is quick to get their hands dirty. Her home could easily pass for a personal museum with as many of her art pieces gracing the space.

Kennedy's husband, Socari, greeted me and Nolan at the door. "Welcome to game night," he happily announced. I don't know when Socari and Kennedy met. All I remember is her coming home announcing she was married. Seven months later came Anison— hence the shotgun wedding. I hugged Socari, peeled off my jacket, and tossed it back to Nolan.

"Thank you for having us," I showed my manners because Nolan seemed to have lost his. "What games are we playing?"

"All sorts," Socari looped his arm into mine.

Seconds later, I was being tugged backwards by my belt loop.

"I got her," Nolan's voice filled with intensity.

Socari's face was blank. "Oh—kay," he led the way to the dining room, passing several guests.

I shot Nolan a look, telling him to check his rudeness, which he ignored because he always got pleasure from making it clear to Socari he didn't care too much for him.

At the Hudson's house, Nolan had to play along because his parents did not play about being rude to guests, especially family. But far away from the eyes of his mother and father, Nolan's disdain was on full blast.

Light music played in the background as many conversations happened at once. As we walked by, several guests smiled and waved at us, eliciting me to throw my hand up as well. Nolan put distance between Socari and me. Socari isn't weird or anything; Nolan's just over the top. Sure, Socari is one of those people who likes to hug and touch but so does Nolan—at least Nolan's that way with me.

"We have spades, checkers, a bootleg escape room Kennedy set up and—"

"Chess," my eyes glimmering from the two plastic boards set up at the small table across the room.

"Yes, chess. Thank Kennedy for that. We have Monopoly, Tonk, and Uno." Socari explained.

"Ya'll got any food?" Nolan blurted out.

"Food all you think about?" Kennedy chastised her little brother. "We have plenty. Thank you for finally coming to a game night." Kennedy placed a gentle kiss on her husband's cheek.

"Finally?" I questioned.

"We've been doing this for how long, Cari? Two, three years?" Socari nodded his head up and down, squeezing his wife's waist, "Nolan's invite always seems to go unanswered." Kennedy chuckled, but the humor wasn't present. "Mom said I should've sent them to you." She informed me. The vibe was on point here. Of course, I would've come to like one or two with Harmony. An awkward silence gathered around us, "well, mingle and play a couple of games." Kennedy told Nolan the food was in the kitchen before she and Socari walked away, joining another couple playing spades nearby.

Nolan stalked to the kitchen with me on his trail, "after I fix this plate, I'm busting your ass in chess."

I pursed my lips, "you can try."

Kennedy went all out with this spread. Fresh fruit and vegetables, crab salad with crackers, baked chicken tenders, meatballs from the gods, and a slew of desserts.

The night was going good. The partygoers were friendly—not stuck up like I thought. Kennedy and Socari kicked off karaoke, beckoning me and Nolan to participate, but we were heavily into our second chess game. I could not beat him tonight, which pissed me off. My strategy was tight, but he saw through it each time. Frustrated with the fifth loss, "I have to use the bathroom," I informed him. I needed a second. I wasn't at all competitive—if I won a game or two, but losing all five, oh, I was hot. "He had to be cheating. I'm convinced of it," I said to myself in the mirror.

I dabbed water on my face.

Get it together, Malani.

What the fuck?

I didn't lose, not like that.

Not consistently to Nolan.

The doorknob twisting snapped me out of the feelings going through my head. "Just a second," I called out to the impatient guest on the other side of the door. It was not the only bathroom in this big ass house.

"Lani, open the door," Nolan's voice vibrated through the other side. I opened it, taking a step to exit, only for him to gently push me back in by my waist. He looked me up and down like he was drinking me in—maybe I imagined that. A wide grin on his handsome face while I posted up against the cabinet that housed the wash plane sink—not looking at him. He stepped too close, snatching my breath away from me and staring deep into my eyes, "the fuck you mad for?" Placing his hands on either side of me, trapping me within the comforts of his muscular arms. He pulled his bottom lip between his teeth, studying my face for a moment.

Words jumbled in my head, not able to formulate a proper sentence or a response that may add coldness to the warmth his body was illuminating onto me. The bathroom was hot. I swore sweat beads would drip from my face at any moment. I folded my arms across my chest in an attempt to hide my painfully hardened nipples—that wanted soothing from Nolan's tongue. "I'm not mad," came out, not loud, but not a whisper—just enough for him to hear and smirk because he knew I was. I silently prayed the courage clear or dark liquid provided would jump into my body—if it did, oh my God, if it did.

He backed away from me, leaving me cold and wet. "Let's go. Kennedy's wrapping the party up. No time for a rematch. You were going to lose anyway," he taunted.

I rolled my eyes at him leaving the bathroom fed up in more ways than one.

Nolan drove to his house, not asking where I wanted to go. All I could think about the entire ride was releasing the sexual tension he built between us, but that wasn't happening tonight.

Because how could I pleasure myself in his bed?

"That was fun," I said, making small talk.

He undressed down to his boxers and t-shirt, tossing the clothes in the corner of the room—the hamper was literally inches away.

"Yes, surprisingly. I could do it again. Maybe invite Ezeke and Harmony."

"I was thinking the same thing." I undressed, too, sliding against the cool sheets of his bed in my t-shirt and panties. He didn't come to bed right away, saying something about needing coffee. My eyes were heavy as I positioned myself in a spot comfortable enough to close them. Pretending I was asleep when Nolan sunk into the bed, close behind me, cradling my body as I relaxed in his embrace.

"TELL ME I'M CRAZY," my phone was glued to my ear as I awaited Harmony's voice telling me I was indeed crazy. I had to be crazy to think something was happening between me and Nolan. Why else would he hold me last night? We've slept in the bed together plenty of times, but him cuddling me never came about unless I was sad, which was rare. I don't know, since that kiss—it's like something changed between us. I feel the difference. The only thing is, I'm at a cross between knowing if it's a good or bad thing.

"Was he drunk?"

"No, he doesn't drink."

"But you were horny?"

"What does that have to do with it?"

"Because your ass was probably giving off pheromones."

I laughed at her stupid behind, "whatever. I'm telling you, Harms, I know Nolan, and I think he's finally feeling me." The sound of Nolan turning his key in the lock ended the conversation with Harmony. "I'll call you back," I whispered like he was already in the house.

Nolan went to pick up the breakfast order we placed at *The Lounge*. Helping him plate the food, we sat at the kitchen table, scrolling through our emails at first. Seeing the email, I was anticipating generated a smile on my face.

"What happened? Nolan asked, taking a bite of his waffle.

"Nothing," I lied. I wanted to keep this information a secret just in case for some reason it fell through.

"Grant got you cheesing like that?"

Was that a hint of jealousy in his voice? Looks like I've answered my own question—I'm not crazy.

"No," I avoided his stare because I would have given in and told him exactly what I didn't want to say to him.

"Eat up. I'm hitting the court with Ezeke soon."

"And I can't stay here?" I clasped my hands together sitting my chin on top of them to stare at him.

He ran his hand over his face, "you can if you want. I thought maybe you wanted to get your car."

"Oh—right," I said, completely forgetting I rode with him last night.

I didn't have anything to do today. Christmas shopping was on the agenda, but with Harmony working—that's out of the question. I be damned if I go alone or ask Nolan's impatient ass to go with me. I should've gone Black Friday shopping with Kennedy and Mama Steph, but I was too busy nursing a headache.

And reeling from sharing that kiss with Nolan. His lips were soft; everything I'd imagined and craved. I clenched my thighs as I thought back on that day. I haven't brought up the kiss and neither has he. Clearly, we are still very much best friends. It seems like the kiss didn't happen or affect our friendship. Furthermore, it lets me know we can cross the line of friendship.

But why hasn't he ever looked at me as more than a friend?

Never once had Nolan ever approached me outside of friendship lines. Why?

I appreciate him respecting our friendship, but I want him to know me enough to see how I look at him isn't friendly anymore.

The way I light up when he enters the room isn't noticeable to him?

In front of my brick apartment building, Nolan reached over to unbuckle my safety belt then he exited the truck to open the door for me to climb out. "See you later?"

"I don't know. It depends on your busy schedule."

"I'll be over later tonight," Nolan gave me a quick hug I craved lasted longer than it did.

chapter
ten

Nolan

"Ezeke, pass the fucking ball." I yelled across the court. I don't know why I continue to play basketball with this ball-hogging ass nigga. Every game is the same. He's hogging the ball—trying to make baskets to impress the women on the sideline. Hitting the rim each time he put up a shot. I don't bet on games anymore because I know if he's my teammate—we're losing.

"My bad," Ezeke apologized after missing the last shot. I'd worked hard to get us tied with the other team only for him to do some showboating shit and risk it all.

Much like Lani, I hated losing, too. I showed mine differently. Mental notes helped me through, like not being paired up with Ezeke the next time—friend or not, I want to win. Lani was a sore loser, but it was sexy as hell when she walked off from our chess game—hips swaying with each step.

Damn, did I just say that?

By game two, I knew she was pissed. She has a hard time hiding her emotions. I read them all—at least, I thought I did. Lately, it's been weird between us. We are still on good terms but weird. I felt it more at Kennedy's spot. I've been looking at her in a way I shouldn't, and it's scaring me.

70

"Are you going to Lani's after this?" Ezeke asked, sitting beside me while I unlaced my sneakers.

I glanced at him. When I first met Ezeke, I was sure he wanted Lani. Then after a while, he started pressing on Harmony, but still, I have this nagging feeling he feels a certain way about Lani. I know for a fact she only sees him as a friend, so his best bet is to keep on Harms.

"Nah," I placed the sneakers in my gym bag. "Willow's coming over to my place. I might chill at Lani's after that, though."

"Why?" He asked. I didn't like his tone, but I could be imagining things. Maybe I'm just thinking all the niggas I met in college want Lani because Grant all of a sudden does.

"Well damn, my nigga. Do you want to go over there?"

Ezeke held his hands up in defense, "relax. I'm just asking questions, my boy."

I chuckled, "too many questions, but I'll answer because you're my nigga. I like falling asleep next to Lani," I admitted. He shot me a confused look, and I explained further, "we've been doing this shit for years."

"Not when ya'll dating other people?"

"I mean, not when *she's* dating. I'll date and still slide next to her. I guess it's a security thing. She's my security blanket, and I'm hers."

I tried to put it in simple terms for Ezeke.

On the outside, looking in, nobody understands our connection. My friendship with Lani is the most significant relationship I've had in my life. We've grown up together, shared secrets, and built trust between us. I've never had a deeper connection with anyone other than Lani on this earth. She'll be my best woman at my wedding, and I'll be her man of honor, shit—thinking about marriage made my stomach drop.

After leaving the gym, I ended up texting Willow the address to my house. She looked good, the tight uniform was replaced by tight jeans and sweater that exposed a bit of her midriff. I couldn't keep my hands off her and I didn't try. I buried myself into Willow, sinking deep into her core while she called my name mercilessly. She wasn't shy during sex which I appreciated—a woman well attuned with her body. Taking her to reach her peak two more times before I came into the condom. I was spent, between basketball and going rounds with Willow. I needed to take a nap before going to Lani's. Willow's head rested on my chest, "what about next Friday?"

"Huh?" I had no clue what Willow was talking about. She was saying something when we got into my apartment, but I stopped listening when she dropped to her knees, taking me into her mouth.

"You've met my friend, and I want to meet yours."

Willow's friend was a weirdo; she giggled after each sentence. 'It was nice to meet you,' hehe. 'I hope to see you again soon,' hehe.

"Meeting my friends is equivalent to meeting my family. You will officially meet them when the time is right."

Willow huffed but accepted the answer. She had no choice really. This shit was new. I wasn't keen on introducing women to my crew. "Can you tell me about your best friend. The beautiful girl who sat next to you when we first met, right?"

"That's Lani. She's my right hand, my Queen is what I call her sometimes."

"Why do you call her that?"

"Our favorite game is chess." Willow nodded in understanding. "She's been my friend since we were about four years old."

Our parents were neighbors, working hard to provide for their families. Each having children, they connected because my mom was working, and my dad needed to go to work. My mom wasn't going to be home in time to trade us off with him. My dad couldn't miss work, so he asked Lani's parents to watch us. Since that day, they took turns watching all the kids. All of us forming friendships.

"You and Lani always only been friends?" The question I knew was next fell from her lips.

"Yea, best friends."

"What is she like?" Usually, I would get aggravated with these types of questions, but Willow was genuinely curious. I could talk about Lani for days, but I definitely didn't want to have this conversation after drilling her down.

"Stubborn." Willow giggled as I climbed on top of her, laying her back against the soft pillows. "Enough about Lani," Willow reached between us, stroking me until I was hard enough to enter her. Sliding a condom over my erection, a squeal escaped her throat as I pushed myself deeper. I had one more round in me.

My eyes couldn't focus on the bright screen of my cell phone, answering the call without knowing who it was or what time it was.

"Hello?" I answered, clearing my throat.

"Hey," Lani's voice brought me from my land of slumber, the softness causing my dick to tingle. Willow was asleep next to me—rubbing my eyes I looked at the time on the phone. Eleven p.m.

"Damn, I've been sleep."

"I figured. I've been trying to call you."

"My bad," I yawned, tossing my legs over the bed. I went to the bathroom to relieve my full bladder. "Why are you up?" I asked as I washed my hands. Putting the toilet seat cover down, I sat on the lid. "Were you waiting for me?"

Lani smacked her teeth, "no. I couldn't sleep. Then, I remember you said you were coming over, but you're not here."

"Don't I always keep my promises?"

"Do you really want me to answer that?" Lani laughed.

I laughed, too, remembering the one time I broke a promise to her in high school. She was trying out for the varsity cheerleading squad, and I told her I would be there after practice to cheer her on. But unfortunately, I got tied up, too busy doing—well, what I was doing now—chasing ass. She made the squad, though. "Nah, don't answer that."

"Are you coming or not? Harmony's working late tonight. I need to know if I need to lock both locks."

"You should have those locked anyway."

"Nolan," she blew out an aggravated breath.

"Stop pouting. Let me take a shower. I'll be there soon."

IT WASN'T hard getting rid of Willow; she's so understanding.

I grabbed two sodas and a bag of chips with French onion dip from Lani's refrigerator. All requested from her via text.

"You're lazy," I tossed the bag of wavy chips over to her. She caught it mid-air, setting it on the bedside table.

Then, she lifted her shorts to expose her bruised upper thigh. A purple and black oval shaped bruise extended from her thigh stopping short of her knee.

"What the fuck happened?" I grimaced while examining the mark.

She sucked in a breath at my touch, "stupid shit at work."

"Somebody did this shit?"

"No, it's embarrassing, I don't want to say."

I cocked my head to the side, "explain, or I'll be out there first thing in the morning."

"I ran into the conference table, literally ran into it."

When she covered her face, I couldn't stop laughing.

"It's not funny, everybody was laughing at me. I didn't think it would bruise this bad."

"Does it hurt?" I straightened up, rubbing the bruise gently. Positioning myself between her legs to get a better look.

"It's a little sore."

"How about when I touch it?" My thumb ran over the line in the middle of the bruise, the impact point.

She put her hand over mine, attempting to move it, "uh huh."

"Stop," I pushed her hand away. "I got it. I'm not going to hurt you," I massaged the area through her labored breathing. Before I could stop myself, my lips kissed her bruised thigh. "Does that feel better?"

She stared at me with her mouth ajar. Shit, I couldn't believe what I just did. But it felt right.

chapter
eleven

Malani

I stared at Nolan wondering if I imagined what just happened.

Then, he did it again, so tenderly.

I couldn't focus on the slight pain of my thigh because I was so turned on. Getting wetter with each passing second. It felt so awkward sitting there, unsure of what to do with my hands. Coaching myself to not touch. I didn't know what was happening.

Was this sexual?

Is he feeling the same chemistry?

Honestly, I never thought about what it would look like if he started to feel the same way as me. It's been one sided for so long.

Closing my eyes, I drifted away, freeing my mind from anything that distracted me from him. Nolan continued rubbing his fingertips over my thigh like the bruise would magically disappear from his touch.

"You're getting goosebumps."

"It's cold," I countered too quickly.

"Is that what it is?" He sat up leaving me void, going into the bathroom to relieve himself.

My attraction to him pleasurably suffocated me. I was overwhelmed by the attention I was receiving from him. Had he not been standing inches away from me, I would've made myself cum from the thought of him. The thought of his lips on my skin. This is what I yearned for.

After he finished his business, he glared at me from the doorway. "Imma go."

"You don't have to. It's late. And I kinda don't want to be here alone."

Nolan's mouth got my attention when he licked his lips. He chuckled lightly, not laughing at anything in particular. "Slide over."

I did, kind of hurriedly. I had to slow my ass down.

He undressed down to his black boxer briefs and slid against me, his arm wrapped around my waist, holding me in place adjacent to him.

Pushing the limit, I pressed my butt into his crotch—thinking he would pull away, but when he didn't, I couldn't stop the smile that spread across my face.

"How come you always smell so fucking good?" He said lowly into my ear, his soft beard resting against my cheek line.

Then, I felt it, his dick twitched. I was a fucking tsunami now.

I wasn't imagining it. Nolan *is* into me.

The kiss—that kiss, since then he's been different. But since he hadn't talked to me about it, this is only speculation. I feel the shift, but I second guess it every time. I don't want to be rejected, so I'll keep my mouth closed for the sake of our friendship.

The next morning, Nolan kissed my forehead then left my apartment. I wished he'd stayed longer, maybe we would've watched a movie before being forced to face the real world. I hated sitting around. Harmony and I decided to make today our Christmas shopping day by going downtown. "I don't know why you wait to Christmas shop so late." She rolled her neck.

"Because they put all the good stuff out last minute."

"No, they don't. They literally put out all the good deals after Thanksgiving." She chuckled like she's the Queen of Deals. Had I not told her about certain sales at the retail stores, she would be buying last minute gifts right along with me.

"Well, good thing I don't gift for a good deal. I gift from the heart!" I put my hand to my chest and smirked at her.

"You're better than me. Your money is longer than mine anyway."

"Whatever," I replied with an eye roll. "I've been thinking about spending Christmas at home."

"What?" She sang, drawing her head back for emphasis. "Instead of going to the Hudson's? You always go there, ditching *me* half the time."

"Girl, I invite you every year, and you decline, every year. Anyway, I'm thinking about switching it up this year." I thumbed through the clothes on the clearance rack.

"Have you told Nolan about this thought?"

"No. I mean it was just a thought, I kind of just wanted to be in my pajamas and drink wine all day and maybe watch a marathon of Christmas movies."

"Bitch! That sounds like a day for me, but my grandparents would not allow me to stay home. I'm tired of driving back and forth to Greensboro. And your boy is talking about riding with me."

I dipped down low, eye level with the clothes that way Harmony couldn't see me since she was across from where I stood.

"I know it was your idea bitch." She squealed.

"It makes sense."

"To who? Ezekiel's people is way across town from my family. Next time, Imma drag you with me and make you suffer the holiday with my dysfunctional ass family."

"At least——."

"Don't finish that sentence."

I closed my mouth and continued to shuffle through the rows of clothing.

"What do you think about these pants?" Harmony held up a pair of green and black plaid pants with ruffles on the side of the pants legs.

"Cute," I continued to look at more pants on the rack because unlike her, I'm shopping for other people, not myself. "Why couldn't we go to Private Place. I don't like this store."

"Private Place is too bougie for me," she turned her nose up.

"Mama Steph loves all the outfits I buy her from there."

"I'm sorry, but Nolan's mom is bougie as hell. We can go if you want, but I'm grabbing ice cream from Cinnamon Kissed first."

Me and Harmony walked a few doors down to the ice cream parlor. She ordered a double scoop of chocolate, and I got a waffle cone of banana foster. It's something about cold weather that makes you crave ice cream more than a bowl of soup or chili.

"Well damn, look at this." She walked towards the back of the shop to the seating area. Thinking she was finding a place for us to sit until I saw something that almost made the avocado toast I had for breakfast spew from my mouth. "Hello Nolan!" Harmony sung.

"What's up, Harms?" He said annoyed until his eyes bounced to me.

The girl sitting across from him was the beautiful waitress from *The Lounge*. The way she held his hand from across the table let me know it wasn't a friendly encounter.

I stared at the embrace and the familiarity of the two. Trying to will myself not to let a single tear drop.

He looked into my face. He saw my line of sight and moved his hand slightly. "Lani?" He called my name and I never felt so disgusted to hear it fall from his lips.

I've been avoiding Grant since I kissed Nolan and for what?

Clearly, it didn't mean anything to him.

I can play this game. If friends is what he wants, friends will be what he gets.

I smiled, putting on my best face, "hey, friend."

His brows formed a line. His date cleared her throat, snatching his attention. "Do ya'll remember Willow?"

"The girl who had you slobbering all over your breakfast? Of course, we do," Harmony extended her hand to this Willow. "I'm Harmony," she said as she and Willow shook hands.

I followed Harmony's lead, "I'm Malani. It's nice to meet you."

"The best friend?"

Not anymore.

"I've heard so much about you." Her smile was beautiful, inviting, but I wasn't in the mood to receive it.

"I'm sorry it's been one sided. Nolan hasn't mentioned you." That wasn't a jab, it was the truth. We're together every fucking day. I could scream, but that'll just be me overreacting on situations and feelings I've made up in my head.

"That's okay. I'm a firm believer that everything happens for a reason." Willow smiled, grabbing Nolan's hand.

"Bitch, I can't," Harmony said only so I could hear. She walked away claiming she needed to grab more napkins to catch the dripping chocolate.

Nolan didn't look me in the eyes, "come over tonight. I'm cooking dinner, and it's about time you and Willow get acquainted."

He did not invite me to have dinner with him and this girl.

Instead of declining, I said what any friend would, "I'd love to, text me the details."

BEHIND CLOSED DOORS, emotions flooded my entire body. I had tears that could fill three one-gallon jugs.

I've been so stupid this entire time. Fooling myself that he felt for me what I felt for him. He didn't have the decency to tell me he was dating her, even as his friend.

Oh, my God! He was with her last night.

"Are you okay," Harmony knocked on my room door. I was sitting on the floor with my back against the door hoping I could cry in peace.

I don't know what hurt the worst… the betrayal, the thoughts I was having, or the secret I still keep. Honestly, I can't be mad with Nolan. I take responsibility for allowing my mind to wander to what I already knew wasn't real. I psyched myself out, and that's my own fault.

I brought my legs to my chest and wrapped my arms around them. "I'll be okay. I'm about to get ready."

"You're really going?" Her concern was laced with shock.

I nodded like she could see me. "That's what friends do," I chuckled lightly.

Friends—the word at the moment seemed so overrated.

"I'll go with you."

"No, thank you, though. I'll be fine. I promise."

"Can you let me in?"

Harmony's worry projected through her voice. I hated being this fool. When I opened the door, she embraced me tightly. I held the tears, only because I didn't want to go to Nolan's apartment with puffy eyes.

I took a deep breath before knocking on Nolan's door. I could smell the familiar aromas from outside the frame. Nolan's a one-trick pony when it comes to preparing meals. Of course, spaghetti is his meal of choice, but he does it so well. Sautéed onions, peppers, and mushrooms with a homemade sauce. My mouth watered, and I couldn't wait to taste the perfectly cooked pasta with the seasoned sauce.

Willow answered the door pulling me into a hug like we'd been friends forever.

I stiffened at her touch. Nolan never dated the overly happy type. I didn't think he was attracted to women like that. My judgements off though because I thought he was attracted to me.

"Babe, it's Lani!"

Babe?

Lani?

She's too comfortable and why is she answering his door like she lives here?

Nolan's been holding out, but that's okay. He's entitled to do that.

His face dropped the same way mine did earlier when he entered the room. Grant took my coat hanging it on the coat rack with his. I grabbed Grant's hand leading him into Nolan's living room.

"What up, Nolan," Grant greeted Nolan but was greeted with Nolan's clenching jaw.

"Lani, help me set the table?"

"Nolan, I didn't come here to work."

"Lani," he said sternly.

"Okay," I groaned. I slid the remote into Grant's hand before excusing myself.

Instead of following him into the dining area, he pulled me into his bedroom.

"What the fuck are you doing with him?"

"I didn't want to be a third wheel."

"Bring Harmony. You should've asked me first, Lani. I don't like a lot of people in my house."

I stared at my feet, "I'm sorry. We'll leave."

Nolan blew out a breath and ran his hand over his face, "I want *you* here, but I don't want him here. He has to go."

"He's not welcomed as my plus one? So, I'm supposed to sit here and watch you fawn over her all night? If Grant goes, I go."

"Why the fuck..." he paused like he was combing over ideas in his head, "then go."

We looked at one another for a minute. He was serious. His face was screwed up like I'd just spit in his face. He glared at me with anger, a look I've never seen pointed towards me.

"O—Okay," my voice cracked as I walked out the room. Nolan tried to grab my wrist, but I pulled away. He's so fucking selfish, and I'm sick of it. "Grant, I don't feel so well. Can you please take me home?"

Grant quickly stood to his feet, "yeah," he grabbed our coats helping me into mine.

"Do you need any medicine?" Willow offered. "I'm sure Nolan has something you can take."

"Lani?" Nolan called me from the hallway. His eyes were softer. I ignored him.

"No, I just need to rest," I answered Willow.

Grant ushered me out, and I took a deep breath once I was on the other side of Nolan's door.

It's like I've lost my best friend, but this is what we need.

Distance from each other to explore other avenues in our lives.

This entire day has been shitty. Being blindsided by Nolan and

Willow. My heart caved in my chest watching her in his space and him being so open with her so soon.

She's slowly taking my space in his life.

It wasn't like this with other girls. No dinner to meet them or hold friendly conversation with them. It was understood that Nolan was dating, and I occasionally waved or spoke to them but never had to be forced to spend time. We respect boundaries.

ME AND GRANT stood at the landing of my apartment. It wasn't as cold as last night, but that's how North Carolina weather is. One day it'll be sunny but chilly. Then, the next day is a damn icebox.

"Are you coming in for a bit?" Harmony was at work tonight, and I didn't want to be alone.

Grant huffed, "do you want me to come in?" I looked down avoiding his eyes. He stepped to me, closing the space between us. "I get the feeling something's going on with you and Nolan."

"Something like what?" I asked defensively because Nolan always coached me to be. 'Our relationship is nobody's business,' he would say.

He shrugged, "I don't know. He wasn't happy when he saw me with you."

"That's just Nolan being Nolan."

"The way tonight went makes me think it's something more than what ya'll are letting on."

I didn't speak maybe because he's right, but obviously there is nothing between Nolan and me except years of friendship.

"I promise it's nothing."

"Malani, I know history more than anyone. I know it's powerful, and it repeats itself. I like you," he cupped my chin into his hand making our eyes connect.

"But?" I questioned waiting for the excuse of friend-zoning me.

I'm so cool to be liked, but too cool to make it as someone's girl-friend. I'm the homie and I've accepted that.

"No buts. I like you." A smile spread across his lips.

He leaned down, brushing his lips against mine. His tongue parted my lips and tasting his tongue with my own rendered me temporarily foggy. It shouldn't feel this good. I shouldn't be kissing him, but I didn't want to stop. His hands respectively ran up and down my back. Breaking away, I held his gaze.

"So, are you coming in?"

"I really should get going," his mouth said as he followed me into my apartment.

"Can we watch a movie before you go?" I took the smile as a yes. I battled with my head and common sense in allowing him into my room. Ultimately, I pushed it all aside and motioned for him to sit on my bed. The bed that a day ago I laid on with Nolan as he kissed my thigh. Those feelings rushed to the forefront of my mind. As quickly as they came, the quicker I made them go away. I'm done fooling myself.

My phone buzzed signaling I had a text message. I read the message and replied.

"I thought that smile was only reserved for me." Grant stared at me intensely. Under his gaze I felt glued, he was definitely into me, and I should be into him but Nolan.

Ugh, Nolan.

I bypassed the messages and missed calls from Nolan, scrolling to Harmony's name to call her.

"Do you want something from *The Lounge* or not? Bobby is flirting hard as fuck. At this point, I can get whatever I want."

"What's the special?" I put Harmony on speaker, so I could run into the bathroom to change into pajama pants. She suggested nachos. "Not at this hour. I'll take a cinnamon roll." Coming out of the bathroom, I asked Grant, "do you want anything from *The Lounge*? My roommate can pick it up."

He shook his head while scrolling on his own phone. I ended the call with Harmony opting to give Grant my complete attention. "I just ordered something I think you'll like." I hated being surprised, but I didn't tell him.

Forty-five minutes later, Harmony barged into my room as she typically does, not even speaking to me. "Do you have any brothers?" Harmony bluntly asked Grant. He gave her a smile shaking his head. "Cousins?" She pressed.

In my opinion, Harmony was not ready to be in another relationship, situationship, or anything regarding the opposite sex. The last one ended with her so hurt, it hurt me. She hasn't always had the best of luck with guys. Neither have I, but Ezeke wants her badly. I took the bag from her hand as she continued to grill Grant about his single friends and relatives.

The doorbell to our apartment chimed through the air causing Harmony to stop the interrogation. Grant stood, "do you mind if I get that? It's our food." I nodded as I sunk my teeth into the warm, gooey, cinnamony cinnamon roll.

"What happened tonight?" Her voice was low and irritatedly smothered with concern.

"Nolan called you?" I rolled my eyes to the ceiling, taking another bite, this one just as pleasing as the first.

"Called me pissed, talking about, 'talk some sense into your girl,'" she said, mocking him. "And what's his beef with fine ass Grant?" Harmony tossed herself onto the foot of my bed.

"I don't want to talk about Nolan anymore. As far as I'm concerned, we are no longer friends." Shrugging my shoulders, my stomach turned. I went to his contact and blocked him. Fuck him for basically throwing me out of his home. Grant came back with food smelling so good. "That came from *The Lounge*?" I asked identifying the gold bag.

"Kind of," Grant handed the bag to me as he went into the bathroom to grab a towel to lay on my bed. He kneeled by me, and I helped him put the clam containers on the towel, opening each one revealing samosa, chicken curry over a bed of rice, and naan with hummus. The spice crawled up my nostrils and hugged them tightly. The food smelled amazing, but the question still lingered. I looked over at Grant who only smiled at me. "Harmony asked if I had any cousins; well, I got Bobby."

"What?" Harmony and I said in unison.

"He's experimenting with Indian cuisine. I called in a favor."

"Damn, that shit smells good. You mind if I try?" Harmony perched up on the bed.

"Of course, the more…"

I cut him off, "bye, Harmony."

Harmony rolled her eyes, "okay, Mom. I'll leave you two alone." She walked off like she was mad but winked her eye at me when closing the door.

"I love Indian food," I said, and from the way he looked at me told me he knew that already. "How do you know things about me I haven't told you already?"

"What's one of the first things I told you when we first met?"

"I'm beautiful?" I giggled.

He smiled, "besides that."

He waited for my answer not throwing me a bone at all, quizzing me to see if I paid attention to him. "You said you did your research."

Grant nodded with approval, "I like to know all the facts."

"But what if I like to be asked?"

"Then, I'll ask you instead." We dug into the food before it got cold. Bobby did a good job recreating the spice level of each dish. I laid on the bed rubbing my full belly as Grant discarded the empty containers.

"That was so good, thank you." I gushed.

He laid beside me resting on his elbow to look at me. "Would you believe me if I said it was all vegan?"

I laughed, "leave it to Bobby to get me hooked on all the vegan food."

For the remainder of the night, Grant shared stories about his childhood. He's an only child to parents who still lived in Greensboro and worked for the school system as well. Grant's career goal was to become a principal. He had a five-year plan and everything. His goals were intriguing, and I admire a man who knows what he wants in life.

It was close to midnight when he said, "I really should go."

"Or you could stay."

"I don't know if sleeping next to you would be a good idea."

"Why not?"

Grant stood to put his shoes on, "my actions are unpredictable around you, and I'm trying to be a gentleman."

I huffed, "I'll walk you out then," were the words that came from my mouth but not the words I meant. I wanted to lay with him, maybe even cuddle, but if he can't restrain himself then it's good. He's choosing to go.

Sometimes all this girl need is strong arms wrapped around her body. A warm leg to put my cold feet on in the middle of the night. It'll be me and my weighted blanket tonight. Reluctantly, I walked him to the front door.

"Goodnight," Grant lifted my chin bringing our lips together. I instantaneously surrendered my tongue to him, standing on my tip toes and wrapping my arms around his neck. He groaned into my mouth appreciating the effort and access I was giving him. Grant broke the kiss, whispering, "damn," into my ear. He scooped me from my feet. My legs snaked around his torso as he carried me back into my room.

We ended up talking more between kissing sessions. His lips were just so soft and inviting.

With him, I didn't have to worry if he liked me. I also didn't have to hide my attraction to him. It felt good to totally be myself around a guy.

chapter
twelve

Nolan

I called Lani for the fifteenth time today, she's been ignoring my phone calls and text messages. Shit, I even sent her stubborn ass an email that went unanswered for the past couple of weeks. My calls immediately go to voicemail, so I know she blocked me. I fucked up by coming off hard that night about Grant but damn. We've never gone longer than a couple of hours without speaking to each other. I feel like she chose being with that nigga over me, and shit like that don't sit right with me. I've popped up at her house several times, but she never answered the door. Sometimes his car was in the parking lot. Using the key is useless when she's pissed. I attempted to contact her again for the final time before shoving my phone into my pocket.

Lani and I always spend Christmas Eve together, exchanging gifts, watching movies and baking cookies. It seems like this year will be very different. My mom's been bugging me all week about confirming the dish Lani is supposed to bring to Christmas dinner. Every year my family does an organized potluck for Christmas dinner. This year I was in charge of the drinks which I already dropped off to my parents' house. Knowing Lani and I are in a bad space, I'm not sure if she will keep her obligations to my family.

I don't know how to make it right between us if I don't know what the fuck is wrong. She couldn't possibly be mad over me not wanting Grant at my house. Had she told me he was coming I would've had a different reaction but being blindsided, she knew I wouldn't like that shit. I took out my phone to call her again, voicemail.

"Is she still not answering?" Willow lay naked across my bed.

I didn't respond to her because my business with Lani isn't any of her business. With any girl I've ever dated, I never talked about my friendship with Lani. I let them know she's my best friend. If and when she needed me, I was there, but conversations concerning her role in my life and the extent of our friendship was off-limits. I got a lot of pushback from several girls, which ultimately ended our relationship. If they couldn't accept the one female that's been in my life since knee-high then fuck them. I'm not a complete asshole about the situation, though. I do let them know we're friends and nothing sexual happened between us. It's just something about telling females that tidbit made their mind wander to other things, other things I didn't care to discuss because when I say nothing has ever happened between us—that's exactly what the fuck I mean.

The next number I dialed was Ezeke's, "have you heard from Lani?"

"Man don't tell me y'all still haven't made up?"

"No, she's not answering my calls. Have you heard from her?" I repeated myself.

"Yeah, I just had lunch with her and Harmony at *The Lounge* exchanging Christmas gifts."

"Why wasn't I invited?" Over the past couple of weeks, I've noticed they'd been moving shady, and I don't like that shit. Lani and I should know not to put them into the middle of our shit.

"Baby girl wanted it to be just us. She said she would give you your gift on Christmas. Yo, man. Talk to Lani. I can't keep being an errand boy."

"Bro," I walked out the room for more privacy because I can see Willow's ears on high alert. "I don't know how many times I've called Lani over the past couple of weeks. She's not budging. And I don't know what this Christmas day shit is about, but she knows we spent today together, every year no exceptions."

"Well, I guess you're gonna have to pop up on her, my boy."

"Did she say anything to you?"

Ezeke sighed, "come on, anything that girl tells me stays between me and her, you know that."

I did, but shit, the least he could do is help me out. If she was mad at him, I would help his ass out, but I see how it is. "Where is she now?"

"She mentioned going somewhere with Grant, but that's all I can say."

"She's spending time with that nigga on our day?"

"Nolan, Imma say this one more time—"

"I know, I know," I cut him off, "talk to her. I got it."

"Don't you got the baddie from *The Lounge* over there? Spend time with her, and try to talk to Lani tomorrow. This day is done. Let me know when you're free, so I can drop my gifts off to you because I'm staying in tomorrow."

"What happened to going back home?"

"Doing different things this year."

"You're welcome to come to my parent's house."

"I got something set up for myself, so I'm going to enjoy that," he chuckled, and I could only imagine what he was talking about.

All my friends have been very cryptic since me and Lani's little falling out. They don't tell me shit. I feel like I'm the black sheep of the clan. I took Ezeke's advice after calling and texting Lani one last time.

I **WOKE** up late as fuck on Christmas Day to missed calls from my mother asking was I still coming for breakfast. Looking at the time, that ship had sailed. Fucking around waiting for Ezeke to show up last night had me up later than I wanted to be. He finally came around one a.m. We sat outside talking, him mostly about Harmony. I dozed off a couple of times because it's always the same shit. All he has to do is step to her correctly and let her know how he feels. It's not hard if you ask me. But as his boy, I listened and offered advice until four in the morning.

I got dressed and threw all the family gifts into one bag tossing them in the backseat of my car and headed to my parent's house. I called Lani. Again, no answer. No response to the text from last night either. Once I got to my parents' house, I placed my keys by the door and the gifts under the tree. My mother stood in the kitchen staring out the little window over the kitchen sink that looked out into the backyard. I gave her a warm hug and kiss on her cheek. I shifted my eyes to look at all the delicious dishes that graced the modern white marbled island. One dish in particular caught my eye, "Lani's here?" I got excited, hoping to lay my eyes on my best friend. She didn't stand a chance staying mad in my presence.

"No, she's not," my mom busied herself with the dishes, "she stopped by earlier to bring the potatoes and gifts."

"Did she say anything else?" I quizzed, taking a spoonful of Lani's potatoes.

"Did you fuck up?" My father entered the kitchen, "she said you knew she couldn't stay."

"What happened, Nolan?" My mom's tone was way softer than my father's, but it was just as accusatory. They were downright blaming me for Lani not being here when it's her decision. I never uninvited her. She's family. She knows this is where she spends holidays.

Kennedy came in saving me from my parents' unsatisfied glares, "What's going on?"

"Lani's not coming over for Christmas dinner," my mom announced, pitifully.

"Aunt Lani's not coming?" Anison dropped his head, "she always gives the best presents."

"That's not the meaning of Christmas, young man, but she dropped all the gifts off," my dad informed him.

"Nolan, what's wrong? Is she okay? This isn't like her." Kennedy fired questions at me, too.

"That's what I'm saying. My baby looked so sad when she came by this morning." My mom shook her head.

"What did you do, son?" My father glared into me.

There was too much noise filling my ears, too many voices asking questions I didn't know the answers to. I couldn't enjoy Christmas like I wanted because of the drama with Lani. She'd completely turned my family against me, all of them looking at me sideways because she wasn't there. The unknown was my fault no matter the reality. I should've been the bigger person. I should always be the first to apologize and never let Lani stay mad for longer than an hour. I'm exhausted from trying to please them and talk to Lani. The question, 'what did you do?,' replayed in my mind like a broken record.

What did I do? I invited Lani over to get acquainted with Willow. Lani came over with Grant. I didn't want Grant in my personal business, and I wanted him gone. Then, she got all in her fucking feelings and hasn't spoken to me since that night. Before that night we were good, hanging and doing what we always do.

Oh shit, the kiss.

Did that drunk shit mean something to her?

I pulled my phone out, impatiently waiting on the call to connect, "Harmony, I need to ask you a question, and you better keep it one hundred." I sat in the dark in my father's office. It was the only place I could get peace of mind while enjoying the crumb cake Kennedy prepared.

"Hurry up, I'm about to smoke with Ezeke."

"It's just ya'll?" I asked, curiously. It must have been the plans he was referring to.

"Yeah, you know we love cannabis, especially on Christmas."

"What's up, Nolan?" Ezeke said from the background.

"Put me on speaker."

"Already on it, you have two minutes," Harmony sassed. I hated calling her when I couldn't reach Lani, but Harmony answered every time.

"Did Lani say anything to you after we kissed?"

"Wait, what the fuck? *You and Lani* kissed? Ezeke, call her from your phone right now!"

Seconds later I heard the voice I've missed but remained quiet. "Merry Christmas, Ezekiel." Lani chimed into his phone.

I'm glad she's in good spirits, meanwhile I'm racking my brain trying to get us right.

"Merry Christmas, Baby girl—" he said back to her.

"Bitch, fuck that, why didn't you tell me about the kiss between you and Nolan?"

"Harmony?! What are ya'll doing together?"

"We're—" Ezeke started.

"Cut the shit, we're asking the questions here."

"Who told ya'll?"

"Not you and I feel some type of way."

"I—I don't want to talk about it right now. We can talk when you get home."

"I'm good on that. Ezekiel, you talk to her."

"Are you alone?" Ezeke asked Lani. For some reason, I didn't like the way he asked her.

She blew a breath before responding to him, "yes," I was out the door, heading to her place. She was going to talk to me today. My mom stopped me, handing me a grocery bag with a plate I assumed was for Lani. I stayed quiet on the phone as she and Ezeke continued the conversation. "Nolan told you about the kiss?"

"Yeah, why didn't you?" Ezeke pried, not that it was any of their business.

"Because he doesn't…."

"Nolan, we'll call you back," Harmony hurriedly whispered into the phone.

"Nah, wait…" I tried to say, but she had already disconnected the call. I wanted to hear what Lani had to say. I don't what? I sat in the parking lot, getting my thoughts together. I've been angry at Lani for shutting me out all these weeks, and I wanted the anger at bay before I approached her. I feel abandoned by her and don't like the space she creates between us. I've often told her to talk it out before shutting me out.

After twenty minutes of staring at her window, I exited the car. Knocking on the door, I prayed she didn't shut it in my face. Not having Lani in my life makes me appreciate our time together. I needed my friend more than I knew.

"Hey, Queen," I pulled Lani into my arms as soon as she opened the door.

She was stiff for the first few seconds, then wrapped her arms around me. We sat silently next to each other in the living room. Lani tried to hide her misty eyes.

I took her hands into mine, automatically interlocking our fingers. "I'm sorry."

"Nolan, I don't want to be friends with you anymore," her trembling lips said. The words were like staples in my heart. After twenty-eight years of friendship, Lani and I had never spoken those words to each other. It felt like she was breaking up with me, and shit, I could feel my heart breaking.

I looked her over, not knowing what to say, and I didn't want to say the wrong thing. Us not being in each other's lives is non-negotiable. We're locked forever. "What do you want to be, Lani?"

Her eyes finally met mine, "what do you want to be?"

"Is this a trick question?"

She nervously chuckled, "no."

"It's not fair to shut me out for weeks."

"It's not fair we kissed, then you're serious with another girl so quickly." She slid her hand from mine dropping them into her lap.

"Lani, you kissed me!" That did not come out how I said it in my head. It wasn't until her eyes glossed over that I knew it wasn't how she expected I'd react. "Lani," I tried to explain.

"No, you're right. I kissed you, and I shouldn't have. For that I'm sorry."

"I'm not trippin' off the kiss. But I feel like it's something you're not saying."

She shrugged, moving to the opposite end of the couch. I moved right along with her. She's not running from me. "I was thrown off by your relationship with Willow."

"Does me being with Willow bother you?"

"Does me being with Grant bother you?" She fired back at me, ignoring my question.

"You know it does, and I'm not cryptic about it. What's the real issue?"

Lani shrugged her shoulders, "I feel like you hide things from me."

"I tell you everything important. I'm getting to know Willow on a personal level. I promise to tell you every detail from here on out. Now can I have my friend back?" I poked her in the side and was awarded with a smile. I draped my arm around her shoulders to pull her closer to my chest. Kissing her forehead before reaching into my pocket for her Christmas present. I handed her the black velvet box, watching her eyes light up with excitement.

Lani opened the box revealing an eighteen-carat necklace with a lock. Inside was a picture of her and I when we were four years old. Her parents were the ones who provided the photo I needed. On the back read, 'Checkmate, Queen.' Lani wrapped her arms around my neck so fast I fell back onto the armrest. "Thank you so much! I love it!"

"I love you, Lani, for real. I never want to lose us. Do you understand me?" She nodded her head, and I put the necklace around her.

A fire ignited inside me when my eyes zoomed in on the passion mark on the left side of her neck. "What the fuck is this?" I rubbed my thumb over the mark.

She quickly turned her head, "it's nothing."

Why she felt the need to lie to me, I don't know. It only made the anger growing inside of me worse. "You letting him touch you like that?" I bit my lip, holding back what I really wanted to fucking ask.

"We've been spending a lot of time together."

"That's not what I asked."

Lani rolled her brown eyes, leaving my question unanswered, "did you get the gifts I left for you?"

I held out my wrist with the Cuban link silver bracelet that read, 'Mr. Hudson.' I loved this gift and the outfits and shoes she purchased for me. I went to my car to get the gift bags with her clothes and shoes.

Lani and I spent the rest of the night together, recreating Christmas Eve day. We played chess. She whipped up more mashed potatoes and smashed the plate from my mom.

An unnerving feeling kept bothering me the entire night. I didn't like seeing that mark on her. I didn't like knowing someone else had their mouth on her.

Earlier, I wondered if the kiss meant anything to her. Now, I think it solidified something within me.

chapter
thirteen

Malani

Nolan's head laid across my thighs. He was holding onto my waist tightly in his sleep. I ran my hand through his charcoal black coils pulling a smile from him in his slumber. His embrace brought comfort to me, so I didn't move. Instead, I allowed myself to enjoy his touch just a little while longer. There is so much I wanted to tell Nolan, but I would rather hold the words to myself. I can't break our bond when it's already on unstable ground.

I was fifteen when I realized I was in love with Nolan. We were going into our first year of high school, and I was nervous about the first day. He walked with me to each class and sat with me at lunch. Nolan was popular, but I wasn't. I was the girl they knew hung around Nolan, but they saw it more as pity. I hadn't blossomed, so guys weren't looking at me. Girls only wanted to be my friend because they thought it would get them closer to him. Nolan would drape his arm around my shoulders as we walked in and out of school. I felt secure with him. We started hanging out more and more around this time. He'd spend the night at my house when my parents worked late, and I'd spend the night at his when his parents worked late. I would get mad if I couldn't hang with him. I'd watched enough romance movies to know what love looked like, which was what me and Nolan possessed.

I knew I had to keep it a secret. One day when I was hanging out at his house, he'd invited some of his friends from class over. A loudmouth, Seven Miller, sparked a conversation with Nolan when I got up to get snacks for the group of four. "What's up with you and her? She clearly likes you, man," he cackled along with the other boys.

I stood by the door and heard Nolan laughing, "nah, she's just a homie." My heart split. I vowed to keep it to myself until I met Harmony and Ezeke in college. Nolan went to college in the same town but a different college, so we spent many weeks not being around each other. When we spent time together, we always lay on my dorm room bed because it was our norm. Our closeness was second nature, but it raised questions for Harmony. Nolan hung out in our dorm so much he and Ezeke, whom I met in Art Appreciation, started to hang out. Our duo became a foursome, and we've been solid ever since.

***

"WHAT ARE YOU THINKING ABOUT?" I hadn't noticed Nolan looking at me until he spoke. He nestled closer to me, his long body draping from the small sofa. I could tell from the dark spots under his eyes he needed a few more hours of sleep to be completely rested.

"I was thinking back on our college days."

He touched the corner of my mouth, drawing attention to the dried drool from my slumber. I turned away shyly, but he caught my chin guiding me to look down at him. "Are you wondering why I never introduced you to Grant?"

"No, because our entire friendship we've only shared my friends."

"Why do you think that is?"

I shrugged my shoulders.

"It's because I trust your judgment. You don't allow too many people to get close to you, taking your time to feel people out before you call them your friend. I always admired that about you."

My lips curled into a smile.

He admires me. That within itself rendered me to gush.

"Do you have an extra toothbrush?"

"Yeah, I think so," I bounced my knee, so he could lift his head for me to rise from the sofa. I rummaged through my cabinet in my bathroom until I found an unopened toothbrush. I was down to my last one. I needed to remind myself to get more. I could hear Nolan opening and closing cabinets in my kitchen. I was directly behind him when he opened the refrigerator. "Here you go," I said, extending the toothbrush to him.

"You must be hiding the food somewhere because your shit is bare. What the fuck Lani?"

I was ashamed because I hadn't been shopping. Harmony's been working so many overnights. I always order from *The Lounge*. I've missed a few trips to the grocery store, so what? Grocery shopping is supposed to be done with him anyway. I bet he has food. Did I cross his mind when he was shopping?

"Lani, you barely have milk. Go get dressed," he demanded.

"I'll order and have it delivered."

"No, we're going out."

I didn't have any intention of leaving my house today. The day after Christmas is always my cleanup day, but Nolan insisted.

Shopping was fun. Spending time with Nolan was what I really enjoyed. Laughing and planning meals together for the week. If only we were doing this as a couple, I would be completely over the moon. After getting essentials for my house and Nolan's, we ended the day at his place, eating popcorn and watching horror movies. Laying in his bed felt weird because I knew Willow had the pleasure of experiencing him in a way I'd only dreamt.

I leaned against Nolan's bare chest, and he reacted by tossing his arm over my shoulder, pulling me into him. He rested his chin on the top of my head. "I like when you wear your natural curls."

Wearing my hair in its natural state was pure laziness because I didn't feel like straightening my hair or going to the salon for a blowout. Wash and go's and twist-outs have helped me for the past weeks.

My fingertips circled Nolan's abs, and his heart rhythm deepened under my touch. He grabbed my wrist, "you can't be doing that." His tone was direct. I would bet all the money in my bank account—I heard a bit of flirtation. I wasn't hearing things, not this time.

"Well, can you put on a shirt?"

"Nah, keep your hands to yourself." He dropped my wrist, focusing his attention back on the movie.

My brow creased as I adjusted in the bed away from him. With a slight change in my mood, I, too, focused on the movie. Constant rejection from this man, although the touch was innocent.

"Do you want to watch another movie?" Nolan asked.

"No," I stretched, faking a yawn. "I'm getting sleepy. I should go home. Plus, Harmony is coming home later, and we have to work out why I didn't tell her about the kiss." I rolled my eyes at him for divulging the information.

What was I going to say to her anyway? I kissed Nolan, but he acted like it didn't happen. It was embarrassing to me, and I felt even more rejected. The kiss was powerful, but it sucks harder than the vacuum attached to the cannula when you're the only one to feel it.

"Why didn't you tell her? I thought ya'll shared everything."

I shrugged, "I never got around to it."

"Bullshit, Lani, I know you better than anyone. When something happens, no matter if someone says to not tell anyone. You will at least tell one person. What's different with the kiss?"

Here we go.

"Did the kiss mean anything to you, Nolan?"

"I don't know."

I stood defeated because how could he not know? He, who knows me better than anyone on this earth, doesn't know.

"Did it mean something to you?"

"You tell me," I countered, sliding my feet into my boots.

Nolan sat at the edge of the bed, inches away from me. He took my hand, and I stood between his parted legs, looking down into his brown eyes. Nolan held my gaze as he stood, towering over me. "I think it did," he flicked his tongue out his mouth to wet his lips. My eyes immediately dropped to those succulent lips, compelling them to touch mine. "How long?" Nolan's hand caressed the back of my neck, quickening my breaths.

"For what?" I pushed out, closing my eyes for a brief moment when he stepped even closer to me.

"How long have you been feeling me?" His eyes spoke to my soul as I melted into his arms. My legs felt like they were going to give out at any moment. I must be dreaming. I had to have fallen asleep while watching the movie. But, Lord, if this is a dream, please don't wake me until it's complete. Nolan's hands were on either side of my face drawing me near to his, "how long?" He whispered.

I succumbed to Nolan's presence, close to me, intimately. The smell of his cologne invited me to breathe it in over and over again. His soft hands warmed my milky brown skin and his voice traveled to the depths of my being, vibrating throughout my core.

"I'm not feel—" his mouth against mine interrupted the lie that was going to spill from my lips. I pushed up on my tip toes as he slid his tongue against mine. My knees buckled, causing Nolan's arm to circle my waist to keep me steady against his hard chest. I suckled on his tongue, cementing this moment in my mind. I wanted to leave a lasting impression if this was the last time we kissed. Breaking the kiss momentarily, Nolan sat on the bed, pulling me down to his lap. I straddled his waist, returning to his unbelievable lips—my heart pounding in my ears as our lips enjoyed each other's. A flood of familiarity and heat crawled up my back. His lips were pillow soft and his tongue tasted of the buttery popcorn. I tried to consume the taste from his tongue—replace it with my own essence. It wasn't enough, I wanted Nolan to taste me every time he swallowed. I wanted his scent coming out of my pores so I could enjoy the smell every day.

Nolan gently bit my bottom lip, pulling a moan from my throat as the pleasurable pain passed through my body. I was more than wet, damn near climaxing. He attacked my lips once again, and I folded into him as his hands roamed my body, squeezing my butt between rubs.

The doorbell halted his movements, and he cursed under his breath. I planted slow kisses on his neck, "Lani, that's Willow." I reared back to look him in the face, his eyes exposing disappointment, "I forgot she's spending the night."

Fuck!

Willow was nonexistent in this world we created around us.

My brows furrowed as a frown appeared on my face, "you're kicking me out? After..." I stopped myself from further embarrassment. Sliding off his lap I bit my bottom lip as I gathered my things.

Nolan grabbed me before I could get out the door. He put his forehead against mine. "I don't want you to go."

"Are you going to get rid of her?" A glimmer of hope passed through me, but it was gone as soon as it came.

"She's already here. I can't do that." He cupped my chin, trying to kiss me again, but I put my hand on his chest, stopping him.

I stared up at him with glossy eyes before walking away.

I gave Willow a quick smile letting her into her man's apartment as I walked out with my tail tucked between my legs. Anger seeped through my pores as I drove home, alone with his scent all over me.

I hate this.

When will this end, Malani?

You cannot keep putting yourself through this.

After years of not knowing how I feel about him, he finally gets it but kicks me out when she comes. It was supposed to be our day. At least, that's what he said. How could he forget she was coming over? Why am I accepting being second in his life? She isn't the problem. He is. I hope Willow can be all he needs because I can't be anymore. I parked in front of my building, but instead of going in— I let all the emotions pour out my eyes.

Might as well call me unlucky Malani.

I called Harmony for support, "what bitch?" She said with attitude, still mad with me about not telling her about the kiss.

"Harmony," I sobbed into the receiver.

"I'm on my way," she said. I reclined the car seat as I waited for her to come home. My eyes were heavy and sore. "Get out of the car," Harmony tapped on the glass. Opening the door, she gave me the hug I needed. My cries grew louder the tighter she hugged me. Just a few weeks ago this was me consoling her. "Do I need to fuck Nolan up?" I shook my head as we went into the apartment. Her already knowing the reason for my tears was an issue. I've been on an emotional rollercoaster with Nolan this year. I'm ready to get off. Especially if he's unwilling to be what I want him to be. "What did he do?" I went on to tell her about the day with Nolan when my phone rang. It was him. "Answer it," she urged.

I didn't want to, but I did. "Hey, Nolan," trying to sound upbeat but failing miserably as my eyes watered.

"Hey, I didn't want to have any bad blood between us. But we do need to talk about what happened tonight."

I sighed, "there's nothing to talk about. Enjoy the night with Willow."

I sounded bitter—bitter as fuck, but shit, I was.

"Lani, we crossed the line tonight. I don't…."

I interrupted him, "you don't what? Want to be with me like that? Cool, I understand."

I didn't understand. I expected this to be his reaction, though. Crazy thing. He kissed me tonight. He initiated the moment and now he's reneging in the aftermath. Warm tears rolled down my neck, "you asked how long I've been feeling you, and the answer is —I've always wanted you. When I realized I loved you more than a friend was freshman year of high school, but Nolan I can't do this anymore." I hung up before he could say another word. I laid my head in Harmony's lap and cried again, tossing my phone onto the coffee table. I wasn't eager to answer his call.

"Are you really done?" Harmony asked after the tears and sobs subsided. I nodded my answer. "Are you done being his friend *and* pursuing him?"

I nodded again, "why?"

"I'm making sure because we've been down this road before,

and Nolan always does something to catch you up again. This isn't love."

Sitting up, I asked, "what do you know about love?"

Harmony chuckled, "enough to know, this ain't it."

A fire rose in my belly, and I spit it from my mouth, "you don't know shit about love. Love looks you in the face every day, and yet you look the other way. You are just like Nolan. You are the desired one. You don't understand my pain. You don't understand how hard it is for me to give him up. The pain of rejection and not being good enough for the one you want. Your words are useless to me." I stormed towards my bedroom, leaving Harmony with a stupid look on her face.

She didn't know shit and fuck her for thinking she did.

WHEN I AWOKE, my head felt like someone was literally walking on it the entire night. Nolan's calls didn't stop last night. I had to power my phone off to charge it. Harmony was still on the sofa when I dragged myself to the kitchen for coffee. We had matching dried tears on our faces.

I called Dr. Cooper, requesting to come in later this afternoon when the headache subsided. He instructed me to stay home but to log into the portal to confirm appointments for tomorrow. The fact he's a chill boss brightened my day a little.

While I prepared the Kona coffee my parents sent me from Hawaii, I returned the call from Ezeke, informing him of what transpired between me and Nolan last night as well as me and Harmony. Of course, he was concerned about her. I let him know she would be fine. People like her and Nolan always bounced back.

Grant called while I was on the phone with Ezeke. Ending the call with Ezeke, I answered as cheerfully as I could muster. "Hey!" I held the mug to my lips, sipping the hot, dark liquid. "I thought you lost my number," I teased. After the night of the disastrous dinner party and the night we spent together, Grant basically ghosted me. Then, he invited me to a play but canceled at the last minute. It should've been a red flag to me but reeling from Nolan—I need this distraction.

"I apologize. I've been sick. That's why I couldn't take you to the play."

"Oh no, are you okay?"

"I am now. I wanted to talk to you. I thought about texting, but I would rather hear your voice." I blushed, taking another sip. "Please tell me you're free later because I miss your face."

Harmony stirred, so I took the conversation into my room. "I can be free. It depends on what you're planning."

"Dinner at my place?"

"When?"

"What time do you want to eat?"

"Send me the address. I'll come over after I check things off my work list."

"See you soon, Malani."

Confirming appointments was the most annoying part of my job. Patients never answered the phone or responded to the text and emails I sent from the office but would get mad if they missed the appointment. Dr. Cooper has a strict policy. If patients are five minutes late, he asks me to reschedule them. They wouldn't get mad with him but with me. I've been called every name in the book by patients who switch all the way up when the handsome surgeon walks into the room. Looking over the schedule, we have busy weeks coming before the conference. Women and men want to be snatched before the new year. I emailed Dr. Cooper the time I spent working so he could enter it into the system. He responded immediately, asking me to reach out to a patient who claimed she had a bad experience in our care. It was his job, but I'm a team player, so I called her and listened to her complain about me, to me. It was hard, but I kept my composure and professionalism as I apologized and offered a free consultation in the future. Most of the complaints consisted of the women wanting to be alone with Dr. Cooper during the consultation, and my presence bothered them. I literally say nothing during the consultation, even when Dr. Cooper asks me a question. My job is to ensure his professionalism stays intact because some patients throw themselves at him. I've been called the 'body-guard' since he arrived at our hospital and chose me to work under him.

I took a nap before getting dressed for dinner at Grant's. His house was conveniently around the corner and down the street from me. Taking my coat at the door, he welcomed me into his place. His home was beautiful, with marble flooring, high ceilings, and vast open space between the kitchen and living room. The place had renovation written all over it, and I appreciated the aesthetics gracing the walls. Grant put his hand on the small of my back, guiding us over to the candlelit table. I sat in front of the white crystal plate as he rushed to the kitchen.

"Close your eyes," he requested, and I obliged. I could hear him putting the food onto the plate and wanted to peek, but I behaved. "Open," before me were two slices of pizza.

"Fancy," I laughed. "Did you prepare this yourself?"

Grant joined me in laughter, sitting in the vacant seat across from me, "you see what happened was—I tried cooking a pasta dish recipe I got from Bobby. I put on the pasta and forgot about it. I'm sorry."

"Never be sorry for trying to impress me. This is perfect!"

"This just means I get a re-do," Grant smiled.

I find myself enjoying every conversation I have with Grant. He cleared my mind from Nolan. I didn't think that was possible. The upside of this evening was *The Lounge's* cinnamon roll he got for dessert. Grant's attentiveness earns him brownie points. "You know what I couldn't stop thinking about?" We sat on the brown leather loveseat.

I shook my head.

He pushed his glasses up the bridge of his nose, "your smile, it's beautiful like you. I want to see more of it."

"You will," I smiled at him, becoming more relaxed and comfortable in his presence.

chapter
fourteen

Shit! I couldn't focus on Willow.

My mind was strictly on Lani. That kiss fucked me up, and now she's being stubborn and taking what I said out of context. Her lips are fucking insane though. I could still feel them on mine. Crazy shit is Lani never showed or verbalized any attraction to me. Why now? Lani has been very selfish this holiday season. This year I've struggled the most I've ever had since losing Liam. Every year is different, but the weight of it all pulls me down further as the years go by. Lani has been adding to that stress. Chasing her, calling and texting her all day long, only for her not to answer. When I need her, she ignores me. A simple conversation could solve every minor infraction we go through. I hate she pushes me away.

"Did you hear me?" Willow's hands planted on her hips as she stared into my blank face. "I said they called me into work this morning. Will you come by to see me later?"

I nodded, "How long are you working?"

"I don't know. Mr. Bobby said it's really busy, which is unusual on a Tuesday." I wrapped my arms around her waist from behind, kissing her neck as she wiggled free from the hold. "Please come see me later. I like you being there." She kissed me before rushing out of my apartment.

Willow had my attention as long as I could keep my mind from wandering to Lani. She's a cool woman—freaky like I like but also conservative. The more time I spend with her the more I like her. From our conversations to the sex. Then, there's Lani, not like I have to choose between the two because the choice would be obvious.

I called Lani again. No answer. I hear her voicemail more than I hear her actual voice. I threw on some clothes and headed to the hospital. I needed to put my eyes on Lani and also discuss what the fuck happened last night.

"How can I help you, handsome?" The mahogany-toned nurse at the desk asked when I made it to the hospital's third floor.

"I'm here to see Malani Dawson."

"And you are?"

"A friend."

"No baby, what's your name?"

"Nolan."

"All right, Nolan, Miss. Dawson is in surgery. She will be out shortly. I'll show you to her office." I followed the nurse to Lani's office.

Stepping inside, I realized I hadn't been to her job in a long time. Lani periodically comes by the school to watch a lecture, but I haven't been a supportive friend by coming to her place of business. Pictures of us throughout the years adorned her walls and desk. Nostalgia ran over me as I browsed pictures I hadn't seen in a long time. I should've shown up with flowers or some shit. Maybe that would've been too much.

Lani's voice made my ears rise—I sat on the edge of her desk, awaiting her entrance. For some reason, I was nervous as fuck. As my eyes roamed her in those pink scrubs, the nerves instantly went away. She's always been beautiful; there's no doubt about that. Knowing how she tasted made me want to explore more parts of her body.

She rolled her eyes when she saw me. "Hey," she leaned against the closed door. She looked exhausted from the dark spots under her golden-brown eyes.

"Come here," I held my hand out to her.

She accepted. I pulled her close to me. I didn't know what the fuck I was doing, but it felt familiar. I've never been the guy to shy away from a woman, especially Lani. Had I known she felt a way about me, things could have been different a long time ago. I hugged her, and this hug felt way different from the many hugs we had shared in the past.

"What are you doing here?" She stepped back and slid her hands into the pocket of her scrub pants.

"I can't come see you?"

"Nolan," a warning in her tone told me to cut the bullshit.

"I'm sorry about last night."

"Which part?"

I looked into her eyes, "the part when you left."

Lani scoffed, "you mean when you kicked me out."

"Chill on that. I didn't kick you out. I felt like shit when you left, so I came to take you to lunch."

"I already ate."

"Coffee then," I suggested.

She sat down in her office chair behind me. "I'm okay, really. I have a lot of work to catch up on before the conference next month. Dinner is at your house tonight, right?" I nodded, "are we having guests?" She switched up quick. I hated when she did that.

I rounded the desk and stood beside her chair, "just us." I lifted her chin to meet my eyes, "I'd love for you to tell me how you feel about me." She swallowed hard, "I want to hear from your lips." I ran my thumb over her bottom lip.

Too much? I didn't fucking care. Her not saying shit all these years got us here.

"Not here," her voice was barely audible.

"Nah, right here." I spun her chair around and then dropped down in front of her. "High school? Why didn't you say anything?"

"Because you didn't feel the same."

"How do you know?"

Lani chuckled, "I know *you*, sometimes better than you know yourself. I've always been your best friend first. I couldn't tell you and mess up the relationship."

I thought about my next words before I said them. I didn't want to hurt Lani's feelings or cause more friction. I placed her in the friendship box because I thought that's where she wanted to be, and she never fought her way out. We've had plenty of opportunities when we were younger. She just didn't take advantage of them. I'm not a fucking mind reader. I've always operated the same, tell me what you want. It goes to show, me and Lani don't know each other like we think we do.

Truthfully, I'd never seen Lani more than a friend up until that first kiss. We've been close physically, mentally, and emotionally; that's our friendship.

"How do we move forward?"

She shrugged, "maybe, we'll stay friends."

My eyebrows became one with my hairline. "Friends? Are you saying you don't want more than a friendship from me?" I was genuinely insulted while I pointed in between us. "You don't want to explore this?"

"I'm saying, you have Willow, and I have…" she paused, looking away. "I have Grant, and it's unfair to them."

I breathed air, scrubbing my hand over my face, "Lani, I want *you*. I'll choose you over anybody, Willow included."

"Friends," she replied with finality. "I promise nothing will change with our friendship. We can still hang out and do what we always do." I scratched the back of my head as her words hit me like a stack of textbooks.

Why the fuck would she kiss me? She got me thinking about us then shut me down like a regular nigga in the street. Lani and these games got to go. We're too old for this dumb ass back and forth shit.

Allowing her to have this moment, I left the hospital feeling like shit. At least I was able to talk to her, though.

I fucking hate this arrangement. Even more I had no choice but to go with it.

It's like I'm on a deserted island, mouth dry from lack of water, then someone dangles a glass of iced cold water on a fishing hook, but when I go to grab it—something knocks my hand down.

How can I continue to hang with Lani when I want to kiss and hold her all night? This must be how she felt all the years she wanted to be with me.

Damn, life is so fucking crazy. I needed someone to talk some sense into Lani and see that giving us a chance is best. I called Harmony only to be sent to voicemail, not once but twice.

Ezeke's the next best thing to get through to Lani. "Ezeke, I'm feeling Lani." Blurting the shit out felt foreign.

"What? Run that by me again," his cackling filled the inside of my truck. I repeated myself but realized how foolish I sounded since she basically friend-zoned my ass. "Have you told her?"

"Yeah," I turned into *The Lounge's* parking lot staring through the dim windows hoping Willow hadn't seen me pull in before I could get my mind right.

"What did she say?"

"She wants to stay friends. Spitting me some shit about it not being fair to Grant and Willow. First off, fuck Grant!"

"And Willow?"

"That's complicated."

"How?"

"I like Willow," I admitted.

"More than Lani?"

"Hell no, I love Lani."

"As a friend or something more?"

I honestly couldn't answer that. All this shit is new and being conflicted with my feelings for her is also new. There's no question in my mind I love Lani.

"I don't know, man."

"Do you think she deserves you waffling with your feelings for her? My boy, she put you in the friend-zone because she doesn't trust it yet. Make her trust it."

Shit! That psychology degree is working out for my boy. He's right. I have to fight for Lani.

He put me on hold to answer a call from Harmony. "I'll call you later. She's upset because she and Lani got into an argument."

"Last thing," I called out before he could end the call. "Talk to Lani for me."

"I got you."

I felt I was making a mistake with each step I took toward *The Lounge's* entrance. It almost feels like I'm cheating on Lani. What am I to do with this newfound interest? Willow greeted me with open arms, kissing me, then guiding me to the booth I shared with Lani on many occasions. Willow scurried off, returning with a plate of pancakes she placed in front of me.

I don't eat pancakes. Willow didn't know that, but Lani does.

"What time do you get off?"

"Three. It has calmed down a lot since I first got here."

"What are you doing later?"

"I was hoping to come back to your place," her cute ass licked her lips making my dick twitch.

I pushed the plate aside, "I'm actually having dinner with Lani tonight."

"Cool, we can play chess. I've been waiting to see if she's as good as you say she is because I think I can beat her."

Willow was so eager, which I like about her, "not tonight. We're laying low."

"Well damn, don't you think you spend enough time with her?" Her question was innocent, but it still rubbed me the wrong way. "She was just at your house last night. I want to get to know her, but I have the feeling she doesn't like me."

"Lani does like you." Well, I think she does.

"Then, why hasn't she rescheduled the dinner to get to know me? Babe, I want to bond with your best friend." She held my hand, "I'm sorry if I'm laying all this on you."

"I'll ask her if she wants to meet up with you later this week, but tonight it's just me and her, okay."

"Okay, let her know I'm off on Friday. What are ya'll having for dinner?" I ran down the menu with Willow and chatted with her until Bobby called her back into the kitchen. I left on that note, texting Lani to pick up the fries we forgot when we were grocery shopping.

SCHOOL RESUMES NEXT WEEK, which meant I needed to look at the upcoming lesson plans. My students surpassed the timeline I set for them at the beginning of the school year. I could add a lesson they will learn in high school. I love preparing them for the next level and growing their minds so that when they get to high school, they will already have exposure to the material beforehand. I combed through the plans before Lani walked into the apartment carrying more grocery bags than I expected.

"What's all this?" I asked. We'd just gone shopping. I didn't need anything this soon. "And why didn't you call me when you pulled in?"

She sheepishly bit her lip, "I had a taste for brownies, then I wanted ice cream, so I got it all." Lani unloaded the bags onto the counter and pulled out all the dishes she needed for our dinner. "Are you helping?"

I shook my head, "I'll find a movie. I'm not cooking shit."

"How did I know that? Can you at least wash and season the chicken so I can make the brownies?"

I felt a magnetic pull to Lani, wanting to touch her every chance I got. I stayed with her in the kitchen the entire time as she fried the chicken wings, cut the potatoes for French fries, made the homemade ranch sauce and brownies with marshmallows and chocolate chips. Even though she was in my presence, jealousy itched my hands when she received the phone call from Grant. I made so much noise in the kitchen, tossing pots and pans into the sink and shuffling the silverware until she ended the call.

We basically ate dinner in silence, only making small talk about how good the food was. The doorbell rang, and I glanced at Lani. If she invited Grant over to my shit again, he and I were going to have a serious conversation.

She shrugged as she dipped the chicken wing into the ranch

sauce before taking a bite. A small amount of ranch dripped onto her chin. I swiped her chin with my thumb, removing the ranch and licking the contents away.

"Check, Queen," the ball is in her court regarding us taking it to the next level. The doorbell chimed again, and irritation flooded through my body as I went to see who was on the other side of the door. "Fuck," I mumbled when I looked out the peephole to the person standing at the door.

"Who is it?" Lani asked with a mouth full.

I regretted the words I was about to say because I knew our night would end. "Willow."

Lani chuckled, "let her in."

I wanted to pretend I wasn't home but didn't want to hurt Willow's feelings. Shit, I didn't want to hurt Lani's feelings either. Having never been in this situation before, stuck between someone I knew I loved and someone I'm getting to know and like. The extra people in our lives complicate Lani and I being together. In a way, she's right; it's unfair to Willow and Grant, but also, at the end of the day, we need to put our needs and wants above someone else's. Against my better judgment, I opened the door as my heart rate climbed to the roof.

"Hey, baby," Willow greeted me with a kiss. The plastic chess set and a bottle of wine she was holding poked my chest. "Am I too late for dinner?" I stood there in silence, both appalled by the cheap ass chess set and her presence.

I made myself clear tonight was me and Lani only.

"You kind of missed it, but Nolan eats slow. He still has food on his plate," Lani said from behind me. I noticed she had her coat and shoes on with the pan of brownies wrapped in foil. "I'll leave you two lovebirds alone." I gave her a look that asked her where the fuck she was going. "I'll see you on New Year's Eve?"

"Are you leaving already? I thought we could get a game of chess in." A frown crossed Willow's face.

Lani observed the box of chess and looked at me. She nibbled amusedly on her lip, then looked back at Willow. "Another time." Lani walked out the door as Willow came in.

I stepped out with Lani closing the door behind me, "why are you leaving?"

"I have work early in the morning." She started to walk away but turned back around. "Nolan, I don't wanna make it seem like you have to choose between spending time with me over spending time with Willow. But, of course, you spending time with her is a priority. When the plans we make can't be fulfilled, I understand."

"Why are you saying this?" I shoved my hands into my pockets as the cool air cut through us.

"Whenever we hang out, I feel like I'm taking you away from her. So, we can hang out when we can. It'll be like every other time you had a girlfriend."

"Swear me and Willow didn't have any plans tonight. She just popped up."

"Which is fine, she can do that." Lani inhaled and closed her eyes on the exhale, "I'm not mad with you, I'm mad at myself. We had to physically connect for you to show some type of attraction to me. I knew I wanted you without that because you're you. Don't think you're doing me any favors by claiming you like me back. I'll be okay either way."

"But I do, and if the kiss cleared my vision, so what? I see it now."

"That's not good enough for me," her eyes met my gaze. "Checkmate."

"Nah," I grabbed her elbow, pulling her back to me. I leaned down close to her ear, "you can't run from me forever." Pulling up to stare into her eyes, tears were falling onto her face.

Shit, I wanted to kiss her tears away. I wanted to hold her until she recanted her statement of only being friends. I could never be that type of friend to her again. Her concern is valid. I didn't know, but also, I didn't know that was a line I could cross. If she'd 'Red Rover' me, I would've come full speed—not caring to break the chain because I would've willingly joined her.

Each of our older siblings coupled off when we were younger, but me and Lani built mountains on our already strong friendship.

How was I wrong if I thought our bond was different from our siblings?

"Lani, you're mine, always have been, always will be."

"Show me," with that she walked away. I swore a smirk replaced the drying tears.

She might not know it now, but I planned on showing her just how the romantic Nolan gets down. I will get Lani by any means necessary.

chapter
fifteen

Malani

Nolan's face flashed in my mind as I slid my panties down my thighs. Wetness was already forming between them, thinking about the kisses we shared. I licked my fingertips before caressing my bare flesh. His smile invaded my thoughts as I circled my swollen bud, applying enough pressure to make my legs tremble. I whispered his name repeatedly until I climaxed, a temporary high only to be left empty.

Turning over, I cried silently in the darkness of my room.

Nolan didn't understand how I was feeling, and I didn't have the energy to explain it to him.

Grant's a good guy—right? He likes me, and he's caring and intelligent. He has all the qualities that made me fall for Nolan, but why can't I focus on him? I usually seek advice from Harmony at times like this, but since the other night—I haven't seen or spoken to her. I assume she's crashing at Ezeke's since she had to call him crying. Ezeke would welcome her with open arms. When will we stop looking out for the ones that knowingly deny our love? I love Ezeke, but he's a fool if he keeps waiting on her.

This new year, I will not shed any tears over Nolan Hudson. I promise my career will be my main goal for the new year since Dr.

Cooper was opening a private practice and asked me to join him. After he told me his plans, he couldn't get the entire question out before I said yes. He still wants me to consider becoming a surgeon, but I enjoy working with him. I'm not convinced about the whole surgeon prospect.

I dialed Grant, hoping we could catch a movie or dinner before he went in. He's been working on activities for his class for the upcoming semester. History isn't a fun subject, especially in middle school. I remember falling asleep in class so much the teacher called my parents. Gladly enough, I wasn't failing the class due to Nolan giving me his notes.

"Another night in?"

"Only if you want it to be," I could hear papers shuffling in the background. "Where are you?"

"Home. Have you eaten?"

"No, my stomach was just growling. What do you have in mind? And don't say *The Lounge*."

"I wasn't."

I definitely was.

Continuing, I suggested, "how about I grab some pizza and come over."

"That sounds fantastic. See you in a bit."

I ordered pizza from *The Lounge* then freshened up, but before leaving, Harmony walked in.

"Can we talk?" She asked somberly.

Without a word, I sat on the couch, folding my arms across my chest.

"I'm sorry. I should've been more considerate of your feelings for Nolan."

Yes, she should have.

She glared at me with her big eyes.

"And I'm sorry for coming at you so hard. I appreciate you being by my side since day one and putting up with my Nolan drama. You've been privy to everything, and I can't expect you not to have an opinion."

"But I failed to support you, and that will not happen again."

I smiled accepting her apology, "I meant what I said about Ezeke, though."

Harmony pulled me in for a hug, "oh, I know."

I canceled the order from *The Lounge* because Harmony and I spent so much time catching up. So much had happened in both of our lives in the last couple of days. She was surprised to find out I friend-zoned Nolan. If only I could keep my promise. "I'm trying to be better. I may not like Ezeke in that way, but I was always open with him about it. We are great friends."

I nodded. Maybe they are like me and Nolan—better off as friends.

"I need to make a store run, and I ate all your wheat bread on purpose." When she opened the door, Grant raised his fist like he was about to knock. "Well, hey, Grant." She looked at me side-eyed.

"Hey, a certain someone was supposed to show up at my house with a pie of pizza, but she never showed. Have you seen her?" His humor brought a smile to my face.

Harmony smiled back at me, "I think she's in here somewhere." She stepped aside, allowing him to cross the threshold of our space. Harmony gave me an appreciative grin as she closed the front door.

Grant looked so fine, dressed in gray basketball shorts and a black t-shirt. He sauntered towards me, taking Harmony's spot on the couch. "Did you forget about me?"

I shook my head, "no, I lost track of time. I'm sorry."

"Don't be. I found you."

That rolled off his tongue so sexy, I clenched my thighs together. I'm too horny for this. "Do you want to go back to your place?"

"No, here is fine. I needed to get out of those four walls. I've been so swamped with lesson plans—my apartment looks like my classroom."

"Are you planning for the entire semester or the month?"

"Entire semester, that's the way to do it. The work-life balance is why I choose to do it that way. The more I plan now, the more time I can spend with you." This man has a way with words. "Tell me more about your work."

I sat crisscrossed facing him, "I'm attending a conference in

Miami with Dr. Cooper. Never been to Miami, so I'm excited to go. He's launching a private practice featuring yours truly."

"That's dope! Isn't a private practice hard to get off the ground in North Carolina?"

"A little but it's achievable with the right business plan. I asked the same questions as you, but Dr. Cooper assured me a friend of his family works miracles."

"Tell me more about Miami."

"It's a surgeon's conference. I've never been before."

"Your doctor's going, too?"

"Yes, Dr. Cooper is attending."

"Are you sharing the same room?"

"No, I booked separate rooms but requested they are side-by-side."

Grant looked perturbed, which was the same reaction I received from Ezeke. "I'll be honest. I don't like it at all. But it's for work, and I have no business telling you not to go."

If that was Nolan saying those words, I would be slobbering him down. My ghetto ass heart wouldn't let me take it there with Grant. Although it feels different with him. I feel different. I'm still the Malani that's madly in love with Nolan. But with Grant, I'm also someone else, someone I don't quite recognize, but I like her. I like her with Grant. I like the way he kisses her, kisses me. But I still craved Nolan.

"When is your friend coming back?" Grant asked, his face held a grin that I couldn't quite decipher.

My phone buzzed with a notification from Nolan making me regret reaching out to Grant. "She'll be back soon.

"Do you still want to grab a bite?"

"No, I'm okay. If you want to grab some food, I won't stop you."

My flashing phone impatiently reminded me of the message from Nolan.

Nolan: I'm coming over

Grant stepped away to place the order for his food. I took that opportunity to call Nolan.

"I'm almost there," he said instead of a normal greeting.

"You can't," fuck, I didn't want to say that. I wanted him here so bad.

"Why the fuck not?"

"Grant is here."

Nolan chuckled, "and? I'm coming Lani. I don't give a fuck."

"No, I don't interrupt your time with Willow. I leave in peace."

"We're two different people."

"Nolan," I sighed while watching Grant pace back and forth with his phone glued to his ear.

"Queen, I'm sleeping beside you tonight. Either tell that nigga to get the fuck on, or we're having a slumber party. I'll be there in five minutes."

He ended the call.

Minutes melted into seconds. Nolan and Harmony walked in simultaneously. The smile on his face met my scowl. Harmony smirked then tossed me the candy I asked for before retreating into the kitchen.

Grant sat closely next to me, "what's up, Nolan?"

"Not shit, what up with you?" Nolan stood with his arms folded across his chest. He licked his lips when he noticed me staring at him.

I couldn't help it. He commanded my attention.

Grant said something about spending time with me, then he rubbed my thigh.

Nolan's jaw clenched, "Lani, why are you still sitting?"

"Something wrong?" Grant asked.

"Yea, you don't mind leaving, do you?" Nolan helped me from the couch, positioning me behind him. In my peripherals, Harmony was watching from the kitchen.

"No, of course not, Malani is everything okay?"

"Yea, she's good. She might call you later," Nolan held the front door open for the scrambling Grant.

My mouth damn near touched the floor. Grant was looking at

me, but I didn't know what to say. Nolan had spoken. I waved at him on his way out.

"Damn, Nolan, you get down like that?" Harmony shrieked with excitement.

Glaring at Nolan only made him grab my hand and lead us to my bedroom.

I was so turned on and wet. If he breathed on me—I would cum.

"Don't be mad. I warned you."

"That was so rude," my back was to him because a smile adorned my face.

"Are you ready for bed?"

"What did you do with Willow? Fuck her then sent her home?"

His eyes lowered, "damn, you think I'm like that?"

"No, I'm sorry." I offered him a pleasant smile.

"Let's go to bed." He climbed in first, holding the covers open for me to slide in, too. I've only shared a bed with Nolan these past years. It would have been weird to wake up next to anyone but him.

"Good morning," I held my hand up, shielding his eyes from the harsh sunlight beaming through my window.

"Good morning," Nolan stretched, wrapping his arm around my waist. He nestled his nose into my neck. "Are you sure you don't want this?"

I turned to face him, giving him my first smile of the day. For a minute, I let myself revel in his touches that felt more like a potential lover's than a friend's. I didn't miss his fingertips brushing along the small of my back. He was always fine, even in the morning with morning breath. "I always wanted it, but now it's complicated."

He held my hands, "it's not though."

I buried my head into his chest, cuddling against him. I could stay in bed with Nolan all day, but we had plans with the crew that couldn't be rescheduled. He left an hour after we woke up. Sharing a cup of coffee with him makes me look forward to the many other cups we will share in the morning.

NEW YEAR'S Eve festivities started as planned. Harmony, Ezeke, Nolan, and I poured into Nolan's living room in our pajamas. We've had this tradition since college. We would get together, cook our favorite dishes, and share our goals for the upcoming year. This was my favorite of all the holidays because I held everyone accountable to their goals throughout the year. Harmony and I spent the morning preparing our dishes. She oversaw the black-eyed peas, and I was in charge of the collard greens.

I also prepared mashed potatoes and Harmony made a cookie dessert. Harmony helped me organize all the food on the counter, even the store-bought cake Ezeke purchased. Nolan prepared the jasmine rice and the cornbread recipe from his mother. I smiled, looking over the kitchen and the new year decorations for tonight.

"What's got you so giddy?" Nolan surprised me, poking me in the side.

"I'm just happy and love bringing in the new year. It brings new beginnings and feels like we get a reset." What I didn't say was I was looking forward to riding the wave of this shift that occurred in our friendship.

"Are you going to stay up until midnight?"

I nudged his arm, "Wake me up when the clock hits 11:59."

As much as I love the new year, I could never stay up until midnight. Even as a little girl, it was something about the festivities and food. We would eat, which tired me out every single year. I always had high ambitions of staying up, but it never worked out.

Nolan tossed his arm around my shoulders, pulling me into the living room, "I'm excited for the new year, too," he said as we sat on the pillows surrounding his coffee table. Harmony and Ezeke were playing a game of spades as me and Nolan watched them go back and forth. We watched movies as we ate. Nolan's arm rested around me the entire time, and I couldn't help but melt in my seat. Harmony peered at me with a question in her eyes. This is the side of Nolan they didn't see all those years, the side that I saw and read too much into.

Around ten, my eyes were getting heavy, but they were at attention when Willow walked in.

Does she have a key to his place?

My eyes shot to Harmony, who hunched her shoulders. I jealously watched as Nolan guided her to the couch where he and I were sitting. Willow sat between us, and it seemed so fitting. Their fingers were laced like she was claiming her man.

Her man.

"Hey, girl," she said enthusiastically, tossing her hand up to me.

"Hey, Willow," I smiled before darting my eyes at Nolan. "Nolan, can we talk?"

I led the way to his bedroom, fury running through my body but displayed on his face.

"What's wrong now?" Nolan crossed his arms.

"Since when do we do plus ones on New Year's Eve?"

"Willow's not a plus one," he had the nerve to look confused.

"She's outside of the circle, so she's a plus one," I said matter-of-factly.

"She heard us talking about it and asked if she could come. I didn't see a problem with it because we're still friends and all. Do you want me to tell her to go? I'll tell her to go."

"*Now* you'll tell her to go," I mumbled, reminding myself of the night she showed up after that perfect moment between us.

"What's that supposed to mean, Lani?"

"She can stay. It would've been nice to know that others outside our friend group were invited."

"Are you jealous?" Nolan started towards me, closing the distance between us. He already knew the answer to that question but wanted to taunt me instead.

Hell yes, I was jealous.

Sometimes I wished I was the girl who liked to cause drama because I would be all up on her man in public, like he's all up on me in private.

But I'm not that girl.

I believe in good and bad karma.

My lips curled into a smile as his scent hit my nostrils. "No, if these are the games you're going to play, she can have you."

"Have me?" He stepped closer, causing me to back up until my back pressed against the door. Nolan leaned down to my ear, "don't think I don't notice how you stop breathing when I'm near you. Quit that tough girl shit because I see you now, Lani." Closing my eyes, I steadied my breathing, "do you want me to tell her to leave because I will—for you."

I exhaled sharply, screaming yes in my head, but it didn't actually come out my mouth. "No, she can stay." He stood back to see if I was serious. "But I'm leaving at eleven."

"That's not the plan."

"The plan is fucked up now. Nolan, I'm not watching her kiss you when the clock strikes midnight."

"Then let me kiss *you*," he was close to me again, causing my breathing to be unstable and my thoughts to become foggy. It sounded perfect, but it wasn't real.

"Nolan, you like her."

"But I'm not in a relationship with her. Lani," he scooped down to meet my eyes, "I want you, no bullshit."

"I can't tell," I put distance between us the best I could. Walking towards his bed, he caught my wrist, bringing me to him. "I've been dealing with you rejecting me for years. We get to this space, and you invite her on our night."

Jealousy pulling from my core—unwantedly. I wanted to hold those thoughts to myself, but he was pissing me off.

"You never opened your mouth to say how you felt about me. I'm telling you I want you, and you're fucking around for shits and giggles. This is not a game, Lani."

"You want me how? To fuck me, or do you want to be in a relationship with me?" His eyes shifted to the window behind me. "Exactly what I thought. The only thing I want from you is a commitment. If I can't get that, your heart, I don't want it. We can kiss a million times, but it's not worth it if you don't love me like I love you."

"I never told you to love me, though—not like that," his words were like venom ripping through my skin.

"You're absolutely right," we stood with silence filling around us.

I didn't have any more words to say to him. He had all the answers, so I'll leave it at that. "We can return to the party."

"Nah, Lani, I do love you—"

"As a friend, I get it."

"Let me fucking talk," he reached out, grabbing my waist pulling me closer to him again. "This shit is new, let me catch up."

"Take as much time as you need, just don't expect me to wait around anymore." Wiggling free from his hold took a lot of willpower.

Nolan glared at me before opening the door. Another random person had joined our party, a friend of Willow's who was flirting a little too hard with Ezeke. A look I didn't see often rested on Harmony's face. She was jealous.

"Anybody want a Perc?" The girl asked.

Willow laughed, "girl, I told you not to bring that. It is not that type of party."

"I'll take one," Nolan responded, and my head whipped so fast in his direction.

My heart hit my chest, tumbled then dropped to my stomach.

I'm dreaming. I have to be.

His angry eyes met mine, he took the pill from the girl and downed it with the sparkling juice in the wine flute.

Shaking my head in total disapproval, I said goodbye to Harmony and Ezeke. I was not about to sit in Nolan's house and watch him down pills his brother died from. If he wanted to go out that way, it would not be in my presence.

After the tears I shed from Nolan's recklessness subsided, I called Grant. Liam invaded my mind, the times Nolan cried in my arms about how unfair it was that he was taken at a young age. Then—he goes to do some shit like that. The look of satisfaction in his eyes when he popped that dangerous pill in his mouth sickened me to my stomach. It hurt me, and I don't think he cared.

"Please tell me you're up, bored, and hoping I come over."

"I'm up, extremely bored, and hoping, no praying you'd come over."

"Open the door," seconds later, I was surrounded by the warmth of Grant's apartment. "Did you have plans tonight?" I looked him over, "Oh my God! You were asleep. I'm so sorry."

He shook his head, "I'm glad you're here. How was your night?"

"Let's just say, I'm glad it's over."

Grant helped me out of my coat. "Are you finally spending the night with me?"

"Yes," I took his hand and followed him to his room.

My conscience screamed at me for my wrongdoing of using Grant to take my mind off of Nolan. I've been so consumed with Nolan I'm missing out on what a great guy Grant could be. This thing between me and Grant is morphing into a friendship on its own and who am I to deny it.

My heart belongs to Nolan, whether I place it into his hands or he rips it out my chest.

chapter
sixteen

Nolan

I swallowed another Percocet before crossing the threshold of the schoolhouse. I had to get through this day, and it wasn't going to be without that little pill.

The first day back from a break was always the hardest because the kids were too busy discussing what they got for Christmas rather than wanting to learn about math. I wasn't feeling today and needed to be numb from all the bullshit. I haven't seen Lani all year, literally. She called herself doing something storming out of my apartment on New Year's Eve, but I'm done chasing her. If she wants to talk—she will have to seek me out. Tracking her down to talk to me was left behind last year.

"Settle down, kids," I held my fist in the air, signaling them to cease all conversations. The final bell had rung, and it was my time. In the first half of the class, we reviewed last semester before I introduced new material. I had so much energy I couldn't stop talking about quadratic equations. The kids were tired of my shit. They thought this was going to be a chill day but fuck that. We have goals to reach and materials to go over before our focus shifts to the standardized test they complete at the end of the school year.

Grant was in the teacher's lounge. It brought a smile to my face thinking about the night I kicked him out of Lani's shit. He nodded in my direction, "what's up, man?"

I shrugged, "what up, have you talked to Lani?" I cut the theatrics, genuinely curious to know if she was still seeing this clown. That's her M.O running to another nigga instead of facing issues with me head on.

"Yeah, I saw her this morning."

"Ya'll met for breakfast or some shit?" Deep breath filled my lungs, I tried to calm myself.

Grant chuckled like something was funny. His eyes darted around to the other two teachers engaging in their own conversation. "Malani spent the night," he said, lowly. The implication in his voice pissed me off.

"Hmph, ya'll getting serious?"

"A little," he chuckled again. "She says that a lot, a little. I guess it's rubbing off."

"I guess so," I bit my tongue, counting slowly to ten in my head. "Tell her I said to call me."

"Well, she's leaving for Miami in a few hours."

"Miami?"

"The surgeon's conference."

Lani didn't mention shit like that to me, "who is she going with?"

"Dr. Cooper."

"Same room?" My nostrils flared.

"No, separate. She didn't talk to you about this?" I didn't like the look he was giving me. My best friend purposely omitted telling me shit, which didn't sit right with me.

"Hell no because I wouldn't approve of that shit."

The rest of my school day was spent worrying about Lani's stupid ass decision to go on a fucking vacation with her boss. I counted the hours, minutes, and seconds until the school day ended. I dialed Lani's number as soon as I got home.

"Well, hello, my long-lost *best friend*. How are you?" She answered on the first ring.

"Lani, where the hell are you at?"

"Say hello first," she demanded.

I blew out a breath of air, "hey, Lani. Now, where are you?"

"I just got to Miami for a conference. I'm a little jet-lagged, to be honest with you, but I'm so anxious at the same time. I've never attended anything like this before. What if they see me as an inexperienced nurse practitioner?" Doubt was in her voice. "Like what if they ask why a NP is even on the roster?"

What irritated me the most was she spoke like she'd told me this information. I wanted to call her out, but it would have to wait because she didn't need that from me right now since she was miles away from home.

I softened my tone because it's what she needed, "Lani, you've got this. You wouldn't have been invited if your boss didn't believe in you. I believe in you."

"Thank you," she took a deep breath. "Nolan, have you taken any more pills?"

"Did you spend the night with Grant?"

There was a brief pause on her end, "I did."

"Have you—"

"No, I haven't slept with him."

I couldn't tell if she was lying or not, but I hoped she wasn't.

"Nolan, the pills, it upset me. Liam—"

"I know. Hey, be good, see me when you get back. I miss your lips since you denied me access on New Year's Eve."

Despite her reservation about us and how she complicated our relationships with Willow and Grant, I wasn't going to allow us to fall too deep back into friendship. I wasn't lying when I said I wanted her. How I wanted her was important because my track record wasn't sweet regarding romantic relationships. I have too much respect for Lani not to handle her delicately.

"Shut up!" The falling shower stream filled her background.

I imagined her naked, sitting on the side of the tub. "Imma let you go."

"No, I can talk to you and shower."

"Yea?" My mind went to her fingering herself while in the

shower. I could've sworn I heard her moaning softly. Continuing to talk about nothing, I stroked my length until my seed spilled onto my hand.

chapter
seventeen

Malani

Talk about a beautiful city. The pictures and videos I've seen of this beautiful place did it no justice. After masturbating in the shower, I took a short nap. It was still early in the evening. I decided to tour a little.

Our hotel had direct beach access, along with a courtyard and the most exciting part was the rooftop pool. I walked to get ice cream from a shoppe that reminded me of Cinnamon Kissed. Albeit expensive, it was good. Besides this wasn't on my dime anyway. Dr. Cooper instructed me to save all itemized receipts to submit for reimbursement.

"I asked you to call me." Dr. Cooper stood behind me. It seemed like we both had the same idea. He was dressed in shorts and a beach like shirt that was only buttoned from his abs down. His chest was glistened from what I only imagined was baby oil.

I wore a two piece, the top was black and the bottoms were printed sunflowers, the coverup I wore matched the bottoms. There was no other way to walk around this city except in a bikini. I was just blending in.

Embarrassed, I responded, "you said for dinner. This is a quick snack."

He smiled, taking the barstool next to me. Dr. Cooper always smelled divine. "What did you get?"

"Guava Sherbet, want to try it?" I extended the cone to him, he licked the creamy fruit dessert. "They sort of gave me a look when I asked for it on a cone."

"Because it's sherbet, a bowl and spoon type of dessert."

"Says who?" We laughed. Dr. Cooper ordered the same as me along with an order of French fries. "Dr. Cooper, can I ask you a question?"

"Only if you call me Jamel."

I cringed but nodded, "how fake do I have to be at this conference?"

He laughed, "on a scale of one to ten, a high twenty. It's not as bad as you're thinking. We come to the conference to make connections. The boring parts are the speeches and presentations. We'll have more fun later that night."

It was intimidating, but I found myself wondering what kind of fun Dr. Cooper meant.

We ate at a high scale restaurant in the heart of downtown. Dinner first, then the drinks started pouring. In the back of my mind, I pictured Nolan shaking his head with each shot I chased with Dr. Cooper. I cut myself off after the sixth shot of tequila. If I wanted to be present at the conference tomorrow, I had to end the fun.

We walked back to the hotel, well he walked, I stumbled. With my phone in hand I climbed into the queen-sized bed to call Nolan.

"Hello, Mr. Hudson." I slurred when he answered.

"Don't tell me you're fucking drunk."

"I won't." I laughed. "What are you doing?" I struggled to get out of the bikini that was restricting me from getting comfortable on the bed.

"Nothing, where are you?"

"I'm in my hotel room."

"Alone?"

"Alone. How was work?"

"You called me to talk about work?"

I turned over, pulling the pillow from the head of the bed with me. "I called to talk to you."

"Well, talk to me about what you really want to talk to me about."

"Are you alone?"

"Yes, Lani. Have you been drinking?"

"You told me not to tell you," I giggled uncontrollably.

Nolan sighed, "you need to go to sleep."

"But I want to talk to you."

"And I want to talk to you too, but not while you're drunk."

"Can you wait until I fall asleep before you hang up?"

"Of course."

THE NEXT MORNING, Nolan's call was still connected. He was softly snoring. A smile formed on my face. I like this. Too bad it caused a lot of doubt. He was still very much seeing Willow, and I'm sure Grant conjured me and him being an item in his head.

Just like he didn't hang up on me, I didn't end the call with him. I showered and ate breakfast all while nursing my phone to my ear.

"Good Morning, baby," was the next words I heard.

My toothbrush dangled out my mouth.

Baby? Damn, that made me swoon where I stood. Chill bumps covered my arms.

"Good Morning, sleepyhead. Sleeping in this late you act like you don't have no business about yourself."

"Shit, I don't. What you doing?"

My room door opened, and my head jolted towards it. In walked Dr. Cooper, dressed in a tailored suit. "I expected to find you asleep; that's why I got a copy of your room key. You recover well."

I smiled at him. He looked exhausted. "Thanks to a good night's sleep."

"Let me borrow some of your energy," he walked further into the room, placing the keycard on the nightstand.

"Lani?" Nolan called my name.

I handed Dr. Cooper the bowl of strawberries, mangoes, and grapes. "Try these."

He nibbled on the mango first, throwing his head back like it was the cure to his hangover. "I'll see you later, no more wandering."

I nodded in agreement. My attention returned back to Nolan when Dr. Cooper walked out. "I'm getting dressed," I answered his previous question. The nerves continued to float around in my stomach. I'm not equipped for this. I should be back home, letting the patients know Dr. Cooper was out of town for the weekend. Yet, I'm here—in over my head. "I wish my mom was here to talk me off the ledge, I don't feel confident at all," I admitted to my best friend.

"Talk to me," he insisted.

I did.

Words spilled out my mouth like vomit to him. Aside from being in love with him, one of the reasons I fell in love was because he listened. At this moment, I needed my friend to tell me it was all in my head.

"Name something, anything that Dr. Cooper knows how to do, but you don't."

That was easy, "we know the same." Dr. Cooper trained me in his role, 'just in case,' he would often tell me. I couldn't do surgery alone, but he'd let me take the lead.

"That's why you're there, Queen. I didn't carry your ass through college for you to constantly throw a pity party."

"Shut up!" I laughed, sometimes I needed reassurance from him. I liked the way he broke it down to me.

It was time to jump over another hurdle. The conference started at noon, although Dr. Cooper said I could skip the earlier events, I wanted to get the entire experience.

The conference was being held in a huge space that took my breath away. Nerves tickled my spine as I stood at the door staring at the hundreds of people and tables. I slowly walked to retrieve my badge from the table at the front.

"You lucky bitch," the lady at the table said with a smirk.

"Excuse me?"

"You work under Dr. Cooper, and I'm trying to get under Dr. Cooper if you know what I mean."

"I know if you speak that way again, this will be your last year at this event." I met the eyes of the woman who rightfully scolded the girl.

"I'm sorry, Dr. East." She continued to the next person in line, hanging her head.

Pulling the lanyard over my head, the woman was directly looking at me. Her gaze was intimidating. She extended her hand to me, grasping it firmly. "I'm Dr. East."

"Malani Dawson," I cowered.

"Dr. Malani Dawson," Dr. Cooper corrected from behind me. "She's modest." He placed his hand respectfully on my back.

"It's nice to meet you," her smile was as beautiful as she was. I didn't miss the eyes she was giving Dr. Cooper. "All the way from North Carolina. How was the flight?"

I couldn't tell if she wanted the answer from me or him. I could tell she was trying very hard to be professional.

"J.J., can we talk privately?" She was close to him, and her eyes were glossy.

"Malani, would you be okay?"

"Yeah, I'll go around all the tables to get the free stuff."

The conference was open to the public, it was information regarding all types of plastic surgery. I stood by the abdominoplasty and liposuction table the most making sure they were giving correct information. I circled the room two times before everyone was called into the auditorium.

The panels were broken up in different sections, facial— including head, face, mouth, teeth, chin, cheek, jaw and eyes. Breasts, Abdomen, and Skin. I was all ears during the breast panel, I've only seen one augmentation performed during my time in med school. It always piqued my interest, but I placed it deep in the back of my mind because it wasn't Dr. Cooper's specialty. Listening to the doctors speak so highly of happy patients and testimonies from patients, I composed a plan in my head to present to Dr. Cooper.

Adding breast implants, decreases, lifts, deconstructions, and augmentations to our roster would be beneficial to our practice. I texted him since his panel was next. He sent back a thumbs up, then the next message said exactly what I knew he was going to say.

Dr. Cooper: Only if you become certified.

chapter
eighteen

Nolan

I took pills to get through the day. One a day turned into two a day, and sometimes, depending on how stressful my day was, it turned into three pills. It's euphoric, nothing matters. I know why Liam chose these little pills.

Staring at the ceiling and feeling good as fuck. Willow was putting on a show. Too bad I was missing it. Her mouth was on me, pleasing me. Normally, I would be all into it, but lately, her mouth and sex didn't compare to that little pill. Finally, I closed my eyes, dozing off into the blackness.

The more stressful the work week got, the more pills I chewed. I need an escape—a mind-altering escape. Sunday came, and I stayed in bed all day dodging calls from Ezeke.

I was preparing a sandwich when the front door swung open. Lani walked in dressed professionally in a cinnamon-colored blazer suit and a pink floral blouse. Her heels clinked on the hardwood floor. The smile on her lips faded when she looked at me. The briefcase she held fell to the floor with a thud. No words came from her lips while she wrapped her arms around me. I lifted her onto the island, stepping in between her legs.

"You have to stop," I looked down, focusing on anything other than her eyes—only for her to grab my chin to meet her teary gaze. "How many pills did you have today? It's all in your face, Nolan, so don't deny it." Lani fussed at me like only she could.

I scrubbed my hands over my face. I didn't want to have this conversation right now. I wanted to eat the sandwich, shower, and watch TV. "Four," I answered after a minute passed.

Her eyes grew wide, "four?! Nolan! Where are they?" She tried to push off the island to search my apartment, but I held her in place with a tight hold on her thighs.

"Lani, I'm not a fucking addict like—" I was close to saying something that will make her look at me funny, but it's how I truly felt. I also felt empty, and I'm drowning because I couldn't get over this fucking winter hump.

Her next words were carefully measured, "I never said you were. Those pills are not okay to have if you don't have a prescription. Shit, even when they are prescribed. Will you give them to me?"

"I don't have any more."

"Nolan," she didn't believe me, but I was telling the truth. I did run out.

"I promise. Tell me about your thing. How was it?"

Lani let out a frustrated breath. She closed the sandwich I was making and then took a bite before placing it back on the styrofoam plate. "I'm worried about you."

I squeezed her thighs, pulling her closer to the edge of the island —she held onto my shoulders for support, but I wasn't going to let her fall. My thumb slowly outlined her bottom lip. "I've missed these," I bit my lip, meeting her intense gaze.

"We can't—."

"Fuck Grant," I said above a whisper, enunciating every syllable.

"Nolan, you're high."

"And?" I captured her lips, not giving her room to refuse me. No matter how many pills I'd taken today, I felt this. Her skin felt like fire. The rigidness of her tongue toying with mine sunk me deeper into her. My hands were rubbing her thighs until they weren't. They unbuttoned the buttons on the high waist slacks sliding them and her panties down her legs. It felt like I was going in slow motion—so eager to see her.

I scanned her face, although her breathing was accelerated, she gave me an unsure look. I knew she didn't know whether to stop me or allow me to keep going—I kept going. I inserted my middle finger into her, immediately her wetness dampened my finger. Arousal was painted on her face while I hooked another finger in her and swiped my thumb across her clit, over and over again. I watched her beautiful, contorted face when she released the orgasm.

"Lani?" My lips trailed to her neck—I sucked, licked, and nipped the tender spot with my teeth. I couldn't believe I was sliding my hand under her shirt, squeezing her breast until her nipples pebbled. Biting my lip, suppressing the groan that dared to escape my mouth. "How long has it been since you've been touched?"

"Does touching myself count?" Her breathing hitched, embarrassed to share she'd been giving herself orgasms.

"No," using my tongue to slither down the length of her neck.

"Why not?"

"Because you won't take yourself pass your limit. You'll cum, then stop," I took her chin in my hands guiding her eyes to mine. "I'll take you well above your limit and have you cumming nonstop."

I've never imagined this moment with her, let alone speaking to her in this manner. Sexual words leaving my mouth towards Lani never happened before, but we're here now. We were both unsure but committed to the act. Once I started touching her, I knew stopping would be a task. She tried to close her legs to create friction from the building ache. My dick was just as hard, as much as I wanted to be inside her, I wanted to taste the sweet nectar that moisturized her inner thighs.

I dipped down, covering her with my mouth as she arched her back, giving me more access and licking her again and again until her essence coated my tongue. Having her taste inside of my mouth was fucking insane. I spread her legs as far as they could go with her satisfied moans falling deep into my ears. Either the pills were causing me to hallucinate or I was dreaming either way I'll deal with the aftermath when I wake. Lani felt real and if I'm being honest, she tasted just like I thought she would. I cursed myself for not indulging in her before. I should've been drinking from her fountain years ago. Lani's sweet melodic whimpers encouraged me to continue while she rotated her hips against my tongue. Her hands fell onto my head, pushing my face deeper into her pussy. I smothered myself in her, she smelled good and tasted even better, with her lower lips just as hypnotizing as her top. I licked her through another orgasm, letting her legs fall over my shoulders. Her pussy was pretty, begging me to taste it.

I could have had this all along, our mental connection paired with her good ass pussy. Shit! I've been depriving myself.

Watching her chest rise and fall as she came down from another orgasm. I bathed in her juices because I wanted her scent so far up my nostrils I'd smell her every time I breath. I stood to my full length, pulling my dick from my pajama pants. Pre-cum rose, lubricating the tip. Her eyes were wide, and I realized this was her first time seeing me completely bare. I had to calm myself from diving straight into her. Her face was unreadable because she was probably experiencing the same emotions that ran through me. I was the advocate of male and female platonic friendships, but I now stand in this kitchen as a hypocrite and also not giving a fuck that we're about to continue enjoying this new phase. Lani's legs wrapped around my waist when I lifted her from the island and I carried her to my bedroom.

nineteen

Malani

Nolan never left my mind during the entire Miami trip. I made my way to him the minute I drove into our town. What happened after seeing his face was pleasurably unexpected.

When we got to his bedroom, I started to have cold feet. The fact that he was high from the pills should have turned me away, but I've wanted him for so long. Lust overruled logic. What would having sex with him mean for our friendship? Would he toss me aside after we have sex? No, he wouldn't do that. I know him better than that—right? We were crossing a dangerous line but the more he kissed my lips, neck and breasts the more the walls of doubt tumbled. Embarrassing enough, it's been a long time since a man has touched me in this way, and years of masturbation left my body reacting in ways it hadn't before, missing a man's touch and welcoming Nolan.

I wanted this.

I've always wanted this.

He laid me on his bed so carefully and stripped me from the rest of my clothes. It felt like my eyes were closed the entire time. I was in a dream, afraid I would open them and he'd be gone. This would be a figment of my very active imagination.

Nolan's lips returned to mine, "everything about you is beautiful," he groaned against my mouth. The accolades were appreciated, but not needed. Nolan had me.

I reached between us, stroking his dick. It was so heavy and hard in my hand that I could barely grasp it. He seemed to get harder as I guided him to my wetness, rubbing the head against my throbbing clit. His smooth flesh felt so good and I used my juices to coat his tip.

"Shiiiitttt," he hissed. "I can't wait anymore, put me inside of you, baby."

With my eyes closing briefly, I positioned him directly at my opening. This was it, the moment our lives and friendship would change forever. I stared at Nolan's lust-filled face, he was staring at me too and I wondered what was on his mind, besides us taking our years of friendship to a completely different level. The second his face changed a shade darker when he pushed himself deep into me I savored that into my mental bank. My breath was caught in my throat as we physically connected. I thought I could handle his length and thickness, but I was dead wrong. My sex gripped his shaft tightly as he perfectly filled me giving me each inch dangerously slow.

His name fell from my lips repeatedly as he slid in and out of me feverishly. The building pressure in my core was too much. I was getting ready to release, but he pulled out of me dick swinging from side to side. Nolan knew what he was doing. He wanted me to be delirious, and I was. I was so fucking close to cumming. From the wicked grin on his face told me he knew it.

"Show me how bad you've been wanting me, Lani," he laid on his back pulling me on top of him. I slowly eased down on him, gasping when all of him was buried inside of me again.

Nolan's fingers dug into my hips, rocking into me slowly but deliberately. I balanced my hands on his chest as his dick explored every nook and cranny of my pussy.

"Nolan, mmmm," I moaned, his dick was so good I was close to tears. I've imagined having sex with him, but this was better than I could've imagined.

His hand gripped my neck bringing my face to him. "You're not right Lani. You've been holding this good ass pussy from me." He grunted while capturing my mouth, tasting myself on his tongue sent me over the edge. Nolan wrapped his arms around my body, pumping rapidly into me. I was near my peak, each stroke filling me to the rim until I exploded all over him.

He was right. I would've stopped after the first time I came. My body was in overdrive from the multiple orgasms that left a smile on my face. Nolan wasn't done. He rested between my legs, lapping the mixture of our bodies from my pussy. My clit was so sensitive causing my legs to quake with each swipe of his tongue. He was making me feel things I've never experienced before and I was falling deeper in love with him.

"Don't tap out yet," he thrust back into me, snatching my breath from my lungs. Going deeper this time, into my heart and my soul. My eyes snapped shut as I took him all in. I invited him to embed himself into my heart forever.

Reality set in when I awoke from the sexually-induced coma with Nolan arms around my body. I was naked, so I wasn't dreaming. I nestled closer to him, smelling my scent mixed with his on him. Lifting the cover, I stared down at his massive tool between his legs.

"He likes being touched rather than looked at." Nolan's eyes were daring, and I almost took him up on that offer if I wasn't due at work in less than an hour.

"Are you going to work?"

"Nah, it's a holiday. You should consider skipping, you know, jet-lagged and all that shit."

I really wanted to stay in bed with him all day, snuggle close because I feared if I leave it wouldn't be like this when I return. Maybe he'll come to his senses and realize I'm only good for sex and being his best friend. Maybe he'll ghost me or find excuses to shut me down.

Nolan pressed his lips against my forehead. "Stop thinking so hard, baby," he said like he was reading my mind. Hearing him still call me 'baby' could've caused another orgasm within itself. Last night I thought it was induced by sex talk so I didn't revel in it as much, now I'm indulging. But still I was unsure on how we would navigate from here. Years of holding myself together in his presence didn't prepare me for this moment. The tears fell on their own. I was unraveling. "This wasn't just sex for me Lani."

His words echoed in my ears. I wasn't sure how to respond because how I was feeling inside was beyond words.

"I know you had reservations at first, but I really want you." He tilted my chin to look at him. "Did you hear me? I want you, I want this with you."

"Yeah," I nodded, his lips met mine, sealing the deal. He thumbed my tears away.

Was this the right time? I could've bet millions that I'll receive a sign regarding us—nothing came. Just this moment of truth, the moment I prayed for. My heart will forever belong to Nolan, whether intact or broken—it's his to have and hold, to do with as he pleases.

We made love again before I left for work. I wanted to bring up the pills but didn't want to spoil the moment. Nolan's change in behavior does worry me. He's never been calculated, although he does operate with a sense of familiarity. He's different... still my Nolan with a slight twist.

I threw myself into work, helping Dr. Cooper with the office downtown. He was lucky enough to acquire a building in the black-owned area of downtown as Nicoyce's businesses saturated the area. He didn't tell me, but I knew he'd partnered with Nicoyce from the documents I'd filed. Plus, they weren't giving us a hard time regarding our contracts. I put two and two together before the conference. He didn't have to share the news with me because Nicoyce has always been a good company to work for. It was better this way, because it cleared my conscience of turning my back on the company that paid a huge portion of my student loans.

Me and Dr. Cooper met at the new building for last-minute recommendations on the aesthetics of the interior, including my office, then worked on building our client list. Being a respectable man, he didn't want to take clients away from Nicoyce Med. I had a feeling women were going to flock to his practice faster than he could turn around. The practice, still unnamed.

"I got something for you."

He fumbled around in the boxes on the floor. "For me?" He nodded, still going through the boxes. Damn, he didn't say we were getting gifts for each other. Ideas tumbled around in my head on what to get him.

Maybe a coffee mug, or a classical cd, do they still sell compact discs?

Come on Malani, nobody listens to CDs.

Maybe I'll frame the photo of him and I doing a surgery. Yeah, that'll work.

"Here," he handed me a white envelope. No, this man is not giving me any money. "Take it," he urged. I was frozen, unable to move my hands. I didn't want to accept something unethical.

I pulled the envelope from his hand, holding my breath as I opened it. Tears welled in my eyes as I looked at the contents inside. Two round-trip plane tickets to Hawaii. "Oh, my God!" I squealed. I hugged him so tight around his neck he started to cough because I was cutting off his airway. "I can't accept these." I pushed the tickets back into the envelope.

"You can, and you will. The tickets have open dates for you to choose. I'll be returning to Miami to tie up a loose end, so I encourage you to take your trip around the same time. I know how much you miss your parents, and you need to see them because when this practice opens, we are going to be busy for months. Take the time." I hugged him again, thanking him profusely. This small act meant so much to me.

AFTER WORK, I helped Nolan with laundry, dinner, and graded some papers for him. Cleaning for him only reminded me I needed to do the same for my apartment since dropping my luggage at the door. I couldn't wait to tell him about Hawaii. My stomach was in knots as we ate our dinner or rather as I ate. Nolan pushed his food around on his plate and only took small bites when he noticed me looking at him. He ate slow but not that damn slow. I started to get insecure about the quality of my food. But I knew the pills were the cause. Nolan being addicted did not cross my mind until he said it, but I knew if he'd increased the intake, his body developed a craving for the rush rather than food.

I watched Nolan closely, spooning food from his plate into his mouth, and laying in his arms. It seemed so easy to get here. Like we declared our love and now we could revel in it. I can hold him and not worry if I lingered too long or if he heard me breathe in his scent. I don't have to question my touches or his touches on my skin.

Nolan's eyes glared into the side of my face when I declined a call from Grant. "Do you want me to handle that for you?"

"No, we haven't talked much. He's probably wondering what I'm up to."

"Tell him you're with me."

That was so fucking cute. But I'm not in the business of hurting anyone's feelings. Grant is a nice guy, but he isn't for me. Had this been the nature of me and Nolan's relationship months ago, Grant wouldn't be an issue. Had Nolan followed the breadcrumbs I so delicately laid out for him, I wouldn't have to have an unpleasant conversation with Grant.

With my head against Nolan's chest, I could hear his heart racing. The pills.

"Nolan, are you still taking percs?"

He huffed but didn't answer my question.

"I can't be here if you are."

He draped his arm around me, "you're not going anywhere."

"Give them to me. Please."

Nolan stood, heading to the kitchen. When he returned to the living room, he handed me a wrinkled brown bag.

My face was stoic, rattling the pills in the bag, "no more." I said while dropping the bag in my purse.

He nodded and slid behind me again, "I promise, baby."

The next morning, we were still on the couch, and I was

wrapped in Nolan's arms. It was like he never wanted to let me go, and I love it.

"Drive me to school today? I got a fucking headache."

"I can, but I have back-to-back surgeries. It's possible I'll get out late."

"I'm cool with that. I have more papers to grade anyway."

When I agreed to his request, I didn't think about the fifty million parents in the carpool line waiting to drop their little rugrats off. Nolan instructed me to pull into the faculty's parking lot. Since he had a box of graded papers, I helped him to his classroom.

"It's so plain in here," I complained, looking around the room. His messy handwriting on the whiteboard reminded the kids of homework and something labeled 'door buster' written in black dry-erase marker.

"That's the same thing I said," a pretty little, brown-skinned girl walked behind us. "Mr. Hudson needs some color in here."

Nolan smacked his lips, "Lani, you remember Justice?"

"Of course, I could never forget such a beautiful and smart girl. How are you?" I shook her little hand.

"I'm fine. Thank you for grading our worksheets. Your boy has been slipping." My mouth dropped open, "oh yeah, I know it's you. Mr. Hudson doesn't draw smiley faces." She had so much attitude in her little body.

"It be your own kids." Nolan smiled, shaking his head from side to side. "Since you're here so early, put these packets on the desks." Nolan handed her a huge stack of papers. She arranged the papers neatly before placing each one in the top right corner of the desks.

"I don't know how you do it," I whispered to him before laughing.

More students walked into his classroom. The boys shook his hand, and the girls waved at him. I admired the relationships he developed with each child. Their faces lit up when they saw him, then me. He introduced me to the students I didn't meet at the beginning of the year when I came to talk about math in the medical field. He's so good with them, softer.

"After the doorbuster, get started on page three while I walk

Miss. Malani out." A handful of girls awed, and the boys gave Nolan a head nod. These kids were something else. "I wish you could stay. I hate being away from you now." He said when we were in the hall and away from his students' gazes.

His mouth speaking what I've always felt in my heart.

He pulled me into him, close to his chest, "can I kiss you here?" I stared up into his brown eyes.

"Lani, you know how many kids kiss in these hallways?"

"Say yes," I urged. I wasn't the girl in middle school that was kissing boys in the hallways, for one, I was too afraid of getting caught. My parents would've whooped my ass and grounded me for a single peck. In high school, I was engulfed with Nolan, and he wasn't thinking about kissing me.

"Yes, you better kiss me," I fisted his t-shirt pulling his tall ass down to me. I savored the mouthwash on his tongue as he deepened our kiss. Nolan cradled my face between his hands while stepping even closer to me. My heart fluttered. I couldn't believe we were kissing in public. Out the corner of my eye, I saw someone watching us. Grant cleared his throat. Nolan looked at me with a sly grin, then pressed his lips against mine one final time, "see you later, baby." He slid into his classroom with the bell ringing loudly in the hall.

My eyes dropped to the polished concrete floors. "I see he's the reason you can't answer my calls."

"I'm sorry, Grant."

Was I really? Finally getting who I've always wanted isn't a bad thing. Me and Grant weren't even on that level. Sure, I liked hanging out with him only to pass time. Just like the other men I've dated, they were only a placeholder until I got Nolan.

"Now I see why he never talked about you to the boys. He wanted you for himself." I saw the disappointment in his eyes. I should've never gotten involved with him.

I didn't say anything, allowing him to draw his own conclusions as I walked past him.

I DUG IN MY PURSE, fishing for my phone to call Harmony. I needed girl time. I immediately panicked from not seeing the brown bag I confiscated from Nolan last night. I rushed over to his apartment. He did not go into my purse to get those pills. I know he didn't. I tossed pillows and sofa cushions onto the ground in search of the pills. Tears burned my eyes as I came up empty with each spot I checked. I searched the living room, his bedroom, and the kitchen—nothing. I dug in the kitchen trash finding the brown bag but not the pills.

Was he high this morning? I massaged my temples with my fingertips—trying to determine if I missed the obvious signs.

I drew shallow breaths and willed myself from the floor. I made sure everything was back in its rightful place before I left for work.

My mind was wandering all day. It was the audacity for me. He was being sneaky, and I didn't know what to do about it.

Dr. Cooper consulted with the just turned eighteen-year-old who knew without a doubt she needed to be snatched before going to a university in the fall. She was already blessed with nice hips, but she hated the small pudge that protruded from her stomach.

"What do you think, Dr. Dawson," he asked me.

The young girl leaned in, anticipating my answer. Someone of her age, I wouldn't operate on because a few crutches a week would clear her insecurity. But I couldn't say that. She wanted surgery, and it's my job to make her comfortable with her decision. Dr. Cooper also knew I didn't want to have any input in front of the patient, but him pushing me is welcomed.

"It's a long road regardless of the choice. Liposuction will give you the results you want, but overtime you have to maintain it. After clearance, hitting the gym three to four times a week is beneficial."

"I agree," Dr. Cooper co-signed with a head nod.

"Then, what will be the point of the surgery?" The young girl asked.

"Think of it as a head start."

"If you were me, would you get it?"

I took a deep breath, "no."

Her glossy eyes stared back at me. "What would you do if you were in my shoes? Sometimes I hate looking at myself in the mirror."

"I would establish a gym routine, or workout at home. Surgery is a big deal, you have to be committed to the long road of recovery. It doesn't stop when you're healed and off the table. It's everything you do after. Take some time to think about it. We won't operate unless you're one-hundred percent sure."

She nodded her head, "thank you," she said to me.

I nodded, happy to help.

When I stepped into my office, the worry of Nolan consumed me. I thought about calling his parents, but that would betray his trust. And I never want him to lose trust in me. That shit is hard to get back.

The final surgery of the day was a simple lipo followed by a follow-up with a patient who had a procedure six weeks ago. According to the questionnaire she was healing phenomenally, but she scoffed when I entered the room. Dr. Cooper's hand rested on his chin. The perfectionist in him examining her naked body as she stood confidently proud.

He looked over at me, "do you see it?"

Suddenly, the woman tensed like me looking at her was the ultimate sin. Although she could flaunt in front of him with no problem. I stood next to him, trying to see from his eyes. Looking her up and down at the small incision peeking by her abdomen.

"Do you smoke?" I asked her.

"Good girl," Dr. Cooper spoke only so I could hear him.

"No," she snapped her head with attitude.

"Drink?" I queried dismissing her tone because she's not the first and will not be the last to give me attitude in this exam room.

"I may have had a couple of drinks with my girls to celebrate my new body."

"At what stage of the healing process?" I probed with a raised eyebrow.

"I don't know, like three weeks in. What's the problem?"

Dr. Cooper took over, "the problem is, I lay out an intensive healing process. Something I don't necessarily have to do, but I take pride in. It clearly states no alcohol or smoking until the follow up appointment."

"In other words, your incisions aren't quite healed. That leads to risk of infection." I said as sympathetically as I could.

"Infection?" Her eyes ballooned when she realized how serious we were.

"Yes," Dr. Cooper was now gloving up, prompting me to do the same. "Lie down, please," he instructed her.

Tears coated her eyes, and I was over seeing those today. Inside, I was dying. Dreading seeing Nolan and confronting him because confronting him was something I had to do…today. Dr. Cooper talked me through examining the patient. Luckily, she didn't have an infection, and I told her to take it easy for the next couple of weeks. Then scheduled her another follow-up, if only they would listen the first go-around.

It was close to six when I went to get Nolan from school. I drove there and back in silence. When he tried making conversation with me, I didn't respond or engage. I didn't know how to approach the topic without being accusatory.

Nolan hooked his fingers in the waistband of my scrubs and pulled me backwards to him, catching me off guard. He had to hold onto my waist to keep me from falling on my ass.

"What did I do?" He said against my ear. His delicious warmth surrounded me instantly.

I fell into his touch, letting my anger subside a little, "Where are the pills?" I came out with it as calmly as possible.

He chuckled then left me to open the cabinet door under the TV. The pill bottle sat right there, staring at me in my shameful face.

Why didn't I check there earlier?

He tossed the orange bottle towards me, "do you want to count them, too? I bought twenty."

Catching the bottle midair I sat down on the sofa exasperated, "I'm sorry."

He sat beside me, his arm around me, "we have too much trust between us to start losing it. I gave you my word. I'm done with that shit. Trust me, Queen."

chapter
twenty

Watching Lani as she sleeps in my bed is my new favorite hobby. I've slept next to this girl so many times, but it's different now. It feels like I'm in a dream, or I'm doing something wrong when I touch her intimately. I love the look in her eyes when I do touch her—I didn't notice that shit before.

I removed my drenched t-shirt from my body, tossing it across the room. It's been hard for me to fall asleep and stay asleep. I have too much on my mind and too many papers to grade. It's like I'll get a stack down, then another will appear on my desk. It's a never ending cycle.

A pill would help conquer the papers and calm the noise in my head.

I promised Lani, but it's just one pill.

No, a promise is a promise.

One little pill, just one. Maybe a half of one.

It's been a week since I last had a pill, and my body was going through the most. Increasing the amount I took in a day wasn't good. My body became dependent on it almost instantly. As if on cue, Lani stirred, reaching out to my side of the bed. Smiling in her sleep when her hand landed on my chest.

I gently shook her, "Lani?"

"Hmm?"

"I'm having a hard time, Queen."

Her eyes popped open, connecting with mine. "Do you need a glass of water?" Covering her mouth as she yawned. She was exhausted from the hours she's been pulling at work.

"Nah, I need you to talk to me." She closed her eyes, yawning again. "Don't worry about it baby; go back to sleep."

"No, I want to help." Lani sat up trying to sound convincing. "What do you want to talk about?"

"Anything other than what I'm thinking about."

Lani threw her legs over the side of the bed; she left the room returning with my glass chess board set. She turned on the light, setting the board up between us.

My father taught me how to play chess when I was seven years old. 'It's a thinking game, son,' he would often say. We would play almost every night before bed. I lost every time, but he said it wasn't always about winning, it was the strategy that made you the winner. When Liam died, so did our nightly game sessions. I taught Lani how to play since I loved the game and didn't have anyone to play with.

Chess helped clear my mind, like what I desperately needed right now. I liked having Lani by my side because she knew exactly what I needed even if I didn't.

With my legs outstretched at her side, Lani pulled at the hairs on my leg while contemplating her next move. She always played the same way. One of her knights was the first to move followed by the bishop. She never moved the pawn unless she absolutely had to, courtesy of me pushing forward. Her tactics won games between us but not all. I knew how and when to challenge her. That night at Kennedy's, no way was I going to allow her to win. We had eyes around us, and if I was going to attend one of Kennedy and Socari's game nights, I had to set the precedent I was that nigga with this chess board.

I, on the other hand, rely on my Queen. She rules the board, and I explained that to Lani, but she would always say. 'Pawns rule the board because pawns turn into queens.'

Damn, she was dropping hints, and I completely fucking missed it. The shit went over my head for years.

I call Lani my Queen because she's always there for me when I need her, reliable. But pawns were soldiers, fighting their way to the other side of the board, taking bigger, more significant pieces out with the goal of queening.

My eyes traveled to her beautiful face. I get it, and I get her, for real. I pushed the board aside, careful to not shatter the pieces and captured her lips. Catching her by surprise, I guided her onto her back gently, but not breaking our lip lock. I pulled up, watching her eyes glow, "pawns become Queens."

She smiled, throwing her hands over her eyes. Kissing her hands, I positioned myself between her legs, my eyes ran over her body watching her melt under my touch. I planted kisses on her neck, nibbling on her tender spot until she was putty in my hand. I pulled myself from my pajama pants, positioning directly at her opening.

"Wait," her voice was barely audible in the still room. I gave her a look because I couldn't fucking wait. I wanted to be inside of her, engulfed in her warmth right now. My entire body needed to be against hers. "Nolan, I love you."

"I love you, too, Queen," I kissed her neck, slowly trailing my tongue to her chin, then dipping my tongue into her mouth. I pushed into her as she gasped from my girth and length. She was always so tight. Slowly rocking in and out of her, her legs wrapped around my waist sinking me in deeper. The subtle clinking of the chess pieces acted as our musical soundtrack. The sensations from Lani sucking on my tongue and scratching my back had me about to ejaculate prematurely. I leaned down trapping her nipples between my teeth. Lani whimpered as she came wetting my sheets.

This was the distraction I needed. No longer did I crave the pill, but I craved Lani. If I could be addicted to something, I'd rather be addicted to her. Tasting her, smelling her, kissing her—overall being with her. I regretted not being her first. Knowing other guys had the pleasure of being with her, infuriated me, but it was my fault. I had blinders on. But now, no one else will ever touch her in this way again. She's all mine.

Hooking her by the waist and turning her over, I dipped down, spreading her ass cheeks and smiling at the moisture coating her center. She trembled when my tongue slid from her pussy to her ass, and I repeated the act. Sticking my tongue deep in her pussy then suckling on her clit, I smacked her ass as she held it in the air for me. Her juices flowed into my mouth, prompting a deep moan from her throat.

"Baby, I could drink you all day." I spread her again burrowing even deeper inside her, all while grabbing fists full of her perfect ass. The sounds of her sloppy wetness and our bodies colliding filled the room. Lani gripped the sheet, coating me with her liquid again. I continued a steady pace, not wanting to overwhelm her. Plus, I liked feeling her walls contract when she's coming all over me, wetting the sheets with her juices. Marking her spot on my bed and in my life. My hands clutched onto Lani's hips as I buried myself inside her, again and again. Her moans carried throughout the room as I talked my shit. She arched her back trying to match my thrust, only to be stopped by another orgasm.

Grunting loudly, I released inside of her. "Damn," I bellowed, my sweaty back hitting the soft pillows. I stared at the ceiling, getting control of my breathing. Lani laid on top of me with her head on my chest. Needless to say, after that, I don't think I'd ever need that pill. I needed this, Lani asleep with my arms wrapped around her bare skin.

Feeling her, being inside of her was fucking amazing. Touching her and kissing her was a feeling I couldn't explain even if I wanted to. Being her friend all these years compares nothing to being her lover.

Lani is softer, and I see the love she has for me when I look into her brown eyes. I'm not ashamed to admit she's got me hooked.

"Why you smiling so hard, Mr. Hudson?" A nosey ass student asked.

I hadn't even realized I was smiling. Their little asses were supposed to be taking a test. "Probably Miss. Malani putting a smile on that boy's face." Justice cackled from her seat.

"First of all. I'm a man and get back to the test before I fail all of y'all." That statement only made them laugh harder, partly because they knew I wasn't serious.

Grant has been trying his hardest to avoid me. He's tight, but he threw himself into the lion's den. Even when Lani wasn't mine, she still was because her heart belonged to me. Nobody told him to step to her, impatient ass nigga. Sending flowers and shit but look where that got him.

"What's up, man," I said to him when he entered the teacher's lounge carrying a thermos. He nodded his head. "Damn, you can't talk?" I urged, fucking with him. I never pegged Grant for a nigga to have his panties in a bunch because he lost a girl.

Grant smirked, "what's up? You steal my girl and expect me to talk to you? That's low, even for you."

"Your girl?" It was my turn to smirk because this nigga was out his mind. I approached his ass on some cordial shit, but referring to Lani as his girl was a fucking stretch.

"Yeah, my girl. I should've known better than to trust you were only friends."

"We *were* only friends," I defended.

He scoffed, opening the thermos to eat the bullshit ass soup he'd put into it. "Let you tell it."

"Yeah, all right," I turned to return to my class. Regardless, Lani is mine so there's no need for me to explain shit to him.

Grant had the tendency of wanting to discuss personal shit at school. Regardless of what happened outside of these school walls, should stay out. At the end of it all, we have to be civil teachers on school grounds.

"Next time, don't set me up with a bitch you want to fuck."

I could feel the rage brewing inside of me. I bit the inside of my cheek hoping that would help with trying to subside it. I turned back to face him, glaring at his smug ass.

"Yeah, or let me fuck first, then you could have her," he said lowly, so only I could hear him.

My fist connected with that motherfucker's mouth within seconds. He fell back in the chair, and I kicked his stupid ass in the stomach. This nigga is not only disrespectful to Lani, but women as a whole. I thought his ass might have changed since college, but he wore the mask well. I kept kicking Grant until I was being tugged by multiple teachers trying to stop the attack.

Fuck him!

I forcefully pushed my knee in his stomach before landing another punch to his eye. Two men grabbed my arms pulling me from Grant. I realized it was the basketball coach and the gym teacher.

I snatched my arms away from the men, adjusting my shirt and wiping Grant's blood from my knuckles. "Next time, watch your fucking mouth." I left the teacher's lounge going straight to Principal Danders' office.

I **STARED** off into space while Lani fried the chicken for our dinner. I wasn't pissed at her, more at myself for letting Grant get close to her. All day images of them spending time together, him kissing her—touching her flashed through my mind. I wasn't a jealous nigga, but with Lani, I've always been like this.

She was happy, singing in the shower and now in the kitchen as she washed the dishes and cooked at the same time.

"What's wrong?" Lani sat next to me drying her hands on the apron she'd bought from her apartment to mine. She looked at me with concern floating in her brown globes.

"I got suspended today, until further review."

"What? Why?"

"I got into a physical altercation with another teacher." I stared at her long enough for her to read between the lines.

"What happened?" I shook my head because the why didn't matter; it was necessary. "Were you high?"

I scoffed, raising up from the couch, "I told you I wasn't touching them pills so don't ask me that again."

"Then, tell me why?" She stood trying to match my height by standing on her tiptoes. "Nolan, this is your career."

"You don't think I fucking know that? That nigga fucked up, and I didn't care where I was." I softened my tone, knowing my problem wasn't with her. "I didn't think about it; I reacted."

"No matter what, you can't let nobody take you out of character." She held my hand.

I looked her over. She's right, and for that reason, I didn't want Lani to know about me fucking up somebody on her behalf. I hated disrespectful niggas, even more towards her. But, now that she's mine, I feel the need to do even more.

"I hate he touched you," I pouted like a big ass kid.

When something is yours, you want it all to yourself—that's how I feel about Lani. Even when we were friends, I hated when she got into a relationship because I had to share her time with them niggas. Niggas that had a problem with my handsome ass being around her, filling her head with lies and shit. Them, conveniently planning a date when they knew we had plans. I never tripped, though. The only time I had to step to them was when they were disrespectful.

Lani slid her hand into the waistband of my pants finding my dick waking him up with each stroke. "But I love when *you* touch me," she focused on stroking me with her soft hands.

Lani dropped to her knees before me, taking me into her mouth. Her eyes trained on mine as she took me deeper down her throat. She's so beautiful with and without a mouth full of my dick. Lani kept stroking with both hands and sucking. My hands fisted her curly hair guiding her on my shit. She was sloppy, and I love that shit. I loved when a woman didn't give a fuck about saliva and precum painting her face.

"Shit, Lani," I hissed when she relaxed her jaws taking me in deeper. "Look at me," I instructed, staring down into her glossed over eyes took me over. "Fuck, I'm about to cum. You want this nut, baby?" Lani nodded, and I shot the load on her tongue. I groaned because she pulled out all the stops. Pulling her to her feet, I tongued her while she stepped out of her clothes. I sat on the couch burying myself deep into her swiftly; this was home. I didn't want to be anywhere else in this world, only with her. Our connection—this connection will always be important to me. Lani has opened a door I never knew existed, but I knew I never wanted to close it again. My heart's rhythm and my love for her worked in tandem. She moaned as I glided in her slowly, showing her how much I love her with each stroke. I didn't want to rush our moments together. She bounced on my dick until she couldn't anymore. I took control, holding onto her waist sliding her down my length.

Lani buried her head into my neck kissing and licking me there until her hot tongue found its way to my ear. "I've always been yours," she whispered. I didn't give a fuck. That shit went straight to my head, fueling me to slam deeper into her. Saying shit like that to me will make me put a ring on her fucking finger—right now. Lani felt so good as her walls squeezed around me pulling me in; she milked me dry as I exploded inside of her.

We remained connected, my semi-erect dick still pulsating inside her wet goodness.

Her head was on my shoulder. "I love you, and I'll always protect you."

Jealous shit aside, no one will disrespect her and walk this earth saying Nolan didn't do shit. I felt her nod slowly. I smiled while holding her in my arms.

Fucking homeboy up was worth it.

I **WASN'T ALLOWED** on school grounds, but I could still grade papers and send the substitute emails about which worksheets the kids should complete.

Principal Danders said my return was up to the Board of Education, which was total bullshit. Grant wasn't pressing charges, so I didn't understand why they wanted to press the issue.

I'm a damn good teacher, and if they didn't respect that, I would move on to another school district that would.

It felt weird as shit sitting at home all day with nothing to do. I wasn't into watching TV all the time, a movie here and there, but

Lani turned me on to this streaming service filled with Black movies and TV shows. I found so much shit to watch when she was at work. I even cooked, so when she walked in all she had to do was jump in the running shower before coming to the living room to eat. It's been great, and we are closer than ever.

Willow's number flashed on my phone, I deleted her contact once me and Lani became official. Besides, it wasn't a reason to keep in contact with her. I closed the washing machine, turning the dial to its required setting before closing the doors that hid the washer and dryer.

"What's up?" I answered, carrying the basket of Lani's clothes to my bedroom. The more she stayed over, the more I convinced her to leave clothes here. I adjusted my clothes in the walk-in closet to fit some of her work scrubs and everyday wear. I also cleaned out a top drawer for her undergarments. We were that official. I was hoping she would move in soon since she's here more than at her apartment.

"Hey!" She sounded too excited. "What are you doing?"

"Nothing, what do you need?"

"Geez, I wanted to hear your voice. I haven't heard from you in a while. How are you?"

"I'm good, Willow. How are you?"

"Missing you," she cooed. That shit used to get me hard as a rock, but things had changed. I've never been the type to cheat on a girl I claimed as mine, I especially wasn't about to do no fuck shit to Lani.

"Missing me, huh?" I chuckled into the receiver.

Lani cleared her throat causing me to turn meeting her angry eyes.

"Willow, I got to go," at the mention of her name, Lani's eyebrows raised to her hairline and her brown eyes rounded into perfect circles. I hung up the phone reaching towards Lani, "hey, Queen." I kissed her forehead, lingering to inhale her scent.

"We're allowed to talk to our exes?" She followed me into the bedroom, where I ran the shower for her, testing the temperature with my left hand.

"Baby, greet me first." I demanded, glaring into her eyes and taking a page out of her book.

I shouldn't have answered the call, but a part of me wanted to know why she was calling.

Lani's eyes softened, "hey Nolan."

Embracing her I said, "you don't have shit to worry about."

Lani scoffed, "that's not the point I was trying to make."

"I know, and it won't happen again," I pressed my lips against hers, sliding my tongue into her mouth and my fingers up the nape of her neck. She pulled my bottom lip between her teeth, biting down with enough pressure to cause blood to rush to my groin. A whimper released from her lips as I pulled her against my hard chest deepening our kiss.

Lani stepped back to undress. I watched her sexy ass seductively remove the bright orange scrubs. "Are you watching or joining?"

"Shit," I bit my bottom lip. My dick pressed against the fabric of the gym shorts I wore. My shit begged to be freed the moment we inhaled her scent. It was hard staying soft around Lani; my dick had a mind of its own. It thought we were supposed to be inside her every second of the day.

"Nolan, are you seriously thinking about it?" The excitement she previously held dissipated.

Keeping my gaze away from her body, I stared into her eyes. "I don't want you thinking I only want you physically."

She stepped close to me, "you wanting me in any capacity is good enough for me. I know our connection is deep. We've connected emotionally and mentally and explored that for years. This is a new level for us. Sexually, I want you just as bad as you want me. I crave you being inside of me even when I'm at work, there's nothing wrong with that."

Fuck!

I pinned her against the bathroom wall. Leaning down, my mouth attacked her neck, and she let out a squeal. I sucked hard, gripping her bare ass in my hands. "You're so fucking perfect."

twenty-one

Malani

After months of hard planning and going back and forth with the contractors and designers, we were finally at the day Dr. Cooper and me had been waiting on.

A crowd of locals along with family and friends gathered around the small building, "three, two, one..." Dr. Cooper cut the big red ribbon from in front of the door of his new practice as applause filled the air.

Nolan pressed against my back, holding me around the waist, and whispering sweet nothings in my ear, causing my nipples to harden and moisture to pool between my thighs.

The ribbon cutting ceremony became a huge deal when I contacted Dr. Cooper's sister asking her to run an article in the local newspaper, where she worked, about the first black-owned private practice in New Bern.

It was epic, downright historic.

Family and friends of Dr. Cooper congratulated him on his success, he was humble enough to let them know he couldn't have done it without me—although I've only been by his side for four years.

Dr. Cooper reached out for me, handed me the key to the glass door, "are you sure?" I asked because he should be the one opening the doors for the first time.

It wasn't my accomplishment; it's his, but I'm glad he's sharing it with me.

When he nodded, my hands trembled when I reached for the lock. Holding his hand over mine to steady it, we turned the lock and walked into the lobby of the practice with the crowd piling in behind us. Gasps filling the room when they noticed the decor.

Dr. Cooper gave several tours of the space to those that wanted it before we were all enjoying food and drinks catered by *The Lounge.*

Nolan interlocked our fingers as we broke away from the party to my office. A smile spread across my face watching him take it all in. It had been hard being tight-lipped about the decor because I wanted to tell Nolan everything, from the color of the walls to the type of tiles on the floor.

I held it for this moment.

My office was a real live chess board, with the floor laminated as such. In the corner was a huge black resin sculpture of the queen chess piece. Various pieces were scattered about the desk and pictures hung on my walls along with the pictures of me and Nolan. I was happy with this office, but probably wouldn't spend any time in it.

"This is nice as shit, Queen." He tossed his arm around my neck, bringing me into him. The smell of his cologne made me close my eyes and I clenched my thighs together. I was pulsating for him and didn't care if there were over fifty people in the building. I sat on my black, marbled top desk with Nolan stepping in-between my thighs. The black off the shoulder long sleeved dress rose up my thighs. Closing the gap between us, I pulled Nolan by his belt, undoing it as he said, "I didn't like him touching you," Nolan exhaled when I reached my hand down the front of his pants.

"You don't have shit to worry about," I repeated his words from days earlier when I caught him talking on the phone with Willow.

In my opinion, her number should've been blocked like I had done with Grant's number. Nolan thinks he's the only one that could get jealously crazy—I handle mine differently.

I tried to pull his dick out, but he grabbed my wrist stopping me, "I'm serious, and don't pull my shit out unless you want to be bent over this desk with all your co-workers hearing you scream my name." He backed away, adjusting himself. And I was turned on—at any given moment I was ready to be nasty with him.

"Delete Willow's number, then you can talk to me about Dr. Cooper's innocent ass touches," I folded my arms across my chest.

"It's nothing to delete her fucking number."

"Then, why haven't you?" I quizzed.

Nolan stared at me, but words didn't come from his mouth.

Our stare-down came to a halt when Ezeke and Harmony walked into my office. I jumped off the desk, rolling my eyes at Nolan.

"Eww, ya'll nasty," Harmony eyed us with a pretend stank face. She hugged me, congratulating me, followed by Ezeke doing the same. "Lani let's get a drink," before I could protest, she was pulling me out of the office. "Dr. Cooper's single, right?" She whispered after we retrieved our drinks from the open bar.

"I think so. Why? I thought he wasn't your type."

"That was before you know who snatched my heart from my chest and broke it. I'm ready to mingle. I see he has some fine-ass brothers, too."

I chuckled, "all who have dates on their arms."

"What does that mean?" Harmony chuckled, looking through the crowd at Dr. Cooper with his two handsome brothers.

I nudged her, "it means Ezeke is still available," I smiled at her, downing the vodka and coke before asking for a refill and tossing that one back as well.

Harmony smacked her lips, "I already told you. I don't want Ezekiel."

"It looks like somebody does," I nodded towards two females smiling in Ezeke's *and* Nolan's face. I paid more attention to Nolan, noticing his interaction with the female I didn't recognize. She wasn't part of the staff, maybe she's a friend or relative of one. I didn't react because I needed to know if he could control himself. I leaned against the bar, asking for another drink and nursing it while staring at my man laugh and converse without much of a look towards me. That fight in my office wasn't that heavy for him to ignore me.

"Are you okay?"

"What?" I responded to Harmony, reluctantly peeling my eyes from Nolan. "Yeah, why do you ask?"

"Because you're bouncing your leg, babe. It's just conversation."

"But let that be *me* in conversation, and he'll have a whole fit."

"Ya'll are crazy," Harmony commented. "This is why I can't take Ezekiel seriously. One minute he's in my face, then another minute in another girl's face."

"It's just conversation," hitting her with her own words.

Instead of staring at Nolan, I meandered around the party. Greeting and chatting with the staff and their families. Everyone was in good spirits on this joyous night. A few of the staff talked me into giving their family a view of my office. They were impressed with the décor. One nurse asked if we could share offices because she was so in love with mine.

Before ending the night, Dr. Cooper gave a final speech. "Thank you, Dr. Dawson," he embraced me. "I'll see you in two weeks."

I nodded, "yeah, have fun."

Nolan was still chatting with the same girl, so I pulled Harmony out of some guy's face asking her to take me home, and I meant my home.

I peeled out of the dress, showered, and lay naked in the bed I'd neglected for weeks. I didn't like how I was feeling in this moment. Nolan called, but instead of ignoring it like I wanted to—I answered. "Hello?"

"Why didn't you tell me you were leaving?"

"I didn't want to interrupt your important conversation."

"I wish you would've, that was one of Ezeke's bosses talking my head off."

I chuckled dryly.

"Wait, where the fuck are you? I just walked in the house."

"I'm at home."

He smacked his lip, "Lani, get over here. Stop playing."

"I can't. I've been drinking. I'll see you tomorrow." I hung up before he could protest.

Before closing my eyes for the night, I emailed Dr. Cooper his hotel itinerary for Miami. He didn't have time to book, so I did it for him.

I haven't had time to tell Nolan about Hawaii. I wanted to surprise him tonight when I took him into my office, but it didn't work out as planned. His suspension, although unfortunate, fell at the right time for him to be able to go with me. I know my parents would love to see him too.

After hours of tossing and turning, I was unable to sleep, because I missed Nolan's warmth. I needed to be close to his body in order to fall asleep. I called his phone, but it went straight to voicemail. It was going on two in the morning, but I dressed and headed over to his place.

Letting myself into the pitch-black apartment, flipping the light switch on the wall, and setting my purse on the table by the door. I rubbed my eyes, thinking my mind was playing tricks on me. Women's clothes were scattered about the entrance of his apartment. Something moved on his sofa, causing me to yelp. The heifer saw me and started to scream as well, but it was too dark in that space to make her out.

Nolan came from his room dragging his feet. "What is going on?" He saw me, and then I saw something I couldn't recognize glimmer in his eyes. "Lani," I didn't like the way he said my name because I knew bullshit was trailing closely behind.

The floor lamp in the living room flicked on, shining bright, it was Willow—wrapped in his comforter. The same one we made love on this morning. I looked at her then to Nolan, taking in his attire. Or lack thereof. He wore gym shorts, no boxers or briefs underneath. Just thin fabric barely containing his big ass dick.

The clothes on the floor caught my attention again, so I knew she was naked.

My mouth went dry; the moisture traveling to my eyes instead.

My chest tightened as air got trapped in my lungs.

I wanted to say something, I wanted to scream at him, but

nothing came out of my mouth. No words formulated in my head as the scene before me begged me to survey it—telling me everything I needed to know.

Aside from my heavy breathing the room was silent.

Move Malani.

Why are you still standing here?

My feet were cemented to the floor. I was torturing myself by looking between them. Each with a stupid expression on their faces, but neither opening their mouths to explain.

Nolan reached for me, but I stepped back—grabbed my keys, dropping the spare to his apartment on his island before snatching my purse from the table and leaving.

chapter
twenty-two

Malani

"If I eat another pineapple, Imma give birth to a whole tree," Harmony laughed.

We were basking in the Hawaiian sun, eating fresh pineapples, and sipping on kiwi coladas. We'd been here a week, and if she was already gouged out on pineapple, she better suck it up because it's never-ending.

"It's never enough for me," I popped a piece of her pineapple into my mouth.

Surprising my parents was emotional. I actually got to hug and kiss them for the first time in years. I didn't know how much I'd miss them until their arms were around me, squeezing me into a tight hug. I wish I had this every day, and with what I was going through with Nolan, I needed it. I found out my brother, Kolby, was back living in Hawaii with my parents. It was good to see him, too, but not good because Harmony flirted with him every chance she got. I avoided answering questions about Nolan. I knew he would call my dad at some point during my visit.

"I'm not going back," I admitted to Harmony.

She peered at me over her sunglasses. "If you stay, I stay."

"I'm serious," I chuckled.

"So am I," I could tell from the expression on her face and her tone she was.

I was thinking out loud, not sure if I was serious. I liked being with my parents. I missed them.

Why go back to misery?

No one loves me there, not like the love I need, craved.

The unthinkable happened, and I've been left with a million and one why's floating around in my head. Being with Nolan was all I ever wanted—him being with me, not a part of his plans. I'd never known for him to cheat on a girlfriend. Why me?

This is my karma, and I fucking hate it.

The white sand and blue water dancing with the sunlight always had me mesmerized for minutes. Hawaii is jaw dropping beautiful. It was heaven, and I know why my parents moved here. There wasn't any noise. It still looked the same as when we'd visited when I was a kid, but back then I didn't appreciate the stillness. Dr. Cooper and I have been exchanging scenery photos over the week. Mine, in my opinion, being much more serene than his but nevertheless Miami is a beautiful city.

Snapping a photo of me and Harmony in our bikinis—I sent it to Ezeke, unbeknownst to her.

"Why don't you want to go back? What about Nolan?" She pried. The Hawaiian sun kissed her skin, giving it a glow.

I hadn't been quite honest with Harmony as far as the details surrounding our girls' trip because I didn't want to spill tears on warm Hawaii sand. What's going on between me and Nolan has to be handled by me and Nolan, and I didn't want anyone's judgment.

Shaking my head, I simply answered, "I've missed my parents..." I let my words trail off.

"There's something you're not telling me," Harmony glanced over at me for a second then looked down at her phone.

For the first time since being in this beautiful state, melancholy slipped over me—brushing across my face swiftly. I didn't wanna say anything.

She continued, "Nolan only calls and texts me when you're not talking to him. And let's just say he's been hitting me up almost every day this week."

My eyes became one with the ocean, following the waves as they rippled over and over again in the vast water. I didn't care because as far as I'm concerned, the relationship and friendship with Nolan has depleted. I didn't care if he knew where I was. I've posted pictures on social media.

"What happened?" Harmony snapped her fingers in front of my face to get my attention.

Shrugging my shoulders, I responded, "I don't want to talk about it." My phone dinged letting me know that Ezeke hearted the picture of me and Harmony. Spilling my guts out to her was not what I had in mind when I suggested we go to the beach to people-watch and sip drinks. I wanted to enjoy the mai tais and forget my stresses and worries.

"What am I here for if you can't lean on me?"

"Like I've always told you, Harms, what goes on between me and Nolan is our problems. I don't like bringing our shit to our friend group."

"It still affects all of us. I need to know if we are mad at him because I will not talk to him off the strength of being loyal to you. I'm your friend first," she argued.

I chuckled at the sentiment, "I'm not asking you to take my side and be mad at him. I'm mad, but that's just me. Nolan is a good friend to you, sometimes. It's just a lot going on and I don't wanna ruin my vacation by thinking or talking about it."

"Holding that energy isn't good either."

I nodded in agreement.

"Tell me what he did so we can both be pissed at him. I'm sure he told Ezekiel—why don't you trust me?"

I cocked my head to the side, "I trust you."

Harmony folded her arms across her chest.

"It's hard to talk about."

"Have you not held me when I cried? Especially since my heart was broken recently—you were there for me, let me be there for you."

It was embarrassing, but that was my life, an embarrassing ass train wreck with Nolan as the train's conductor. Reluctantly, I told Harmony everything. I cried to her, laying my head on her shoulder. She comforted me as I gave her the energy she asked for.

"Does Ezekiel know?"

I nodded. That night I called Ezeke crying, not caring what time it was or if he was freaking with some chick. He invited me over, and I cried to him. Ezeke is a good listener who offers great advice.

"Why do you tell him but not me?" Harmony asked. I could hear the hurt in her voice, but I didn't have an answer.

I stayed quiet as she rambled off how much I like him over her, and she was my friend first. She would understand why I confide in him so much if she was actually friends with him.

Ezeke's name and picture flashed across the screen of my phone. I wiped my eyes and dried my face before answering. "Hey, Ezeke!" Failing miserably at sounding upbeat and happy. Why couldn't I be happy with this beautiful scene wrapped around me.

"Hey, Baby girl. Are you all right?"

"No," I dug into the warm sand until it was a hole big enough to put my fist in.

"When are you coming back?"

"I'm not."

"Don't do that," his tone was soft.

Sobbing into the phone, I said, "I don't want to come back."

Harmony rubbed my bare back.

I listened intently as Ezeke consoled me. I didn't know what I was going to do, but I knew I didn't want to sit around moping about Nolan. In the back of my mind, I wished we would have remained friends, never crossing that line.

Why did I have to like him?

Why did I have to love him?

PRIVACY FROM HARMONY was getting scarce because she wanted to know my every move and how I was feeling after the meltdown on the beach. My answer was the same each time; I felt like shit. Never in my life had my heart been broken like this. I've never experience pain at this magnitude.

I snuck into the bathroom on my parent's side of the ranch style home. I dialed Ezeke's number, holding my breath until he answered. "Baby Girl?"

I neglected to remember the time difference. It was only nine here. "I'm sorry to call you so late. I needed to talk."

"It's all good, what's up?"

I sighed deeply, "I have something to tell you, but you can't tell anyone."

"I always hold your secrets," he had a valid point. He held my secrets and Nolan's and for some reason that wasn't a problem for me yet.

"I've been really sad lately, like more than usual. The shit that happened with Nolan has me all over the place."

Ezeke cleared his throat, "he swears..."

"I don't care what he swears, Ezeke, I really don't. I know what I saw."

"I'm just saying, do you really think he would cheat on you?"

"No," I admitted, "but that doesn't explain why she was at his house at that time in the morning."

"I don't know."

"You know, but you don't want to tell me, and that's okay." An awkward silence fell upon us, "Anyway, I'm pregnant," I whispered.

"Say that again... Nolan knocked your ass up? What are your feelings?"

"Don't be my therapist right now," I snapped.

"I'm being a friend," he corrected.

I gathered my thoughts, "I feel okay. I'm not sad about the pregnancy. That's actually the most exciting part. Telling him will be the hard part."

"Will you tell him, though?"

"I have to," thoughts of raising my child in Hawaii crossed my mind, but that wasn't fair to Nolan or our baby.

But, then again, he wasn't fair to me or our relationship when

Willow was walking around his apartment naked as the day she was born.

"If you need me to be there, I will. I got your front and back."

"I know, thank you."

Ezeke coached me through methods of relaxation to keep my mind clear. For the remainder of the trip me and Harmony lived it to the fullest by shopping and eating all of my parent's food. Although, I silently cried at night until the last night when I promised myself that Nolan was no longer worthy of my tears. Out of all the guys in the entire world Nolan should have been the main one to know how to treat me, but he didn't.

Like I said at the beginning of the year my focus is now my career because that's what keeps me in New Bern.

Leaving my parents was so hard, they even promised that they will come visit me later in the year. Of course, Harmony left with Kolby's numbers. I rolled my eyes as she hugged him tight.

chapter
twenty-three

Nolan

Ezeke acted like he couldn't open his mouth when I asked about Lani. I'd been calling her and Harmony for over a week trying to get her to talk to me, so I could explain. She wasn't trying to hear me. I was blocked from calling and texting before she pulled out of my apartment complex.

I fucking miss her.

I've buried myself into work, completing all the ungraded assignments and updating each students' grade in the system. That was one accomplishment I was proud of. Although, the investigation was still ongoing. I admitted to fucking him up, what more evidence did they need?

Home life was boring without her. I lay in my bed practically all day, looking through my phone of pictures I snapped of her while she was asleep and videos of her sexy ass in my kitchen cooking us a meal.

This shit seemed final.

Like an asshole, I lost my best friend and girlfriend.

The fuck is wrong with me?

The look on her face that night, I never want to see again.

I was caught in a position I never imagined would happen.

Following her social media, I knew she was back home. I didn't want to be a cliché ass nigga and pop up at her house, although I was tempted until my mom talked me out of it. My mom suggested I come over for a home cooked meal, since she says I've been getting skinny the two weeks Lani's been in Hawaii.

I missed my baby's cooking.

"Stop pouting and help me plate this food," my mom called out to me in the den.

Staggering to my feet, I unconsciously checked my phone hoping Lani's name displayed on the screen. When I didn't see shit, I tucked my phone back into my jeans.

"She will call. Stop worrying." My mom handed me a black paper plate filled with rice, potatoes, and steak.

"Have you talked to her?" I asked my mom.

She busied herself with plating a plate for my dad.

I shook my head knowingly, scrubbing my hand over my face. "Why didn't you let me talk to her?" My heart dropped to my stomach. I needed to hear her voice.

"She's upset. I didn't know ya'll were dating."

"It just happened. What did she say?"

"About what?"

I took a bite of the steak. I wasn't in the mood to play this game with my mom. Me and my dad ate and watched a movie. He was dozing off and shit. Nigga almost dropped his plate in the couch. I fucked all the food up. Shit, they wasn't gone eat all of it anyway. I packed a plate to take home too.

It's like a wall closed around me, everything and everyone reminds me of Lani. Reminders of how I fucked up. They look at me like I'm the problem and they're not wrong. I unintentionally fumbled her. Played with her heart like it was a motherfucking game and everybody else is protecting her—like I should've.

I couldn't take this shit no more. Taking a chance, I made the call. Hoping she would finally answer. After three rings, she did, but the other end was silent.

"Lani?" I called out, my palms were sweaty with anticipation.

chapter
twenty-four

Malani

I got into a rhythm at work. It was much harder being that we were a private practice because I didn't have the cushion of relying on administration as I once had at Nicoyce Med. We hadn't had time to hire any administration. We were just getting off the ground and combing through applications was a task within itself. We have receptionists, but their main task was checking the patients in and out. A temp agency currently employed the billing department for now, but I kept my eyes closely on that paperwork.

We had so many requests for transfers that it made it very difficult to stick to opening at seven and closing at eight schedule. Often times we will be at the office until midnight having to order from *The Lounge* for dinner.

Being this busy kept my mind from Nolan. I've been back for a week, and I hadn't seen him or talked to him. Of course, I blocked his number and persuaded Ezeke to retrieve my house key from him before coming home from Hawaii.

I cut ties at least for right now.

I couldn't help but notice how different Dr. Cooper was since coming back from Miami. He's happy, not that he wasn't before but this was a new type of happy like I was with Nolan. I asked him if he reconnected with that surgeon from Miami, but he said he didn't. That made me more curious at who was putting a smile on his face. Normally, he would tell me, but I have a feeling that this isn't a fling. Guys always talk about the flings but when it comes to someone they really care about they tend to keep their mouths closed. I respect that but it still causes my nosiness to be at its highest peak. I wanted to know. Plus, how my love life's been going, I need to live vicariously through someone else. I just hope whoever it is treats him right because underneath all that handsome hoe-ness, he's a pretty good guy.

I sat in my office as my fingertips fumbled through paperwork that needed to be filed and carefully looked over again, nothing wrong with triple checking. I yawned, rubbing my eyes from staring at numbers and words all day. A hot bath, wine, and a cinnamon roll from *The Lounge* screamed my name.

"I'm heading out," Dr. Cooper stood in the frame of my office. I looked over at the time, noticing it was only nine.

"Are you just gonna leave me here by myself?" I wasn't afraid of staying alone, but it didn't mean I wanted to. The cleaning crew would come in at eleven, but they only cleaned then left to go to their next job.

"How much more do you have to do?" His hands slid into his pockets as he approached the front of my desk.

"Just have to match the numbers to what the billing office recorded this afternoon."

"Can it wait until Monday?"

I sighed deeply, "I suppose it could. I just wanted to get it out the way—one less thing I have to worry about on Monday."

"Yeah, leave it," he smiled, finally looking up at him I noticed his attire. He was in tailored blue slacks with a white polo. He looked like he'd just stepped off the pages of a magazine.

My eyebrows rose in curiosity, "do you have a date?"

"No, I wish. My parents have this anniversary party every year, and I have to go." He didn't sound too excited, but I didn't press. I didn't know much about his family besides what he told me. He has two younger brothers and a younger sister. I've only recently encountered them at the ribbon cutting. I knew his parents were wealthy from the gossip that circled around Nicoyce Med. "This is their year thirty-five."

"Wow, that's exciting. I can't wait till I'm there."

"Yeah, me too. Let's go, my mother hates when I'm late." He helped me shove the papers into the file cabinet, locking it.

Dr. Cooper walked me to my car, after chatting for a bit about tasks we had to complete on Monday, we parted ways. I sat in my car staring at the building allowing the warmth I felt from the sight of it radiate through my body.

Driving away with a smile on my lips, but with nothing to do tonight, the smile faded almost immediately. I didn't have work to obsess over—I was forced to face the sad musical soundtrack of my life.

I needed a good meal and did not feel like cooking at this time of the night, the only food I wanted was *The Lounge*. Saturdays at *The Lounge* are always wall to wall, but I didn't care. I need food, and maybe eavesdropping on someone else's conversation will give me entertainment watching tv shows couldn't provide.

Going home to change first because I would not dare step into *The Lounge* in scrubs. I threw a light jacket over my red fitted t-shirt that I paired with denim jeans. The weather was just getting warmer, but it was still cold enough at night that you needed a jacket. I let my natural curls surround my face, spraying water to hydrate my tresses from the bun it held at work.

I slid into an empty booth overlooking the menu. Of course, I was getting a cinnamon roll, but I needed something else, something different. The waitress came over to take my order talking me into the cream corn fritters to start. Watching the patrons dance and sway their hips to the ambient music saturating the room. Although I would normally feel out of place, I didn't. Nibbling on the fritters while people watching—watching them enjoy their lives to the fullest even though gold and clear liquor enhanced their senses, it was still nice to see.

In historic downtown New Bern, *The Lounge* invited many different types of people to frequent its doors, tasting food from the south incorporated with vegan and gluten-free options. *The Lounge* had everything you needed, good food and good vibes with amazing customer service. All of this is because of Bobby's high standards.

Turning in my seat, focusing more on my phone with my finger hovering over Nolan's number. I wanted to call him, but what was the point? I tapped on his contacts, scrolling down, and unblocked his phone number. I don't know what I wanted, maybe I wanted to see if he was thinking about me like I've been thinking about him. I know I shut him out, but I just thought he would fight harder for us. Then again, my mind drifts off to the fact that there was never an 'us' to him.

Just Nolan and Malani, singular beings roaming this earth and friendship.

A familiar scent filled my nostrils as a hand grazed my shoulder, looking up to find Grant's handsome face smiling down at me.

"How are you?" Slid from his lips.

"Hey," I said with a smile, he was a sight for sore eyes.

"Mind if I join you?" I shook my head from side to side, watching him plant himself into the seat directly across from me. He looked so fucking good, but his face held furrowed brows. "How have you been?"

That was a loaded question but not enough time to unpack it all, "I've been good, what about you?"

"I've been okay, thinking about you a lot."

"What about me?" I placed one hand on my chest and grabbed a fritter with the other.

"Thinking about what I could've done better," his voice went low, "can we go somewhere quieter to talk?" Grant motioned towards the door.

"We can take a short walk, but I need to be back for a cinnamon roll." A smile spread across his face.

Clutching my jacket as we stepped into the cold air. We walked into the thick of downtown, not far from *The Lounge*. Pacing silently, afraid to be the first to speak. I didn't know if I had anything to say to him because our situation had ended so abruptly.

"Grant, I just want to say I'm sorry." I started, "but…"

"The feelings you have for Nolan were much more," he finished my sentence. "I wish you were honest with me. Am I far off from assuming we were building towards something special?"

I paused. He was way off, but why kick a man while he's down?

"My heart called out to Nolan, and when he finally answered, I took that chance." I said instead.

Grant blew a breath, "how are things with ya'll?"

An uncomfortable moment fell over us as we walked past *Cinnamon Kissed*, "So, you approached me wanting to pry into my love life?"

"Not at all, excuse me for wondering if we could pick up where we left off."

Vomit swirled in my throat. If can't read the room was a person —it would be Grant.

Grant stopped, turning to me with the biggest smile on his face. "Do I have a chance?"

I lifted my feet continuing to walk, ignoring his question.

"I don't think Nolan deserves you," he declared, causing me to stop my stride.

Grant's only known me for a hot minute, making his statement bold. Good thing I don't operate by what he thinks.

"Thank you for your concern, but I love Nolan."

"So?" He questioned standing there with folded arms and a grin that creeped me out a little.

My eyes squinted like that made my hearing clearer.

Grant has to be a little loose in the head to willingly pursue a woman who just revealed she was in love with someone else.

"I know you think he's right for you, but I can show you he's not. I am. Think about it."

My feet couldn't move fast enough as we made our way back to *The Lounge*.

I came here for a good meal and got so much more.

Grant departed shortly after, kissing my cheek before leaving.

I couldn't wait to tell Harmony what happened between us because what the fuck?

When I looked at my phone, Nolan's number was on display. Letting air fill my lungs as I grabbed the gold bag with my cinnamon roll and exited *The Lounge*. I answered but didn't say anything.

"Lani?" Nolan's voice caused my breath to shudder.

I closed my eyes, resting my head on my steering wheel.

He called my name again, still, I remained quiet. "Can you let me explain?"

"Explain," I found my voice.

"In person, can I come over?"

"I don't know."

"Please, baby. I promise I can explain it all."

The drive home was long, mainly because I took a long way. I was nervous to see, talk to, or be anywhere near him. Nolan was at my front door when I approached my apartment. He smiled, approaching me for a hug, but I raised my hand, halting him from stepping closer.

"Do you want something to drink?" I asked him when we walked into my apartment.

He shook his head, closely following me to the kitchen.

I felt the heat of his eyes on me, "so, why was Willow at your house?" I asked, glaring at him with evil eyes.

I've been waiting to have this conversation for weeks and rehearsed it in my head many times. Coming up with different possibilities of my own to explain the deceit.

"She broke in," he started.

I laughed, "Nolan, don't insult my intelligence. Try again."

"Queen," he grabbed my hand, but I snatched it away— although, for that second, feeling him felt so fucking good.

"Don't touch me," I warned, "or this conversation will be over. You came to explain, that's all I want is an explanation."

"Lani, I gave her a key when we were talking. I forgot to get it back. That night she used it to get in, I thought it was you. I tried to put her out, then she started crying, saying she didn't have a place to go because her roommates kicked her out."

"Why was she naked, Nolan?" I asked through clenched teeth.

This wasn't making sense to me and when things don't add up, it's because it's a lie.

"Baby, I don't know. I left her with a blanket and went into my room. I didn't wake up until I heard you. I didn't touch her, I swear."

I scoffed, "do you understand this is hard to believe?"

"What reason do I have to lie? If I fucked her, I would've said I fucked her. Did I fuck up by letting her stay there? Hell yeah, sue me. I felt sorry for her, and you were acting like a brat the entire night."

I reared my head back, "a brat? If you weren't in bitches' faces all night, maybe the night would've ended differently."

"Like you weren't in that nigga Jamel's face."

"He's my fucking boss! I didn't take him home and have him naked all in my shit."

"What else do you want me to say?" He shrugged.

I threw my hands up, "Well, I don't know, Nolan. You can say you're sorry. Sorry, you let that bitch in. Sorry, you didn't think of our relationship. Sorry, you didn't tell me she was there when she got there. Sorry, you didn't fight harder for me," tears leaked out of my eyes.

Nolan closed the gap between us. "Lani, I *am* sorry." His hands slid up my neck, cradling my face. I exhaled sharply from his touch on my skin. He took one hand moving my curls from my face and tracing the outline of my jaw. "I am so fucking sorry." Nolan kissed me softly, little pecks until I pulled him closer by his shirt, deepening our kiss.

Tasting his tongue felt like the first time.

He held me close, pulling me deeper into his trance.

My eyes closed tightly, I needed to feel him.

I just want my happily ever after, and I know it's with Nolan.

I want him and only him, but I can't help to ask myself why. He's familiar, he's who I've always loved and wanted to love. I don't have room for anyone but him, but why him?

Pulling away from him, I met his eyes, "I love you, but I can't do us right now."

"I'm not being without you, Lani, you can cancel that."

"We have to go back to strictly being friends."

He scrubbed a hand over his face, "until when?"

"Until it's not toxic."

"Do you think it can go back to how it was before?"

"We can try. I'm not saying we will never be together. I do have to sort my feelings out."

Nolan held my hand to his heart, "I didn't touch that girl, Malani."

"That's not why I'm making this decision. You have to see the distance our relationship caused, right? We stopped having fun and talking to each other. It got hard, and I don't want it to be like that."

He cocked his head to the side, "what the fuck are you talking about? You're dumbing down our shit, and I don't fucking like that. Shit was sweet. The past couple of months with you were the best in my life. Loving isn't easy, relationships aren't easy. Lani, we have a lot of history."

"I don't know."

He sighed, looking me over with a clenched jaw. "No."

"No?" My brows furrowed as he challenged me.

"No, I'm done letting you run away from me. We fuss, but we come right back. It was the same shit when we were friends. I want you, and you want me. We are past this friendship level. I see a future with you."

He sat on the barstool, waiting for me to respond. I didn't have anything to say.

Was I running from him?

He held his hand out to me, and I took it, feeling the magnetic pull from our touch. "I love you, Queen." He said, looking into my eyes.

Conceding, I draped my arms around his neck, "I love you, too." I did, and I hoped he was telling me the truth because continuing to be hurt by him isn't a part of my plan. "Did you get your key back?"

"We're off that subject, baby."

chapter
twenty-five

Nolan

The ticking from the analog clock echoed. Tuning everything around me out, I focused on that sound. *Tick, tick, tick, tick,* the day of judgment. Sitting in the hallway of the cold and empty building facing the unknown was nerve-racking. Had I reacted differently that day, I wouldn't be here. I've pleaded my case and owned up to my actions from day one, and hopefully, that's enough.

I never wanted to be anything else other than a teacher. Despite the shitty pay, I stayed because I loved to teach. Because teachers didn't look like me when I was growing up, they didn't care about black students passing their classes or excelling on standardized tests. They cared more about the shitty paycheck they collected at the end of the month. Shitty paycheck and all, I would choose this career over any other.

Principal Danders' heels broke my attention from the clock, "they are ready for you now," she smiled, but it was forced. She never liked me or my teaching style— I know it brings her great pleasure knowing she was walking me to the end of the road. "Right this way," she instructed when we entered the conference room.

Board members sat at the front of the room, eyeing us until we were seated directly in front of them.

Sitting up straight, I was ready for the outcome. If this was the end of my teaching career, I would have no other choice but to accept it.

"Mr. Hudson, thank you for joining us today. I hope we didn't keep you waiting long." The chairman, whose name I didn't care to remember, spoke. "As you know, we are here regarding the incident of assault against a faculty of Nicoyce Prep, Mr. Grant Burrow. We want to say thank you for your honesty and ownership of the situation, but violence of any kind is prohibited on school grounds. Luckily, students weren't around to witness a member of faculty behaving in a manner we teach them to refrain. But I'm going to be honest with you, Mr. Hudson, the outcome doesn't look good." My head dropped in my hands. "Upon interview with Mr. Burrow, he did admit to provoking you with words, but Mr. Hudson, sticks and stones. Physical harm should've never happened as this caused Mr. Burrow to miss teaching days."

I ran my tongue over my lips, I strongly stand by—fuck Grant's bitch ass. No remorse for Grant. I can't pretend like I feel bad.

"Our initial stance was to terminate your employee, effective immediately—that is until we received an overflow of letters from many of your students, past and present, requesting to give you another chance." The chairman lifted a canvas mailbag filled with letters. "Mr. Hudson, some of these letters are from your first-year students. Students who are now..."

"Some are in their final year in college, some have already graduated college and entering the workforce," I finished for him. I kept up with many of my students from over the years.

"Correct, we don't take that lightly. Judging from these letters, you've impacted these students in a positive way. We appreciate your commitment. With that being said, this *will* be your last year teaching for Nicoyce Prep."

My heart dropped to the pit of my stomach as I scrubbed a hand over my face.

"Principal Danders, you have something you need to say to Mr. Hudson."

I didn't turn to her because I knew her face held a smile. She finally did it, got me out of the school and the career I cherish so much.

"Mr. Hudson, I'm so sorry to lose you as a teacher at Nicoyce Prep, but happy to gain you as my assistant principal next school year."

Applause filled the room as I comprehended what just happened. Did I get promoted? With wide eyes, I looked at each person in the room trying to figure out if this was a joke or not. Principal Danders' smile spread to either side of her face as she shook my hand.

The clapping subsided as they looked to me to speak, "I'm—I'm shocked."

"This is the first time I've seen him speechless," Principal Danders joked.

I chuckled, "I appreciate it."

This moment made a nigga want to cry. A fucking promotion!

"Mr. Hudson," the chairman spoke, "these letters saved your job. It was a good idea to reach out to your students to advocate for you."

"I didn't, sir, if I'm being honest. But I have a feeling I know who did."

"Whoever did, you better thank them. The meeting is adjourned. I look forward to working with you in the future. And Mr. Hudson—" I looked at the small man. "Keep all hands, feet, and all other objects to yourself."

"You got it," I agreed. I walked out of the Board of Education feeling ten times better than I did when I walked in. Assistant Principal Hudson, I didn't think it was possible. Not being physically there for my kids was torture. I missed their nosey asses. Glad I can finally be reunited with them. Monday couldn't come fast enough, give me all the papers to grade.

Lani was standing in the front lobby calling a patient when I caught her eye. She looked beautiful with her hair in a high messy bun and pink scrubs under the white coat with her name embroidered on the left.

I stalked over to her, pulling her to me then brushing my lips on hers. "Thank you," I mumbled against her mouth.

"For what?" She handed the chart to the lady at the desk, who ushered the patient to the back. "Room Number four please," she told her. Lani grabbed my hand, leading me to her office.

"I got promoted because of you. Thank you for reaching out to my students."

"That worked?" A smile spread across her face. I don't know how she did it, but I'm glad she did.

"Hell yeah, Queen. I'm the new assistant principal," I spun around in the middle of her office. "Your boy is moving up!"

"Congratulations," she hugged me, causing my dick to jump against her stomach. "Don't think about it," she said sternly, but I saw the twinkle in her eyes. Since getting back in her good graces, I've been on my best behavior. As time went on, the more I craved being inside of her. If she lets me that close to her, I'd know I'm forgiven for that bullshit with Willow.

"Later?" I raised my eyebrows hoping she would agree.

Lani giggled, "nope."

I slid behind her, holding on tight, "then now," I whispered in her ear. I massaged her through her pants, caressing her as she whimpered.

"Nolan, I have patients waiting," she struggled to say as I pulled her pants down.

"I just want to thank you, let me thank you," I backed us to the corner of the room, out of view of the ceiling-to-floor windows adorning her office. I lifted her, putting her back against the painted walls. Filling her as her pussy walls contracted around me. She was so wet—I knew she wanted this dick. I awarded her with deep, continuous strokes. Her hands gripping my shoulders for leverage. Moans spilled out her lips into my ear. One thing I loved about sexing Lani was if her face wasn't buried into my shoulder or chest, she was making eye contact with me. It's something about the way her eyes change hues when she comes that excites me. I growled as her cum coated my dick.

We collectively ignored the ringing of her office phone, more attuned with each other, lost in the act. I pumped my hips slowly and deliberately, holding the backs of her thighs as I emptied inside her. I gently dropped her legs and feet back onto the tiled floor. Backing away from her only when our breathing returned to normal.

Lani slid her pants back on to answer the still ringing phone. "Dawson, yes, Dr. Cooper. I just stepped away for a quick snack." She bit her lip, holding back a smile. "I'll be right there." She placed the receiver back on the hook. "You are going to get me fired. I have to wash up and go back."

"Nah, let me taste you," I bit my lip easing into her office chair.

Our eyes connected. She was running the idea in her head.

"I promise I'll be quick." Lani was too close to me, and I took advantage by not letting her get so far away from my grasp.

"I can't," she protested, but it was too late. Her pants and panties were back on the floor. "You're so nasty," her eyes darted to the door, probably wondering if we were seen. It didn't matter to me though. I was eating her pussy right now—audience or not.

Sliding the contents on her desk aside, she hopped on the desk spreading wide for me.

My tongue slithered on her clit, suckling with enough pleasure to make her cry out.

"Oooh, mmm Nolan, fuck!"

I hooked one finger inside of her pussy, feeling the mixture of my cum and her juices against my finger. She arched her back, and I slid another finger inside at the same time she grabbed the back of my head as my warm mouth covered her skin.

"You're going to drive me crazy," she cooed with a smile in her voice.

My fingers moved in and out of her simultaneously, watching her chest rise and fall from the pressure building in her core. This was my favorite part. She clenched around my fingers, her knuckles white from the hold she had on the edge of the desk.

Wheeling closer, my tongue flicked her clit. The gush of her orgasm rushing out on my fingers into my mouth.

"Mmm," vibrated from my lips. I didn't think it was possible, but she tasted even better than the last time. Snatching my fingers out of her, I held them to her mouth. Staring deep into my eyes she tasted herself from me. I was bricking up, but we were on borrowed time. She cleaned that shit, her warm tongue sliding up and down my digits. "You better go," I stood repositioning myself in my jeans. I filled her mouth with my tongue, kissing her and gripping her neck. "Now, baby."

She lingered a little longer before pushing off the desk and getting fully dressed.

"I'll hang here for a while, my pants are wet from you cuming all over me."

"That's your fault," she kissed me before leaving the office.

We're back, and I will put it all on the line for Lani.

Ezeke rang my line, "what's up, bro?"

"Not shit, just sitting in Lani's office. What's up with you?" I reclined back in her seat, putting my feet up on her desk like this was my shit.

"Nothing, I got your text, congrats."

"'Preciate it."

"Are you and baby girl straight now?"

"So far so good."

"Have you told her about Willow yet?"

I paused, "nah. I got to wait on that."

"Bro—" a warning in his voice.

"I know, I know. I will, just not right now."

"I'm not covering for you if she finds out."

"I've never asked you to cover for me. I can handle my own shit."

Ezeke was getting on my nerves, being all righteous and shit. I don't give a fuck whose friend he was first, bro code trumps all. The fuck was the point of having a friend I considered a brother if I didn't trust he'd hold my secrets? When questioned by Lani, all he had to do was deny knowing anything. Saying 'I don't know' works every single time.

"Well, handle your shit—in the meantime, put me on with Harmony."

I blew out a breath, "man, step around. Harms is on some bull-shit. I thought you were seeing somebody else anyway."

"Hell no, I want her," Ezeke declared.

"If you want her, you're going to have to get her. I've been putting in a word for you. It's up to you now, my boy." I wasn't sure why Harmony wanted to play hard to get. Ezeke's been on her.

Lani walked back into the office, ending my call with Ezeke. "Ready for lunch?"

After ordering from *The Lounge,* we ate in her office, kissing and talking like we were teenagers. I tried to be on my best behavior, but she ended up riding me towards the end of her lunch break. No longer did we care about eyes watching through the office window.

When my pants were completely dry, I left her office with her receptionist eyeing me. I hated withholding information from Lani, but the situation with Willow was much deeper than I wanted it to be. I can't possibly share with Lani, not now. Not since we were just getting back in a positive place. I can't lose her again, I won't.

twenty-six

Malani

"Don't tell me you're considering talking to Grant again." Harmony fussed over a bowl of peanut butter crunch cereal. I couldn't take her seriously with the flexi-rods sticking out under her bonnet. She took a big bite, talking with her mouth open, "I mean, he's fine, but the fuck he think this is? Plus, Nolan already put his hands on him for talking crazy. He bitched out; you can't respect that."

This was a whole one-eighty because Harmony was so pro-Grant.

"Tell me how you got me saying he invited me to a business party confused with I want to talk to him again?"

"He's trying the same shit my ex does. They will slither their way through the tiniest crack," she took another bite and then rolled her eyes at me. "As your future sister-in-law," I rolled my eyes at her, "I choose Nolan for you."

"That wasn't the question." I laughed like she had a say so in my love life. *I* choose Nolan for me.

"What was the question? I was so blinded by hearing the name Grant come out your mouth."

"Don't make me slap you." I poured oat milk over my bowl of

peanut butter crunch cereal. "I asked if I should go to this event with him."

"As a date?"

"No, silly, as a friend. It's like an event for Black business owners to connect."

Harmony finished the cereal, pouring more on top of the little bit of milk that still rested in the bowl. "What did my good friend Nolan say about this?"

I shot her a look, "I haven't told him."

Harmony laughed, "of course you didn't. Don't go."

"But it may be good exposure for Dr. Cooper."

"Then, let Dr. Cooper's sexy ass attend. But, Babe, going to that event with Grant will cause a problem with you and Nolan. You know that, and I know that. It's not worth it. Tell Dr. Cooper about the event and let him know you have a ticket to go." She shrugged her shoulders, stuffing her mouth with more cereal.

"You're right," I conceded.

"Harmony is never right about shit," Nolan came through the front door of our apartment looking and smelling amazing. Harmony rolled her eyes, "Damn, Queen, I was taking you to get breakfast."

"Should've called, Mr. Hudson," Harmony teased him. I smiled at their exchange as he playfully pushed her. "I gotta get ready for work," she announced.

Nolan pressed his lips against my forehead then I fed him a spoonful of my cereal. "I missed you last night."

"If you'd let a nigga stay over, you wouldn't have missed me."

"Soon, you could've offered me to stay at your place."

"I thought spending the night worked both ways."

Standing against his hard chest, I said, "with a little convincing, I might have stayed."

"I'll keep that in mind," he grabbed a handful of my ass.

"I have a meeting with Dr. Cooper soon. I was going to call you for a late lunch."

"That's cool, I'm heading to the gym with Ezeke." He kissed my forehead, "call me when you're done."

After Nolan left, I finished the bowl of cereal, showered, and headed to the office. I wanted to poke myself in the eye with the pen I was holding and beat myself across the head with the clipboard I was using to cross the names of the applicants from the list. It seemed like we were hosting interviews for the next social media model with how some of these females dressed for the interview. I'm not the one that says clothes provoke certain behaviors from men and women alike, but with all due respect, short skirts, mini dresses, tight form-fitting shirts, and jeans could stay on the outside of this office. I made a mental note to require the administration staff wear scrubs.

Following the fifth underdressed and under-qualified applicant, Dr. Cooper's face held amusement.

"You're enjoying this aren't you?" I said tossing my pen at him.

He smirked, "in a way, yes, but I like having you referee. If you think this is bad, you should've seen me in high school."

"That's the problem, that private school education got these public-school girls acting like they never seen a good-looking man before."

"I went to public school, thank you. But place the blame on my parents, it's their genes. Also, college was worse."

"I could imagine. These girls see a nice-looking Black doctor, and they see dollar signs. Much like the ones that flock to the military bases."

"Let's weed them out," Dr. Cooper suggested approaching the lobby that housed over fifty applicants. "Ladies, I appreciate the interest in the job. We have three spots to fill, but to make it easier on my counterpart and I—please step forward if you have the following qualifications." Dr. Cooper looked over at me urging me to read the list of what we were looking for.

Listing off the most important, tech savvy, respect for patient confidentiality, empathy and compassion, phone etiquette, workspace organization, professionalism, multitasking and at least a year experience in the field. With that said, the room cleared fifty percent. A few were mumbling under their breath as they exited. We resumed the interviews and ended with six strong candidates for the job. I talked him into hiring them all, because one had billing experience and she could be my second set of eyes especially when the contract with the temp agency ends.

I stepped away to call Nolan, "hey, baby. How's work?"

"A shit show, but we're wrapping up. Are you still at the gym?"

"No, I came to my parents' house."

Nolan never goes to his parent's house without me, "is everything okay?"

"Yeah, I came because my mom made a pan of spaghetti then my dad wants to go through Liam's things. Can you come after you finish? I need you here with me."

"Of course, I'll be there as soon as I can."

Dr. Cooper stood in the doorframe waiting for me to end the call. "Are you ready?"

I took a deep breath because this was the moment I've been dreading since waking up this morning. Today was the final exam day for testing to become a surgeon. Dr. Cooper endorsed me and luckily, I only needed to take the two-part exam to enter my new journey. I hadn't shared this information with anyone because I'm afraid I will fail. Soon I'll be Dr. Dawson. I technically am Dr. Dawson, but having the actual certifications is even sweeter.

Three and a half hours later, I walked out of the college doors with a sense of relief washing over me. Now, I play the waiting game, eight to ten weeks of torture await me. Dr. Cooper high fived me when I emerged from the building with a smile on my face. No lie, it felt good. I completed the unthinkable, and I owe it all to this man who believed in me when no other doctor did. Jamel Cooper took me under his wing and invested so much into my career and for that I will always be indebted to him.

"I'm proud of you," he said as we walked to his car. "I have the team on stand-by waiting to add Dr. Malani Dawson to the door."

"Oh my, we will have to change the letterheads," I said getting ahead of myself. Sliding into the passenger seat, I powered my phone on. I wasn't allowed to take much of anything into the examination room other than identification and pencil.

"I remember when I took the exam, one of the happiest days of my life." He smiled as he pulled onto the by-pass.

"Is it pass/fail?"

"It is now, when I took it, it wasn't. I'll get the results, same as you. We can host your celebration at the office if you want."

"Thank you, Dr. Cooper, for everything you've done for me."

Once we got back to the office, I hopped in my own car texting Nolan, letting him know I was on my way. He texted back quickly letting me know he was at home.

My knuckles lightly rapped on Nolan's door. "About time," he pulled me into his chest, kissing me gently on the lips. The scent of his cologne lingering in the air.

"I'm sorry," he helped me out of my coat. "I was hoping to meet you at your parent's house. Did you go through Liam's room?"

Grief is weird. Although Liam wasn't my brother, he was still a part of my life, and his death affected my family as well. I was young, but I experienced it. I never expected The Hudson's to change Liam's room, it was like a memorial to him. It looked the same as it did when he was alive.

Nolan laid against the cushions of the couch, the couch that bitch was naked on. I opted to stand, not wanting to be anywhere near it. I believe Nolan, but the images are seared into my brain.

"I couldn't do it alone. My dad said he was going to help, but he hasn't stepped a foot in Liam's room since he died. He just looks at the door like Liam is going to walk out of it." His eyes were focused on the ceiling, and from the redness of his eyes, I knew he was holding back from crying. He didn't have to hold back with me, I will always catch his tears. I walked over to him inhaling a deep breath before sitting next to him. "I gotta come clean with them Lani," tears spilled from his eyes. "I can't keep holding this shit in," Nolan broke down. My own tears surfaced, sliding down my face as I decided to wipe his. "They're gonna fucking hate me," my heart broke for him.

"Baby, you were eight. Eight years old. You didn't know until much later."

"I should've fucking known," his voice raising caused me to

flinch. With sympathetic eyes, he pulled me on top of him, wrapping his arms tightly around my body. "I have to tell them," he said lowly.

Just like I hated my sister for following Liam, I didn't like Liam for leaving Nolan to fare this guilt. It was only so much an eight-year-old could do, but he wears the guilt that should be placed on the person who was selling Liam the drugs. Nolan didn't make Liam take the pills, he was just a little boy happy his big brother walked him to and from school. We stayed in that position until I grabbed his hand, peeling him from the sofa. I wrapped my arms around his torso embracing him like I knew he needed. We retreated to his room where I laid my head in his lap and toyed with the hairs on his leg, listening to him talk about the good times with Liam.

chapter
twenty-seven

Nolan

Lani shifted in my arms. It was three in the morning, and I couldn't fall asleep. Stress and worry keeping me from a decent slumber. If and when I do sleep, I often wake up from a nightmare. Insomnia overtaking me and dragging me down deeper and deeper into a hole. I find myself not eating how I should because what I'm holding from Lani will unintentionally break us beyond repair. I'd succumb to my own demise if I lose her. The last thing I ever wanted to do was hurt Lani, which is why I never looked at her other than a friend before. I knew I wasn't good for her. Good friend, yes, but boyfriend, nah. We click though, which makes it harder to resist wanting a relationship with her. She knows me and I know her, perfect recipe for disaster.

I kissed Lani's forehead before sliding out of her bed. During this time of the night, there was nothing to do but grade the papers I brought home earlier. I brewed a cup of coffee to keep me focused on the task. Getting through the stack of papers, I arranged them in my bag, preparing to take them for the ride to school. I made another cup of coffee then turned on the TV to pass time by. I arose from the couch when I heard the water running in the shower. It was six now, but to me it seemed like only seconds had passed. I planted my feet at the entrance of the bathroom door watching Lani undress.

"Good morning," I startled her. She held her chest giving me a wry smile. Exhaustion all over her face.

"Nolan," she held her hands out to me, I held her naked body close to mine. "I'm so fucking tired," she complained into my chest.

We did go to bed early, but we made love most of the night. Partly because I couldn't sleep so I selfishly kept her up.

"Do you want to take a sick day?" She shook her head, "then get in the shower, it'll wake you. I'll make coffee." She groaned as she peeled herself from me.

I prepared a light breakfast of bagels with cream cheese and scrambled eggs along with the coffee. Lani didn't look any better when she stepped into the kitchen smoothing her thick, curly mane into a ponytail. With only the thirty minutes of sleep I had, I was pulling it off better than she was.

"Baby, you don't look good." Again, she stepped into my arms with her warm arms snaking around me. Typical Lani, sick and ready to pass it to me.

"I just need ten more minutes of sleep."

"You don't have that type of time, Queen." I reminded her.

"Please, ten minutes that's all I need. Let me lay on you." I sat into the recliner, pulling her onto my lap. She straddled me, laying her head on my chest. She softly snored almost instantly. Ten minutes turned to twenty, then thirty. My eyelids getting heavy enough for the weight to close them. "Shit!" I heard Lani say. She jumped up in a hurry. "Nolan, it's after seven. Get up!" The buzzing of my phone in my pocket caught my attention, too. Focusing my eyes on the screen I saw it was, "Willow? Why is she calling you? I thought you blocked her number."

"I don't know. I'm not worrying about that shit right now. We have to go. Are you driving or me?" I asked, stuffing my phone deep into my pocket.

Lani stood in the middle of the living room with her hands on her hips and her brows furrowed into a scowl. "I guess my conversations with Grant isn't a big deal."

"Are you trying to piss me off early this morning?"

She rolled her neck, "I'm just letting you know."

I chuckled to keep my temper at bay. She had no reason talking to that nigga. "I don't know why she's calling," I lied. "I didn't answer."

"This time," she mumbled under her breath.

"What?"

"Nothing. Let's go to work," she looped her arm underneath mine. Her car was the mode of transportation today. I dropped her off, kissing her before she exited the car. She stuck her tongue out at me before she walked into the building.

I was late for work—my kids knew what to do if I wasn't there. I would leave door busters on the board for them to complete early in the morning. They were allowed to help each other but not give the answer away. Justice was in charge and facilitated well in my absence. Principal Danders pulled my attention as soon as I stepped foot into the school. She handed me a list of important dates for over the summer. I glanced over it making sure it wasn't too many days during the week, the summer was my time to relax and play. Away from kids and grading papers every damn week.

The students were busy with the door buster when I entered the classroom. Proudness running laps over me because this would be the last class I would teach, and I was okay with that. All of them with a bright future ahead of them.

Fucking Grant up crossed my mind as I passed his stupid ass in the hallway giving me a smug smile. I don't know what he thought he was doing by trying to contact Lani, but I didn't have any worries; we're locked in. The antics of this nigga royally irritated me. I initially wasn't the kind of guy to fight over a girl but for Lani —I'd go to war with any motherfucker that threatens our livelihood and our relationship.

As usual, the school day went by quick as hell. I hosted some parent teacher conferences afterwards as I waited for Lani to get off work. I sent lunch over to her job since we weren't able to eat the breakfast that I prepared.

Exiting the school, I answered Willow's call, annoyance lacing my tone, "yeah?"

"We have a problem."

"What's up?"

"Your friend is here."

I ran my hand over my face, "who?"

"Me," Harmony's voice rang through the receiver.

Just my fucking luck for some shit like this to happen. I looked at the digital time on the dashboard, I did not have time for this shit. Lani was about to get off work, time was ticking. "Put Harmony on," I pulled into the parking lot of Cooper's Medical Center.

"Nolan, do you care to explain?" Harmony's tone was venomous.

"Yeah, but not to you. You need to leave from there now."

"Are you kidding me, do you think I'm not about to call Lani about this? Nolan, be for real. Is she…"

"Yes."

"Oh my God!"

"Don't say shit, please."

Harmony exhaled, "you have five hours. That's all I can give you."

"That's all I need," ending the call. I growled, "fuck!" Lani's smile was infectious as she approached me behind her desk. "Baby, we gotta talk."

Her smile slightly faded, "this sounds serious," she sat on my lap wrapping her arms around my neck. "What's wrong?"

I took a deep breath, knowing my next words could potentially end us. "Remember when I told you Willow…"

Lani scoffed, "oh my God! I'm so tired of hearing about her."

"Let me finish," she rolled her eyes, and I contemplated keeping my mouth shut. "She's been living with me."

Her eyes were deadlocked into mine. "For how long?"

Taking the silent approach, I considered lying. Lani deserved the truth, but if that truth hurts her, I'll shield her from it.

"You can't be serious," she tried to get up, but I wrapped my arms around her.

"She had nowhere to go."

"That's not your fucking problem. You're living with a girl, claiming you love me."

"I do fucking love you."

"Thanks for showing it babe. Let me go." Lani managed to get out of my hold.

Holding this shit from her has been killing me. Me and Willow are co-habits. She's barely at my place since her work hours are crazy, and when she is there, I'm in my room. We don't talk unless we run out of paper towels or toilet paper, and we have to decide which one of us will pick it up. I should've told Lani when we got back together, but the fear of losing her overpowered my senses. It was easier to withhold, easier to chill with her at her place, easier to avoid the way she was looking at me right now.

This shit didn't look right, but I pray Lani could hear me out.

Her cell phone vibrated on the desk, both of our eyes snapped to it. Harmony's name slowly scrolled across the screen.

"Hey, Harms," Lani said into the receiver, she turned away from me. "What?"

Fuck, this was all bad.

A good deed gone wrong.

"I heard what you said Harmony, how do you know?" Her eyes landed back on me. "He's right here. Okay, I'm on my way."

I continued to plead my case, not knowing or caring what Harmony told her. Harmony couldn't wait to spread some shit, but why did I expect anything less from her?

"Take me to your apartment," she demanded.

"Nah, listen to me. Listen to what I'm telling you. The shit looks bad, but I swear I'm only helping her out." I stood close to my girl, lifting her chin to meet my eyes.

"Okay."

"Don't brush me off."

"I'm not, just take me to your apartment. Apparently, your little roommate is there, and we need to have a talk. Either take me or I'll find another ride."

I looked her over, trying to read her. "Lead the way."

"If I find out you've been sticking your dick in her, I'm cutting it off," she threatened on her way out.

Even though I was in deep shit, I couldn't help but smile at her feisty ass.

chapter
twenty-eight

Malani

Poker face, Malani. Don't show your hand. I was fucking pissed inside, hurt to the core, but externally—cool, calm, and collected. I held my emotions, but I wanted to burst out in tears. The thought of Nolan doing anything for another woman infuriated me more than anything on this earth. This situation is not okay, especially since we are together and trying to build our future.

One thing for sure, Nolan's seed was growing inside of me. Every day I hold onto the test waiting for the right time to share the good news with Nolan. I wish I had stuck to my plan of wanting to go back to friends. It was simpler then. Now, I'm carrying his baby and questioning his fidelity. I never wanted this for us.

In my head, when Nolan figured out I loved him more than a friend, I thought we would get together, be happy, and continue our journey in life together. I never envisioned us crossing hurdle after hurdle and for what? Why are we being tested so fucking much? Can I really be a Queen and live happily ever after with my King?

Nolan's hand on my knee reared me back into reality. He exited the car, opening my door helping me out.

He's letting her live with him. In his personal space.

Why?

Nolan never wanted me living with him and I'm his best fucking friend.

"Wait," I said, halting my steps. Nights when we spilled into his apartment, tugging at each other's clothes and kissing at the doorway. Did she see? Does she walk around naked? Does she sneak into his room? "I can't do this," words speeding from my mouth so fast, it was like they didn't come from me.

Nolan's brows furrowed as he squinted to read my face, "it's okay. We can do it some other time."

Shaking my head, staring at the building like my execution awaited inside. In a way, it was because my heart was breaking bit by bit. Ticking away as images of them being intimate flashed into my head. Movies nights on the couch. Dinner and breakfast in bed.

I want to be with him, I do. But to what end? I waited years to be with Nolan, and now any and everything is thrown in our path.

Maybe this is a sign.

Maybe, I wasn't paying attention before.

"Lani, don't say what I think you're about to say." He lifted my chin, gazing into my eyes with worry etched in his. "Baby, please," he looked defeated, but so was I.

Who would look out for Malani, if Malani doesn't look out for Malani?

My throat aching from holding back the tears I wanted to shed for us. Us being a more exclusive us—was a little too late.

Nolan held my hands tightly in his. "Lani, talk to me," his pleas fell on closed ears. I've been so obsessed with Nolan that I didn't— couldn't see the bigger picture. Was it always in front of me and I chose to ignore it? Possibly, classic Malani when it comes to Nolan Hudson.

"Were you happy?"

"Lani, when?" He was agitated, shifting his weight from one foot to the other.

"When you were with her." My eyes narrowing at his reluctance to answer an easy question. I knew they shared something deep, because they were moving too fast.

"Yeah, I was, but I'm happier with you. You are who I want to spend the rest of my life with," he declared, but I wasn't looking for a declaration of his love. I know he loves me. He slid his hand up my shirt touching my bare stomach, sending chills through me. "I want you and our baby, together."

Snapping my head, I nibbled on my bottom lip, "how do you know?" My breath hitched in my throat.

"Baby, I know your body, and I know you."

"Do you know me? Because nothing about this situation is Malani approved. If you knew me, you knew I wouldn't be okay with this. I walked in on her naked in your apartment, Nolan. She's your ex for God's sake. I can't keep doing this to myself." I calmed my breathing before I stressed my unborn child. "The way I see it, you still have feelings for her that runs deeper than your common sense. I've never seen you this way. Reckless. And what's even more shitty is you're reckless with me. I don't care what ya'll got going on, but I'm removing myself from being in your way."

Nolan's jaw tightened, "so fuck what I want?"

"Do you give a fuck about what I want? Do you take me into consideration when you're making decisions that could affect us being together?"

"Tell me what you want, and I promise I'll make it happen."

"I want you to myself. It's selfish. I know, but that's what I truly want." I took a step back from him, creating distance between us. " I can't have you to myself, right? I'm always having to share you. That's okay. It's been okay," I said more to myself.

"I'm right here," Nolan took a step forward, and I took another one backwards.

"Are you though? Physically—yes, but mentally—no. Nolan, I see everything, even the things you don't think I see." I held my hand out for my car keys. My voice cracking as my mind caught up with what I was doing—what I needed to do. "We're not meant to be together." I swiped the tears away as I asked for my keys again. Nolan stared at me, almost through me as he dropped the keys into my hands. "Checkmate," I whispered as I left him standing where he was.

Instead of going home, I pulled in the parking space in the park downtown. The moon casting down on the water was beautiful, not how I felt inside. I needed time to think—think about what my life is going to look like since I'm carrying his baby. Focusing my eyes on the river, I let my tears flow freely.

chapter
twenty-nine

Nolan

I damn near broke down like a bitch when the last glimmer of Lani's taillights was out of my sight. Fuck! She carried a piece of me inside of her, and I'll do whatever possible to provide for my child.

"I hope you told my fucking friend about your little situation," Harmony leaned against my front door. I was not in the mood to deal with her shit when Lani's the one person I ever cared about. I didn't give her the satisfaction of looking at her while unlocking the door to retreat to my own bullshit. "This is low, even for you. That girl loves you—." She followed me into my apartment, nagging me like she was the one I hurt.

"Harmony," I rubbed my temples, trying to calm down before unleashing all the emotions I held inside onto her. "Lani knows and she's pretty upset, you might want to be a best friend and go talk to her." My voice was calm as I sent Lani a text telling her I love her. It took everything I had in me not to follow Harmony to Lani, but she needs her space. I respect that. The worst part about having this problem was not having a solution for it. I can't fathom not being able to touch Lani. I tried her cell, knowing she wouldn't answer— but still, I had to try. I called her over and over until I drifted off to sleep, phone in hand.

The faint knock at my room door awoke me.

"Nolan, can we talk?" Willow stood in the doorframe still in uniform.

The light in my bedroom was still on, as my eyes adjusted, I waved her over.

"I appreciate you letting me stay with you when I didn't have anywhere else to go."

I nodded, "it's all good."

"Your friend, Harmony is a real piece of work," she chuckled. "I see you're here so I guess things didn't go okay with Lani."

"Nah."

"Did you tell her why I was here?"

"Yeah."

"Did you tell her everything?"

I looked at Willow, she rubbed her belly. "I didn't get a chance."

"Well, I think it's best if I leave. I've been talking to my roommates and they've agreed to let me come back."

"Will ya'll be okay?"

"We will be okay. I've been able to save up and we will be in our own place soon. I'm truly sorry for causing problems in your life."

"It's not your fault, it's mine."

Willow exited the room, a few minutes later she was saying goodbye with her suitcase in hand.

Not quite an hour later, I drug my feet as I staggered to answer the door for whoever thought it was okay to come to my shit at seven in the morning. Perking up, hoping it was Lani. It wasn't, just Ezeke with a smug expression on his face. "Bro, what the fuck? You told Baby girl I knew about that bullshit with Willow?"

"Why the fuck would I do some shit like that?" I left him standing at the door frame as I retreated to the couch. Tossing the throw cover over my head. I needed a day to not think about this shit, but it seems like that couldn't happen. If I was a drinking man, I would've downed like three bottles of liquor. I wanted to be numb to this shit—I wanted my girl.

"I don't know man but instead of Baby girl taking her anger out on you she's taking it out on me, too, and I don't appreciate that. She's not even answering my damn calls."

I didn't intend on dragging Ezeke down with me. But shit, he's my best friend who the fuck else am I supposed to talk to about these problems I'm having?

Lani should've been more understanding.

I didn't fuck us up on purpose.

One sign of danger and she skates away.

Do I even want to be with somebody that gives us up easily?

Somebody that won't listen to an explanation.

Somebody jumping to their own conclusions.

I stand on. I don't give a fuck what it looks like. I needed her to trust me. The fuck I look like fucking around on her? Two weeks, for two weeks I was miserable without her. Damn, I withheld viable information, but damn. I wasn't cheating.

Roles reversed—I wouldn't be happy about the situation, but nothing will keep me away from her. She's allowing any and everything to take her away from me, somebody she claims she's been in love with for a long time.

"My bad man," I apologized to him, uncovering my face to show my sincerity.

Ezeke values the relationship he forms with people. He didn't have that growing up, same with Harmony. Lani convinced both of them to move to New Bern after college to start their careers. I'm the only one in our friend group that has family at arm's length. Lani, Ezeke and Harmony are a family within themselves—with me as an add-in because of my connection with Lani.

"Lani knows you don't have shit to do with it—you're just guilty by association. She knows I talk to you and is pissed because you didn't tell her."

"Now, we're both fucked. The bad part about it is I know Baby girl's pissed, but she's not the one that called me to fuss my ass out— it was Harmony." He ran his hand over his face.

I sighed exasperatedly, now I've fucked up his chances with Harmony—not that he had a chance anyway, but still. "I can't speak for Harmony," I told him. "She's on some other shit, and I don't even know how she found out. Only person I told was you," I stared at him blankly.

"I didn't tell her," fury glistened in his eyes as I made the statement that's been on my mind since last night. "My boy, as much as I wanted to, I held that secret."

"Nigga don't act like I don't hold yours. And yours hold way more weight than mine and you know that."

"Do they though?" Ezeke stared me down, visibly steaming from the encounter.

At the end of the day, we're boys and that's the shit we do—hold each other's secrets and plead the fifth when asked about it. His loyalty is not in question, but damn if I'm not suspicious.

He slumped deeper into the chair adjacent from me. "What are we going to do?"

"I'm not doing shit, but waiting for text messages. I'm throwing the gloves in with me and Lani being in a relationship. We can go back to being best friends."

"You don't mean it," Ezeke stared at me like I was going to call out April Fools, that never came.

"The hell if I don't, Lani don't give a fuck about me. She doesn't know what the fuck I've been going through. Does she care? I don't think so—so why the fuck should I care? Do you know what, come to think about it—this whole fucking friendship I've been protecting her feelings, looking out for her, but not once has she done that shit for me. Lani is selfish and stubborn as fuck."

"Stubborn yes, but you and I both know Lani is not selfish." He took up for her, "Do you honestly think shit was going to be sweet after she found out?"

"No, but I didn't think she would discard our relationship so fucking fast. We're grown, I've been preaching to Lani for years to talk shit out. What does leaving do? I want her more than anything bro, but I'm not doing the back and forth."

"It wouldn't have been like that if you were honest with her from the jump."

"Don't preach to me about honesty." I shot him a look.

Ezeke tapped on his phone for a minute before returning back to give me unsolicited advice. "Make up with Lani at least and find neutral ground with Willow."

"Willow moved out last night bro, and quite frankly fuck Lani," I spat.

All these years between Lani didn't prepare us for shit. Romantic relationship or not, she's my first fucking friend—my best fucking friend, our bond should be stronger than anything that stands in our way. Instead, she allows these hurdles to deter her away from me.

Life doesn't work like that.

Either she is with me, or she's friend zoned.

chapter
thirty

"She's clearly pregnant," Harmony's words from last night still rang in my ears. Why is Willow's existence becoming a thorn in my side? "But she also looked a fucking mess."

I couldn't help but laugh at Harmony ruffling her hair all over her head, making claims she was imitating Willow. "I don't care. Nolan wants her so bad, regardless of how unkempt she was."

"Nolan doesn't want that damn girl," Harmony spoke like she was inside of Nolan's head. "I hate to say it, but he's soft. That bitch spit him some sad shit and he believed it."

"Well, that's him." I folded my arms across my chest.

"Lani, it's me. You do not have to play hard. I know you're hurt, but don't take shit for face value. Do your research before you break it off with him."

I pursed my lips, little does she know. "How did you find out?" That question slid out of my mouth with ease. I wasn't paying attention, but Harmony was. Why, though? Harmony's eyes darted from me to the front door, back to me, then to her yellow painted toes. "Spit it out," I urged. She was always so full of words, but now she lost them. That could only mean one thing, "you did not go see him." My lips formed a tight line with disappointment.

Harmony's joyous face turned sour, a tear slid from her eyes, but I was not about to let up on the lecture piling in my head.

"Harmony, why do you keep going down this road with him? Him hurting you once wasn't enough?" I closed my mouth as fast as it opened. I'm sitting here going through the same shit with Nolan. "I'm sorry," I apologized.

Her face was full of tears, and I felt like we were back at square one when she first moved in with me.

"I only slept with him one time. I'm sorry."

"Don't be," I held her shaking hands in mine. "I'm sorry for being judgy." I dabbed her tears with the back of my hand, careful not to smudge her makeup. "Was it good at least?" I asked, producing a telling smile.

"Girl, that nigga fucked me like——" her voice trailed off, "like it was the last time." The smile still painted the corners of her mouth.

"Anyway," I changed the subject, "I'm pregnant." I blurted out like I was holding my breath.

"I know," Harmony quipped. "Our cycles run neck and neck. You've been out of tampons for a while, I know because I took the last one. I've been waiting for you to tell me."

"I'm really scared," I admitted.

"I'm here for you and Ezekiel is, too. Can I say something and you not get mad?" Rolling my eyes, I nodded my head. "Talk to Nolan, don't let this shit get between ya'll. Babe, I saw his face last night, and I wanted to hug him. He really loves you."

"I love him, too."

"Then, go to him and don't come back until you've talked it out." I sat still in my seat, not listening to her push me to do something she didn't have the guts to do. An email popped up on my phone, it was my results. My heart pounded and self-doubt flooded my mind. The results are back over a week too early, that's not a good sign. I've failed. "What?" Harmony peered over my phone, but I locked the screen and stored it on the coffee table.

My phone buzzed again, this time a phone call from Dr. Cooper. "Hey!"

"Hey, did you see?" His deep voice was full of glee. I knew he received the same email as me.

"I can't open it," Harmony winked at me, signaling for me to give him her number. I stood from the couch, retreating to my room for privacy.

"I was the same way. Do you want to meet me at the office in the morning to open it together."

I loved that gesture, but I couldn't take more bad news. "Can we wait until Monday?"

He paused for a second, "yes, of course. Come in at six?"

"Yes," I said somberly.

"Great, see you Monday."

After spritzing my hair with water to fluff and moisturize my curls, I painted my face and made the drive to Nolan's house.

"Willow moved out last night, bro," I heard Nolan say from inside his apartment. Reaching the landing I could hear his voice clear as day—partly because his door was cracked. Slowly coaching myself to enter, I stood on the other side of the door waiting to go in to tell him that I changed my mind. That I'm with him until we grow old and fall off the face of the earth. But the next words out his mouth shattered my whole world. "And quite frankly fuck Lani," those words swarmed in my head attacking every thought I had imbedded for us to have a future together.

I didn't know I was crying until the cool breeze brushed the tears on my face. Something wanted me to run inside and confront him, but I went numb. My natural instinct was to get as far away from the situation as possible—to think about what was going on in my head, process it all and come back with a clear mind. I don't run out or distance myself just for the fun of it. I do it so I don't tarnish a relationship or friendship that I care deeply about. I've seen my parents' fuss and fight and say things in anger rather than taking time to step away, get your thoughts together, then come back and revisit the conversation. No matter how long it's been you can still express how you feel.

Deeply wounded by Nolan, I don't know if I ever could recover.

His child growing inside of me but also growing inside of her. "Lani?"

Turning to see Willow, looking beautiful. Not at all like Harmony made it seem. "Malani," I corrected, wiping away the tears I couldn't hide.

"Hi, Malani, can we talk for a second?"

A light chuckle escaping my lips. Before I could respond, Nolan was standing under his door frame. Locking eyes with him, before his travelled to Willow. "What's going on?" It was hard to concentrate on the words I wanted to say because his bare chest was calling out to me. I desperately needed a hug—his hug.

Willow spoke first, "I wanted to have a conversation with Malani. Is that okay to do?" She asked Nolan for permission. He didn't have the say so, but like always I'm sure he's prepared to answer for me.

He looked at me. I couldn't read the look in his eyes. "Lani, is that okay with you?"

Staring back at him caused me to be weak in the knees. Remembering the days when he was a fantasy I loved to dream about. Times when I would secretly position myself under his arm while he slept. Lay in his bed and inhale his scent rendering me intricately smitten. Loving him has been my favorite sport because regardless of all the tantrums he's always on my team. Showing me love his way, and I wouldn't change anything about us.

"Baby?" He gently touched my hand, lacing our fingers. Sandalwood scented skin surrounding us, bringing my attention back to him.

I gave a quick nod, and we ushered into his apartment behind him. Ezeke sat in the rocking chair with his arms folded over his chest. Me and Nolan sat on the loveseat while Willow sat across from Ezeke.

"How far along are you?" Me and Ezeke said at the same time. I looked over at my brother, giving him a smile.

Willow's eyebrows raised, "nine weeks."

I held my palm out, stopping Ezeke from firing questions at her.

My attention shot to Nolan. Two fucking months means he's been cheating on me.

Smiling was the only thing I could do in this moment to keep from bursting out in tears. I stood to my feet pacing back and forth between the coffee table and couch.

Nolan looking at me like he hadn't wronged me for the second time in our relationship. This is a deal breaker, the ultimate low of the low of shitty things you can do to a person. I wouldn't wish this betrayal on anyone. He has to hate me. All these years of friendship had to be a lie. He doesn't care for me.

I was fourteen-year-old Malani all over again. The pathetic lovesick girl that Nolan and his group of guy friends laughed at for having a crush on him. I'm the homie. The one that continuously take all of Nolan's shit and harbors it inside just to have him.

"I've been so grateful for Nolan," she continued her words piercing my heart. "Not too many guys would have done what he did for me and my baby, let alone for a girl he used to date." She smiled lovingly at him, further pissing me off.

If she wasn't with child, I would've reached to scratch her eyes out. Nolan remained silent, my rhythmic breathing replaced the static in my ears. Slowly, I was falling into a pit with no one to catch me. Nolan watching me as I fall, but never offering his hand to help me up.

"Lani, I wanted to tell you, but—"

"Don't insult me by saying you didn't want to hurt me. When have I ever not been able to handle the truth? Don't lie to me," my voice rose with each word I spoke. My head was on a constant spin cycle.

"Can you listen to me instead of thinking you got all the motherfucking answers? Allow me to fucking explain."

"Explain what?" I jabbed my finger into his chest repeatedly. "Explain how you got me and her pregnant at the same fucking time?"

He stood towering over me, eyes blazing with fire, "only person having my baby is you. Willow tell her since her hard headed ass don't give a fuck about what I got to say."

She spoke like he commanded. "Nolan's not the father," she planted her hand on her forehead. "He was supposed to let you know last night when your friend was here. I didn't want any confusion."

I cut my eyes at Nolan, "that doesn't make sense to why she's here."

"I was helping her."

"Get her a room at Black Palace," no matter the anger radiating off of him—I fought the urge to grab both sides of his face with my hands and pull him into me for a kiss. I wanted to feel the softness of his kinky curls against my fingertips. "Seems to me that would've been a win-win since it's close to *The Lounge*."

"I didn't think about that," he admitted.

"No? But you thought about inviting her to stay in your space."

"I didn't think, is that what you want to hear?"

My heart now raced with fury. Closing my eyes and slowly counting backwards from ten calmed me. Or at least I was hoping it did. My mind flashed back to the night I found her naked on his couch. Something deeper was happening here, but I couldn't wrap my head around it. The lies. Nolan doesn't lie to me, but for her, he did. He stumbled his way back into my heart, only to break it once more. I handed it over to him, careless with my own heart because of our friendship.

Nolan loves me. That's what my heart seemed to think, but my mind—my logic tells me something different.

"Baby, stop," the heat of his palms cradle my face, swiping tears from my eyes. I hadn't realized I was crying, lately that's been my reality. Tears pooling at my lids without permission, knowing they needed to escape even when I didn't want them to.

Pulling away from his touch, I didn't recognize my voice when I asked Ezeke to take me home. Nolan called my name, but my mind was far, far away from here. I could hear Willow apologizing to him.

To him?

What about me?

Malani never crossed their minds?

She doesn't owe me loyalty, he does.

My best friend.

Back at home, I planted myself on the couch. Facing the pillows as the cushions soaked up my tears.

"Baby girl?" Ezeke's soft touch on my shoulder caused me to turn over, I pulled him down to me, wrapping my arms around his neck. Emotions coming out of my body like they were being pulled from a Mac truck. He rocked me like a baby, stroking my cheek with his free hand.

We remained like that until my eyelids were getting too heavy to lift.

Waking up to find myself alone on the couch. Tears now dried, but the tightness of the stain pulled at the corner of my eyes.

A coffee cup floated in front of my face, the warmth from the ceramic mug tickling my sleepy eyes. The light brown hand that held the mug by its handle made me smile. Ezeke staying reminds me that he's in my corner.

"Give her some damn creamer," the sassy voice of my best friend calmed my heart.

Harmony thinks of Malani.

I mindlessly fiddled around the couch for my phone, checking in between the pillows only to come up empty.

"I took it," she said, now next to me with the cup of creamer and a tad bit of coffee. Just like I like it. "Nolan kept calling, so I put it up."

Thanks, but no thanks.

I liked seeing his name flash across my screen. Somewhere in my Nolan addicted mind, it showed he cared.

But I didn't say that to her. I weakly smiled before taking a sip of the lukewarm coffee. The bitter taste of the dark roast overpowered the excessive amount of creamer she used. The coffee was shitty, not sure how they'd managed to fuck up a pod.

"How are you feeling?" Ezeke asked with sympathetic eyes.

"How do you think she feels? Niggas ain't shit," Harmony stood from her seat next to me and marched towards the kitchen. I couldn't see her, but I knew she was shaking her head. "Why he have that girl there?"

Ezeke looked from her to me. "I don't know."

"You're full of shit, just like Nolan. What kind of friend are you to Lani? You pick and choose like that bro shit trumps the bond ya'll share. That's the fucked up part about it. Lani will bend over backwards for both of ya'll lying motherfuckers, and for what? A broken fucking heart from Nolan and broken trust from you."

Ezeke's brown eyes darted back to me, "is that how you feel Baby girl? I lost your trust?"

I didn't show him my eyes. I took another gulp of coffee, craving my bed.

"You know I didn't have nothing to do with that, right?" He pleaded for my response, still I had none.

It wasn't like I was mad with Ezeke—not at first. Nolan makes his own decisions. The part that guts me is he knew all along but didn't tell me.

He would rather lose my trust than Nolan's.

So, in reality, Ezeke doesn't give a fuck about our friendship either.

"Don't sit in here and act like you didn't know," Harmony answered for me.

Ezeke opened his mouth, but the knock on the front door stopped his words.

The door didn't have to open for me to know it was Nolan.

I felt his presence.

My hand rested on the cold metal, twisting the knob to find him looking like he didn't flip my world upside down.

"Invite me in," his eyes bore into me while mine was riddled with tears.

"No."

Why was I whispering?

In my head, I said it so forcefully. I meant it.

"No?" He tilted his head to the left like I insulted him.

chapter
thirty-one

Nolan

I pulled Lani to me, closing her apartment door in the process. From the crack in the door, I saw Harmony and Ezeke looking towards the door. They knew it was me, I texted each of them letting them know I was coming over as soon as I thought Lani was awake. Rage ran through my veins when Ezeke agreed to take her home.

She snatched away from me, keeping with this facade like she didn't want me near her. I heard the inhale when I pulled her into me.

"What are we going to do Queen?"

She shrugged her shoulders, that gave me enough room to assume she's conflicted. Lani wants to be mad at something. Punish me for anything, I don't care. As long as I can keep her.

Lani asked the question I knew was swimming around in her head for hours. "Why her?"

"I liked her a lot," I gave it to her straight, no chaser. Her back rested on the door when she took a step back. "I thought she was pregnant by me, that's why I offered to let her stay with me. I wanted to make shit right, but then she told me it wasn't mine."

"Had it been, you would've been with her?"

"Maybe."

"That night of the family and friends night for the practice, did you have sex with her?"

"No."

"Did you want to?"

"She wanted to."

"And you still let her stay?"

I could barely handle the disappointment in her tone, but I desperately needed us to get past this. I fucked up and I knew it, but I wasn't going to be reminded of it every damn day. My heart is with Lani, we're focusing on the then when we should be living in the now. She's got me.

"I did."

"Why?"

"Lani, I just fucking told you."

"No, you told me what you wanted me to hear. Tell me as your best friend."

I huffed, glaring at her. She wanted it to be something deeper but it wasn't. I swear it wasn't. "I told you, so what are we going to do? Do you want to be with me or not because I can slide back into the role of being your best friend then we can focus on raising our child," I forced myself to say. Standing firm and never breaking eye contact letting her know I was serious.

"It's so easy for you to walk away." Her eyes watered and it killed me knowing my words hurt her. Lani crossed her arms over her chest and stared down at her feet.

"No, it's easy for you. I'm here, I've been right here."

Her face streamed with tears breaking me in half, "Nolan, you hurt me."

Taking steps forward, I wrapped her into my arms. Too afraid she would try to let me go I held onto her tight. "I know baby, and I'm sorry." She finally wrapped her arms around me holding onto me just as tight. "Tell me how I can make it better?"

"Never let me go," I tightened my grip without suffocating her.

Lani has always been my right in the face of wrong. The love I have for her runs so fucking deep. We stayed like that for a few minutes, until her tears and cries subsided. Over the years, with her dating she always loved hard. I don't know why I thought with me it would be different, then again I never set out to hurt her. I never wanted to be the cause of tears she shed. My mind trailed back to me holding her—just like this, after breaking up with lame ass niggas. Fuming inside because she gave them a piece of her heart for them to fuck up. Here I am, being that same nigga. Mad at myself for taking her for granted.

I don't deserve her.

I don't deserve the way she puts my needs before her own.

I don't deserve us.

"Imma go, okay," I reluctantly loosened the hold on her. As much as I wanted to be with her, I couldn't allow myself to continue this rollercoaster. I respect Lani way too much to drag her through my shit. My dad and her dad would beat my ass like a nigga in the street if they knew I was out here fucking up with Lani.

"Stay, please." She grabbed my shirt pulling me back to her.

"Come back with me."

"I can't be at your house right now."

I let out a breath. Following her into her apartment, Ezeke and Harmony stared at us. I took hold of Lani's hand as she led us to her room. We cuddled in bed all day, watching movies rather than talking to each other. We took turns choosing the movies. My hands couldn't stay off her stomach, and my lips trailed her neck. Although I had a shit ton of papers to grade, being here with her was more important. She drifted off to sleep around midnight, nuzzling as close as possible to me.

Harmony wasn't in the apartment when I left Lani's room. I grabbed her house key from her key ring, drove to my house to pick up papers then drove back letting myself in. I could never sleep and since worksheets needed to be graded, I set up in Lani's living room. Helping myself to the cold brew coffee in the refrigerator, I was done with both stacks in no time.

———

I DRAGGED MY FEET, *walking slowly to that same blue painted door. Liam was ahead of me, fussing for me to hurry up.*

"If we're late, it'll be your fault and I'll tell Mom and Dad you did it on purpose." He yelled at me from across the sidewalk.

"I want to go home," I pouted.

"And we will. My friend has something for me."

"Why didn't he give it to you yesterday?"

Liam came over to me, "listen, don't worry about things that have nothing to do with you. If we don't hurry, A'Lisa and Malani won't be able to come over, and you want Malani to come over, right?"

I nodded my head.

"Okay, let's go."

Just like yesterday, and the day before that, and the day before that Liam disappeared into the apartment. He came out, then we ran home as fast as we could.

Liam was in the bathroom. I needed to pee.

"Kennedy, I gotta pee," I whined.

Kennedy laid on the sofa watching music videos. "Then, go pee."

I danced, attempting to hold my bladder, "I can't Liam's in there."

"Nolan, Liam's dead."

I AWOKE with sweat beading down my face. Soft hands massaged my shoulders bringing me back to reality. My mind was playing tricks on me because that wasn't how that day went down. Sometimes I forgot the day. The memories would jumble up and appear to me in no particular order. Sometimes it was me finding Liam, then other times it was my mother, father, Kennedy, and even Malani. Truth is, I really can't remember if we went to The Bricks on the day he died. This reoccurring dream alters the reality of it all.

chapter
thirty-two

Malani

"Come here," his voice was deep and low as I straddled his lap. Honestly, what I've been wanting to do all day, feeling his eyes on me untangled the knots of doubt I still held. I knew he'd had a bad dream, but it didn't show on his gorgeous face. His lips brushed against mine hungrily, and I took his tongue massaging it with mine. Tasting him like it was my first time feeling him this way. Knowing he was all mine made him taste a little bit sweeter, and I indulged in him every second. Nolan stood up, holding on to the back of my thighs—my legs were wrapped around his waist. I held onto him with my arms draping around his neck, never wanting to let him go.

I want this—him forever. Nolan placed me gently on the bed, his lips kissing my skin. My neck, then my chest, causing me to strip away my shirt and bra. I wanted to feel the intensity of his love.

Discarding my lower garments of clothing onto the floor, Nolan's tongue ran across his bottom lip drawing me deeper into his trance. I could snap a photo of the look on his face and pleasure myself from that image alone.

"You're my knight," I said to him, meeting his eyes in the dim room.

"Not your King?" He inserted his fingers inside of me, I pushed out a satisfied breath closing my eyes and focusing on him. "Why a knight?" Nolan pulled his fingers out of me, sliding them on his tongue, tasting my essence. He groaned, lowering himself down my body. "Are you gonna tell me?" Before any words could escape my mouth, Nolan covered me with his—snatching the words away with each swipe of his tongue on my clit. Words replaced by moans as he urged me to answer his question. My body shaking from the orgasm he caused and the new one building up in my core. His fingers traveling me down the road to another release that provided unmeasurable pleasure.

"I want you," cut through my dry throat.

Nolan sat up on his knees, pulling his shirt over his head. He wiped my juices from his mouth with the shirt and smiled down at me. "How bad?" Stroking himself before teasing it at the entrance of my opening. "You got my answer yet?" A smirk lingered at the corner of his mouth.

"Because...mmm," he slid into me, again snatching my words and thoughts.

No longer smirking as he rocked inside of me, over and over, fast then slow.

Nolan's eyes were closed, savoring the connection of our bodies —skating the line of being almost too good.

Almost too right.

My nails scratched his back as he took me to a new high.

I couldn't verbalize the words, but the reason he's my knight instead of my king—a king hides behind the other pieces—relying on them to protect him. A knight scourers the board, unafraid to take other pieces out.

Nolan's unwavering, confident, and sexy as hell. Nolan looked at it differently, taking the pieces for face value. Nothing wrong with his way of thinking, I just know each piece was on the board for different reasons, and I respect the ones that work the hardest for the ultimate goal.

I bit down on Nolan's shoulder blade as I came, my pussy contracting around him, milking his orgasm from his body. His tantalizing movements slowing and deepening while he released.

Nolan leaned down to kiss me. I suckled on his tongue wishing it was his lower half inside of my mouth.

"Can you miss the first part of class tomorrow?" I laid my head on his chest as he ran his hand through my moist curls.

"Yes, I just have to make a call. What's up?"

"I'm calling in a favor with a doctor I worked with at Nicoyce Med."

"Everything okay?" He tilted my chin to look at him. "With you and the baby?" He touched my barely there stomach, smiling when I shifted a little from his tickling touch.

"I—We need to find prenatal care, and she's the best in the city," I spoke of Dr. Victoria Roberts. Dr. Cooper speaks highly of her as well as the many patients she treated during their pregnancy. Victoria extracts the baby, and Dr. Cooper and I tighten the excess skin the mother is self-conscious about.

"Okay, I'll call Principal Danders in the morning. Are you nervous?"

"I won't be if you're there."

"Who would've thought we would be going through this together?" Nolan posed the question that's been in my mind since forever.

Secretly, I did. I thought about having his babies and carrying his last name more times than I care to mention.

"Don't you have to work in the morning?"

"Yea, but I'm calling out," looking away from his face. That fucking email had my mind all over the place. I wasn't ready to open it, let alone open it in front of Dr. Cooper. I can't stand to see the look of disappointment on his face.

"Look what I found," Nolan leaned over to retrieve something from the pocket of his jeans. He flipped on the small lamp and held it out to me.

"Where did you find that classic?" I asked, beaming at the picture. The photo was of me asleep on the Hudson's couch—with my arms tucked in a light pink Patty Mayonnaise t-shirt my dad got me for my birthday. They always kept their house cold and never had spare blankets. In the photo, Nolan was asleep at the other end of the couch, snuggled nice and neat under a blanket. We were around ten or eleven years old, probably in a food coma from Mrs. Steph's extravagant afternoon snacks. That lady would damn near cook us a full course meal when it was her turn to babysit. She called it making up time from working all week.

"I apparently always had it. I was looking for another copy of my degree to hang in my future office and ran across it." I could hear the smile in his voice. Looking at us at that tender age filled my heart. Even then we had been through so much, and Nolan always painted a smile on his face for my sake.

chapter
thirty-three

Nolan

Lani never called out from work which concerned me. She can fake like the appointment is the reason, but I know better. If I find out that nigga harassing my girl, it's gonna be a big ass problem.

"She said we can come now," Lani called from the other side of the bathroom door. She'd been in there all morning vomiting. I tapped on the door, handing her a bottled water. "Did you hear me?" She questioned because I didn't respond to her the first time. Lani emerged from the bathroom eyeing me. She definitely didn't look like she'd been puking her guts out for the past three hours. She looked good enough to eat, and if she didn't lessen the intensity in her eyes—I would be doing just that.

"Why don't you want to go to work? Is that nigga..."

"No. This appointment is more important."

"I call bullshit. Yes, the appointment is important. But you just made the appointment this morning, Lani. You're avoiding something."

She smiled, but it didn't match her energy. "It's nothing. Dr. Cooper said it was fine. I will go to work tomorrow." Lani walked past me, but I grabbed her by the wrist pulling her close. I searched her face because she avoided my eyes.

"Check," I kissed her forehead tenderly, lingering there to inhale her scent.

"It's nothing, I promise."

"Okay," I nodded—not believing her for one second. We left for the doctor's office after Lani puked once more.

Four hours later, Lani was still in the back of the doctor's office. She was called to the back immediately after checking in. I opted to stay in the waiting room because I didn't think it would take this long. The wheels started spinning in my head and every possibility of something going wrong clouded my mind. I texted Lani making sure she was okay, but she didn't respond. The fucking message wouldn't send. I hate this reception. I should've gone with her.

Walking to the receptionist's desk, I asked her to check on Lani. She typed Lani's name in the system before looking over her glasses at me, "she's laying down. Her blood pressure was extremely high. Dr. Roberts is monitoring her before she allows her to leave."

"Can I go back there with her?"

"Who are you, sir?" The question she should've asked before giving Lani's personal information to me. So far, I'm not impressed with this office. Lani may have to look into receiving her care from another creditable doctor's office.

"Nolan Hudson. I'm her…boyfriend," I said that shit with pride, poking out my chest and everything. Lani's my girl.

The receptionist granted me access behind the locked door with directions on where Lani was. Seeing her lying in the hospital bed brought back memories.

Memories, the bad ones, I try to fight.

The memories from Liam's last days after I found him passed out on the bathroom floor. We, meaning either April or Kennedy, called the ambulance. Liam was unconscious in the hospital for weeks—they pumped his stomach but to no avail. My parents kept him on life support, desperate for a glimmer of hope for his survival. I remember the doctors letting us see him one last time before my parents made the ultimate sacrifice by pulling the plug. I couldn't imagine what they had to go through—the conversations they had, discussions with each other. I miss my brother, but he was their child

—a child my mother carried in her womb for nine months. The first boy, my dad's first son.

The pride he must have held in his heart when they found out they were finally having a son. I empathize with them because he was ripped away from them. So much promise for it all to end on a fucking bathroom floor.

Was Liam swallowing his hurt? Fear?

I didn't know then and I don't know now, that's the fucked-up part.

When you lose someone, your brain wants to know why? Why had he allowed himself to be pushed past his limit? Why was he taking them in the first place? Why didn't he come to someone—anyone for help? Confide in someone? Why did it have to be him?

Liam's accident is the reason why I push for communication. For my loved ones, I will always stop what I'm doing to talk out any issue we have. Words are important, and I often wonder if Liam felt like he didn't have someone to talk to. I wasn't the one because I was so young, but I'm the one to talk to now. It's something inside of me that can't leave an issue unresolved.

I stopped at the door, looking at her. She was so beautiful, but annoyance was all over her face. High blood pressure? Stress?

I hope I'm not the one to cause it. I'd be lying if I didn't think the whole situation between me and Willow didn't cause some type of strain on her and our baby. I should've been more careful and should've protected Lani first at all costs. Each step towards the bed felt like my shoes were filled with concrete. I didn't hate hospitals but seeing the ones I love in a bed didn't sit right with me. The fact that I didn't know what was going on or how bad it could've affected her pregnancy worried me even more.

"Lani?" I brushed my hand over her flushed cheeks—pulling up a seat in front of her. "What's going on?"

"My blood pressure was a bit higher than it should be, so here I am. I'm sorry, you can go to work if you need to, I'll call Ezeke or Harmony to pick me up.

"I'm not leaving you. What's causing your blood pressure to spike?"

Lani shrugged, "Dr. Roberts says it could be what I'm eating or stress."

"Stress from…"

"I don't know. Just stress."

I took a second to gather my words before I asked, "the baby okay?"

"Dr. Roberts says the baby is fine, but she's happy I came in today." Lani was hooked to a monitor that strapped around her stomach. I noticed the small pudge beginning to form, I smiled. "What?"

"*I* got you pregnant. Thinking about how wild that shit is."

Our conversation came to a halt when someone walked in. Lani tried to sit up and was told to continue to lie down. Dr. Roberts introduced herself, shaking my hand with a pleasant smile on her dark brown face. She moved to inform Lani how the next appointments were going to go. Until Lani's blood pressure normalizes, she wanted her to stop by the office each week for a check. She encouraged Lani to drink plenty of water and gave her tips on breathing exercises. Before leaving the office, Dr. Roberts eased our worries by letting us hear our baby's strong heartbeat. Tears slid from the corner of Lani's eyes, that whooshing sound calming her nerves—and mine.

chapter
thirty-four

He recorded our baby's heartbeat! If I weren't in love with Nolan before, I'm completely falling off the cliff in love with him now. The twinkle in his eyes when Dr. Roberts spread the warm goo over my stomach letting us know what was coming next was priceless. That was four days ago, and I still see that look when I look into his eyes.

My fingers hovered over the email I was dreading to read. Dr. Cooper's patience was running thin with me because I hadn't returned back to work since the email dropped. Why couldn't I just tell him I didn't want to read it? The email coming too soon is a clear bad sign. I know I failed. I didn't want to see Dr. Cooper because in a way I failed him, too. He's been my mentor for a while, teaching me everything he knows and allowing me to see things I wouldn't have if working under someone else. I'm grateful for him but to fail the biggest test of my career is a slap in his face. Like I didn't retain any of the information and skills he taught me. He doesn't deserve that, he doesn't deserve to have a failure as a mentee.

"You gone chew your bottom lip off," Harmony stepped into my room, sitting in front of me on the floor. "What are you thinking so hard about?"

I shrugged, "nothing, everything."

She rolled her eyes, "you're holding back."

"I'm not," my eyes shifted from her to the ring on her finger. "Harms, what the fuck is that?" She hid her hand behind her back with a guilty look plastering over her face. "Harmony," blowing out an exasperated breath, I stood heading for the kitchen.

"Whoa, bitch, when the fuck did that start poking like that?" She said pointing to my stomach, the tank top I was wearing made the small bump appear more than normal. I'd mentally asked myself where it came from when I stared at my body in the mirror.

"Don't change the subject," I folded my arms over my chest. "Who gave you that big ass ring?" She looked away, blinking away tears. I already knew by her behavior. "He proposed to you?" I redundantly asked for a clear understanding. "And you said? Harms, you said yes." I wasn't in the business to tell anyone how to live their life, but what's concerning to me is the tears and somberness presented when questioned about a decision made—a life altering decision. I stared at the wall for a moment searching for the right words to say that wouldn't hinder our friendship. "Congratulations," was all that slipped through my tight lips.

Harmony slightly smiled up at me, "thanks."

"I took the surgeon's test, and I think I failed." Since we were spilling secrets, revealing that to her—somebody, the pressure released from my shoulders with so much ease.

"You know that shit with your eyes closed."

"I know, but maybe I got too nervous. Maybe I didn't answer how they wanted me to answer. Maybe, I didn't finish the test, and I thought I did. Maybe…"

"Lani, breathe," Harmony hands on my shoulders halted the pacing and the overdramatic rant. We sat on my bed, "why do you think you failed, for real?"

"I've failed at everything else, why would this be any different?"

"Why are you so hard on yourself lately?" I couldn't answer. "You're the smartest girl I know. I'm sure you passed the test."

"What test?" Nolan's voice startled me, and my eyes shot to Harmony's briefly before turning to see Nolan and Ezeke standing in the doorway of my bedroom. I wasn't prepared to tell him about my failure—planning to keep it a secret as long as I could. I hated not telling him the other day that the test contributed to my high blood pressure. "Lani, test?" He reminded me, but that didn't make the words form because he repeated his.

"Do ya'll want to have this conversation alone?" My most rational friend asked.

"Lani, only if you want me to leave," Harmony rolled her eyes.

"Everyone can stay." I took a deep breath, sliding my eyes to Nolan, "I took the surgeon's test a few weeks ago, and the results are in."

"Already?" Ezeke asked with the same suspicion housed deeply in me.

"You probably rocked that shit. Where's the mail?" I needed Nolan's enthusiasm when the email first dropped.

"It's an email," clutching my phone to my chest like one of them would grab it from me.

"Baby, open it," he urged.

Ezeke moved deeper into my room, settling around the bed close to Harmony.

This should be a perfect time, it's fitting. I'm surrounded by my closest friends—people I love. What's holding me back? I've failed tests and classes before, but in secret not with my friends staring a hole in my face. It's like I'm under a microscope and afraid of what they would find inside. A fucking mess, a girl that appears to have her career life together only to fail a test on what she does every damn day.

Nolan's hand cupped my chin, guiding me to look up at him. He held his other hand out for my phone. I handed it over to him— almost instantly sliding it into his big hands. The unlocking sound dropped my heart deeper into my stomach. Nolan's thumb sweeping up and down the screen raised my anxiety level.

"Stop," was my last attempt to save face. I should've opened it myself, alone, away from embarrassment. The room was quiet, like everyone was holding their breath on my account. "Not today, I need more time."

"I already see the results," he turned to Ezeke. "Can ya'll step out really quick." Ezeke nodded. Harmony rubbed my knee before they both left the room, closing the door behind them. Nolan's face was stoic. He sat on the bed, gently pulling me to face him.

"How bad is it?" I closed my eyes in an attempt to shield myself from the disappointment I knew was coming. All my emotions washed over me like a cold shower. At this moment, Nolan was silent and I wanted to read his mind. He had to be upset I failed. I studied for the test with Dr. Cooper for weeks, he prepped me and quizzed me every chance we got. First, I didn't want to become a surgeon, but with the idea in my head, a seed was planted and boy did it sprout a big ass tree. It was in my reach, or so I thought.

"Did you study at all?" His words punched me in my gut, knocking the wind from my lungs.

"That bad, huh?" Tears fought to spill onto my face. "Thank you for not sharing my failure with them." I rested my chin in the palm of my hand. In a year, a retest is in the cards for me, and I'll have to share with Dr. Cooper that I failed him. I will retest—I owe that to myself to prove I'm better than a failing score.

"You passed, Queen," Nolan pushed the phone close to my face.

I snatched the phone from him, not believing a word coming out of his mouth. Indeed, the email from The American Board of Plastic Surgery congratulated me on passing level three of the COMLEX and invited me to take the necessary steps to receive board certification. I jumped into Nolan's arms, wrapping mine tightly around his neck. I thought he read the wrong email—the goal of knowing if I passed or failed was accomplished. "I passed! I fucking passed! But why did you send them out?"

"So, I could do this," Nolan captured my mouth, pulling me to his lap. My breath was caught in my throat as I breathed in his scent. "Stop doubting yourself, you're smart as fuck," he said against my mouth. His hand slid under my shirt, squeezing my breast until my nipples rubbed against the fabric of my shirt. I bit my lip, suppressing the moan that dared to escape my mouth. This felt good, so good. Nolan lifted the tank top, dipping low to capture my nipples in his mouth. My hand rested on the back of his head encouraging him to taste me in the way only he could. Passing the test and being in Nolan's arms made my day. I wouldn't want to be anywhere but here. He bit my nipple causing me to moan out in pleasure. My hips rocked seductively in his lap feeling his hardness beneath me.

On the other side of the door, I heard a heated argument, their voices were low but distinct. Nolan groaned and continued his hold on me, "everything good?" He hollered at the door, when the only answer he received sounded like a smack to bare skin. I quickly lowered my shirt and climbed from his lap. Nolan opened my room door. From my seat on the bed, I noticed the redness on Ezeke's left cheek. He appeared paralyzed—frozen in the moment with his head tilted.

Harmony pushed past Nolan, stopping in front of me full of fury. "I'm done being Ezekiel's friend." She threw her hands up in the air. "I'm tired of him fucking judging me and thinking he has a say so in my fucking life."

"Did you hit him?" My eyes were trained on Ezeke, I don't know why—well I do, but tears clouded my eyes. "Nolan..." My voice trembled as I watched my friend like he was in a trance, transported back to his dark days in Greensboro.

"I know. I'll see you later." Nolan had to practically drag Ezeke out the hallway because he was so stiff.

It was only when I heard the front door slam that I spoke to Harmony. "Why?" I asked through clenched teeth. A fire burning within me that not even a fire extinguisher could put out.

She paced back and forth, "he saw the ring. Asked me about it, I told him. He says he already threatened Quentin, now he has to put hands on him. He's always in my fucking business, that's why Quentin wasn't speaking to me this whole time because of him and his empty ass threats. Suppose Quentin and his brothers would've retaliated."

"Why would you hit him though? Knowing what he's been through?"

"I don't know. It just happened. I'm so pissed." She slammed her fist into her hand.

"You can't put your hands on people. What if he would've hit you back? Did you think about that? His trauma is real. Next time use your words. Be mad, but don't let your anger flow through your hands."

Harmony hung her head, "I'm sorry."

"Don't tell me. Tell him."

Ezeke's upbringing was rough as well as Harmony's. It was easy to convince them to move to New Bern because Greensboro was a reminder of all the bad. New Bern was a new beginning, a chance to start over. Our circle is strong because we shared our trauma with each other, Harmony crossed the line by invoking his. But that's for her to figure out, to gain him back as a friend.

"I passed by the way."

"Congratulations," she slid the ring off her hand, tucking it into her pocket.

"Harmony," I pulled her down next to me. "If you want to be with him, be with him. Don't let us decide for you." She nodded her head. I hope she hears me because at the end of it all, I want her to be happy—if it's with him, then it is what it is, and we have to accept her decision.

chapter
thirty-five

I stood in my parent's backyard, letting the sun warm my skin and the breeze run over me. It's a beautiful, sunny spring day we get to enjoy after days of gray and rain. Lani picked today to tell my parents about us. Of course, they've been praying for this day. My mom was floored seeing Lani sporting a baby bump. I was proud knowing I put a baby in there. That moment was one the happiest I had in a very long time.

"You know you used to come back here all the time when you were little. We had a swing set then. You would sit on that swing and swing all damn day." My dad patted my shoulder, reminiscing on the days after losing Liam. Little did he know, I couldn't stand to be in the house without Liam being there.

I pushed my hands into the pockets of my jeans letting that dreary feeling wash over me. "Dad, I have to tell you something."

"Something else?"

Turning to my dad, I saw the worry in his dark brown eyes. I've wrestled with myself for years on revealing this news to my family.

How would they view me?

Would they hate me for not telling them?

I exhaled, closing my eyes, dreading the moment until I pushed it out, "Liam used to take me with him to get the drugs."

My dad's face relaxed, "we know." He released a breath, "we started to pay attention after the second time he broke his wrist." I glared at my dad in confusion, "Liam had 'accidents,'" my dad put his fingers up signaling air quotes. "The first time he broke his wrist, they prescribed the pills—he got a taste for them. He wanted more. I don't think you remember, but for a long time, he would be so angry, he would refuse to walk you to school. He played nice, and we trusted him again to walk you, but we had him followed." I turned around peering at Lani and my mom sitting on the back porch with a glass of watermelon lemonade, laughing and joking like old friends. "A'Lisa told us about the stops in The Bricks."

"So, Lani—"

"Yes, but just like you—she was oblivious. Losing Liam was hard, still hard." He looked down at his shoes. "I'm thankful to still have you, your sisters, and Lani, too. Now, your baby… I'd say we're blessed."

I didn't feel the tears until they hit my cheeks. I've carried this blame—shame for so long. Lani's words repeated in my head, 'you were just a kid.' I couldn't remember the times of Liam acting out. What I did remember was the feeling of being the reason he died. My dad pulled me into an embrace, patting my back as I sobbed. Releasing all that I've held over the years.

My dad and I cleared Liam's room soon after our talk in the backyard. It seemed so disheartening. Memories of him were now enclosed in five big boxes. I kept small trinkets—a necklace and a keychain that hung on his house key. The day of Liam's funeral, I didn't feel like I was laying him to rest. Today—today I have that feeling.

I slid behind Lani, placing my hands on her stomach. She relaxed against my chest. "I was thinking. We've never been on a date."

"Not officially," I turned her around, tasting the exposed skin of her neck. "Where do you want to go?" Sucking, biting, and licking her neck changed her breathing. I backed her into my old room, pressing her back against the closed door. My hand caressed her pussy through her leggings. "Lani, where do you want to go?"

"Anywhere with you," she moaned. I filled her with two fingers, pressing firmly against her clit with my thumb. The circular motions making her body shudder under my touch.

I dipped low to meet her slightly closed eyes. "Anywhere?" I carried her to the bed, pulling her pants and panties down her legs. My fingers returned to her pussy.

Lani squirmed, placing her hand over mine, "not here, your parents are down the hall."

"Fuck that, you said anywhere," I licked my lips, the essence of her skin rushing on my palette. Weird but I've always wanted to have sex in my old room—what a better way for it to be with Lani. "Move your hand," I growled into her ear—gently pulling her earlobe between my teeth. Moving my fingers in and out of her as she whimpered softly. I kissed down the center of her body, draping her legs over my shoulders as I sucked on her clit. Lani arched her back, gripping a handful of my curls while my tongue made love to her pussy. I could lick her all fucking day and not get tired of her taste. My appetite for her is growing stronger. Sometimes I don't know if I could make it through the day without touching her. Even when we're laying down watching a movie, my hands have to touch her—arms have to hold her—lips have to brush her skin.

Entering her, she snaked her legs around me, sinking me deeper into her core. I kissed her, swallowing moans that intensified while increasing my rhythm in and out of her. Our lips never stopped touching the entire time we made love. Lani moaned loud as fuck as she came. I released soon after. My legs dangled off the small bed as I watched her catch her breath. "Where do you want to go for dinner? Or do you want to have dinner and a movie?"

"I want to cook and chill with you, our thing." She rested her back against me and pulling my arm across her.

"Tonight?"

Lani shrugged, "whenever."

"What do you want to eat?"

"You," she sat up on her elbow, stroking me back to life.

Lowering her head, she took me in her mouth. I hissed, drawing in a sharp breath. Her head bouncing up and down—her eyes never leaving mine. Both hands working simultaneously with her mouth. The amount of effort and attention she was giving my dick didn't go unnoticed. Sucking slowly, speeding up, then slow again drove me fucking crazy. I tossed my head back with one hand fisting her mane. She didn't let up, taking me deeper in her mouth every time she went down.

I thrust my hips forward meeting her mouth, "Lani," giving her a warning, I was on the verge of cuming. Groaning, my cum raced to her tonsils. Watching her swallow my shit, I pulled her on top of me. Lani eased down, my length disappearing into her. I held the back of her neck, kissing her deeply. Lani rolled her hips, chasing another orgasm. For a minute, I'd forgotten I was at my parents' house. Forgot we had to be as quiet as we could, so we weren't caught. I sat up a bit, holding onto her waist—guiding her up and down my dick while my tongue occupied her erect nipples. She grabbed the sides of my face, sliding her tongue in my awaiting mouth. She sucked on my tongue while one of my hands continued rubbing her clit and the other squeezing her nipples. Her pussy contracted, and I felt the rush of her cuming again. Rearing back a little, my hands still focused on their actions as I looked at her contorted face. Licking my lips, I said, "you feel so fucking amazing."

She came again, this time her eyes locked on mine. "I love you."

"Fuck," I came, shooting my nut into her, "I love you, too."

LANI INSISTED we go to the store after leaving my parent's house. I was sure I had food that could make a meal for dinner, but she didn't want to take any chances. I was also happy she agreed to come back to my apartment. We grabbed a couple of items for dinner and breakfast in the morning. It's still unbelievable Lani and I are together and having a baby. Her dad was the first to know about us being official—outside of Ezeke and Harmony— I talk to him a lot because he's easy to talk to. After Liam's death, Michael stepped in as a father figure when my dad was broken. He opened that door for me to talk to him about anything, and I continue to use that door even in adulthood.

I washed and scrubbed the potatoes for Lani when I returned from the second trip to the grocery store. The smell of the ground beef was making her sick, so I went out to get plant-based burgers instead. I watched her make her famous mashed potatoes—I've watched her prep so many times, and I still don't know how to make it or make it taste like hers. If I could turn back time, I would have paid more attention to Lani. I would've known the moment her feelings for me started—I should've felt the shift in our friendship. Thinking about where we could've been right now in our lives. Married and going on baby number two Who the fuck am I kidding? We'd have a house full.

"My dad said they used to have A'Lisa follow Liam after school. Did you know about that?" That's been on my mind since leaving my parent's house and even more to and from the grocery store.

Her shoulders tensed, but she continued to stir the concoction in the pot. "Nolan, I was young. I barely remember anything from back then."

"A'Lisa used to walk you home from school?"

"Somedays, yes."

"Did you go straight home?" My question was simple, but the breath she blew out made it seem like it was so complex. "Why are you getting defensive?"

"I'm not. I don't want to relive it."

"Because you should've told me."

Lani turned the heat to the pot off before facing me. "I'm sorry."

"Lani, you've known how long I held thinking I was the only one who knew what he was doing. We shared that, but you made me think I faced it alone."

"We didn't know he was getting pills until we got older. You didn't even know then."

"That's not the fucking point."

"What is the point, Nolan? You want to be mad with me, be mad. You lost Liam that day, and I lost A'Lisa. She checked out, physically and mentally. I haven't had a real conversation with her in years because I knew she watched him crumble. She saw—" Lani swallowed. "When my parents moved, they gave me a box of stuff they thought was mine. The box had A'Lisa's diary. She watched him take pills, even took some with him. In my eight-year-old mind, she was following him because she liked him. I didn't know anything else. I hated walking home, hated going to The Bricks. Watching her mourn him because she held secrets, too, tore her up. I knew, so she couldn't look me in my eyes. I didn't want that for you. I wanted to be there for you like I couldn't be there for her. She pushed me away because I was a part of the secret. Just because I was there watching her—watch him…" fresh tears welled in her face. "You would've done the same," her voice cracked, and she sobbed into my chest.

I harbored so much regret over the years. Always talked about things I should've done differently when I should've been healing. Healing from the hurt and honoring the memories. I've shared almost everything with Lani over the years, but the pain of Liam— that was our disconnect, but it wasn't. She felt it—felt it for me and A'Lisa. She wrapped her arms around my torso, squeezing me into a tight embrace. "I'll never leave you. I wouldn't then and I won't now," I said hoping my words penetrated her heart.

chapter
thirty-six

Nolan

Bittersweet—was the only word that crossed my mind during this last day of school. The kids were at lunch as I stared around the classroom, taking it all in. The walls were bare now. I started removing the wall decor weeks ago, transporting them to my office. A single room, small but enough for three—four people at the most. This step into my new role is serene, and I'm looking forward to the future with Nicoyce Prep.

The light knock drew my attention to the door. Lani stood in the door frame in all black scrubs with pink hearts. "Hey," she greeted me with a kiss as she stepped into the empty room "Are you okay?"

"Yeah, how are you?"

"Hungry," she held out the gold bag from *The Lounge*. "Bobby had drunken noodles today." I smiled practically, prying the bag from her fingers. "Did I come too late? He insisted on making them fresh."

"Nah, it's good. We've been chilling all day." I hated the teachers that made students do work on the last day of school. These kids were not thinking about math on this day; they were thinking about their plans for the summer. "Signing yearbooks and shit."

"Oh, my God!" She gushed, "I miss that. Remember our parents being cheap as hell—going half on the cost of the year-book? Each year we had to share, all the way up until high school."

I chuckled, remembering, "I always got the front of the book for classmates to sign."

Lani rolled her eyes, "yeah, always phone numbers and keep in touch messages. So annoying."

"Now I see why you used to scribble over girl's pictures with a black marker—because you wanted me."

She shrugged, "looks like I got you."

I stood between her thighs, rubbing my hands up and down them thick motherfuckas. Then, grabbing her by the nape of her neck and leaning close to her, "yeah, you do," I gently kissed her, sliding my tongue against hers, tasting her. Damn, this food.

"Eww, get a room," Justice's voice sang. I closed my eyes, breathing deeply only to hear more footsteps approaching. Lani slid off the desk—greeting the students. "Hey, Miss. Malani, O.M.G!" Justice playfully ran circles around the classroom. "That boy did that?" She asked, pointing to me, making all the kids roar with laughter.

Lani's face held a sheepish grin when she looked back at me. "Ya'll settle down," I took control of the classroom. "What do you say to Miss. Malani?"

"Congratulations," they said in unison.

"Can you sign my yearbook?" Justice asked followed by other students. Lani agreed, and I had them form a line. Lani was enjoying this shit, a smile never leaving her face. She stayed for the rest of the school day, the kids convincing both of us to let them watch another movie and eat snacks until the bell rang.

Then, the bittersweet moments came when each student had to say their goodbye to me as their teacher. Special handshakes and hugs had me fighting the tears. I love these kids, man. The bond we've created. To say I will miss them is an understatement—seeing them around school will be different because I'm not actively teaching them the fundamentals of math and life.

"Have they hired your replacement?" Lani took my seat behind the desk, placing the last bit of items in a box.

I nodded, "someone from the public school, but that nigga will never replace me."

"A little cocky, huh?"

"Pure confidence, baby.

"Yo, yo, last day blues," Ezeke strolled in with Harmony. Glad they squashed shit; it was awkward as hell these past weeks. Now I know how much tension it caused the group when me and Lani had it out. I gave Ezeke dap and Harmony a side hug. "How you feeling?"

"I don't know, happy one minute then regretting the decision the next," I admitted.

"It's for the best, though; it's long overdue. I give it a year, and your ass will be principal."

"I still don't know how they let your ass be a teacher. Lani used to do your homework in college."

"Shut up," I nudged her playfully. "What Lani failed to mention is—I used to do her homework, too."

All eyes went to Lani who covered the side of her face with her hand, "Malani?" Harmony stood in front of her.

"What?! I was bad at philosophy." We laughed, "don't act like we didn't all help each other. Ezeke, Spanish and art theory ring a bell? All you did was show up to class. Harmony, I wrote a few of your English papers."

We went around the room naming subjects we helped each other with. Had it not been for them, I probably would've failed out of college. Ezeke with the save for Sociology and Psychology, especially.

"Don't forget I helped you pass British history," Grant said from the door—sucking all the humor out the room. Four sets of eyes looking at him wondering what the fuck he wanted. "I—I didn't mean to interrupt. I heard laughter from down the hall."

"That didn't mean you had to come check it out," Harmony sassed.

"You're right. Hey, congratulations, Nolan!"

"'Preciate it," I said glaring at him, hoping he would take the hint and step off.

"Mala…"

"Nah," I shook my head. "You don't have to address nobody else in this room, my boy. Especially her."

"Right, again congratulations," he threw his hand up then backed out. We erupted with laughter, clown ass nigga.

"I DON'T WANT TO KNOW," Lani and I were laying in her bed after demolishing the drunken noodles and dumplings from earlier. She also had a cinnamon roll, her nightly snack. 'The baby wants it' is all I hear as an excuse to devour sugar before bed.

"Well, I do," we were discussing finding out the sex of our baby. My mom's been itching to buy baby stuff since finding out Lani's pregnant. The excitement of a new baby overcoming her.

"It'll be a surprise. My parents did that with all three of their pregnancies."

"We are not your parents and not knowing doesn't give us time to prepare."

"They make gender neutral baby stuff, Nolan. Also, we can buy diapers because we will need a lot. What about our living situation? That's important. Am I moving in with you, or are you moving in with me? Are we moving in at all or raising him or her in two different homes." She rambled off questions—not giving me a chance to answer before posing another one.

"One step at a time. We have months to figure it out," the hitch in her breathing told me I didn't give her the answer she was looking for. I've never lived with previous partners. The whole Willow shit was different. It did teach me that I like having my own space. I enjoyed having Lani around, being with her, spending time with her. I like the cushion of knowing I had a place of my own to retreat to if push comes to shove. "It's not a 'no' Lani," I comforted her visibly hurt feelings. "And I'm not waiting to find out the gender."

She shifted away from me, not too much but enough for me to notice and pull her ass back. "Okay," was the simple answer, but I knew she was pondering more than that little word.

I never thought about having kids really. I've been teaching for so long that the kids in my classroom always felt like my children. Partly because I was teaching them about life too—giving advice on dating and understanding the opposite sex. I never thought about a mini-me running around. I couldn't imagine waiting until birth to find out the sex of our child. Patience isn't my greatest virtue, but it's Lani's. She waited years for me, so equally, I can do her the solid and wait months until our child is born. "I'll wait," I conceded.

"For what?"

"The gender."

"Okay."

Reaching over, I pulled her close to me—her back resting on my hard chest. I rubbed her soft skin where my baby was growing. "You're so fucking stubborn," kissing her earlobe as she squirmed from my touch.

"I haven't said anything."

My hand went lower—caressing her inner thighs at first then sliding my hand into her panties. "You didn't have to," I pushed two fingers inside of her. "Where do you want to live? With me?" She was so fucking wet for me—sloppy wet. Sliding my wet fingers against her clit she cooed, biting down on my other arm to suppress her moans. My mouth replaced my fingers, yearning to taste her juices. I lapped her from her clit to her ass. Her body shaking with each lick my tongue planted on her tender spots. French kissing her pussy while she creamed over my face, I clutched her thighs pulling her further on my face—into my mouth. Drinking her in—hungrily, avoiding her attempting to push my head away. Her pussy shouldn't be this good, shouldn't respond to my touches and tongue this well. If she wanted to move in, I'll let her. If she wanted me here, I'll do that, too. Pushing off the bed, I turned on the light to admire her. With closed eyes, she was beautiful—everything I could ever need, in my fucking face, but not seeing it. I see her now, and never will I ever let her go. Lani sat up, rubbing her eyes then meeting my lustful gaze. "You never answer my questions," I teased, knowing damn well the reason she's unable to answer. She crawled to the end of the bed, wearing a smirk and her eyes trained on my dick. I hadn't pulled it out yet, but I was hard as hell—she did it for me, stroking me with both hands. My head fell back in satisfaction, groaning when saliva fell from her mouth to its intended target. I fisted her curls, my hips meeting her mouth as she attempted to take me in deep. My shit disappearing in her mouth was sexy as fuck. I've had fire head before but *goddamn*; Lani's mouth is on a different level. I bust on her tongue, trying to hold it to empty inside of her, but shit happens.

Lani sat back further on the bed, clearly satisfied from the job well done, "your apartment is bigger."

"Mine it is," I agreed, pulling her back to the edge of the bed by the back of her calves. Her giggles were replaced by a moan when I slid deep into her.

thirty-seven

Malani

I needed to get out of the house—away from Nolan. Since summer break started, he's been dicking me down, day and night. I'm not complaining by any means, but if I wasn't pregnant now—there's no doubt in my mind I would've been by end of summer. He's not holding back, and I love it, but I do need at least a day without his dick inside of my pussy and mouth.

I managed to sneak away to go into the office for a couple of hours. It was after hours so I knew Dr. Cooper had gone home for the day—at least I thought. When I rounded the building, I spotted his car in its usual parking space. Using my key to enter the center with my briefcase in tow. I only had to file documents and set up the automatic recorded message to run for patients with appointments on Monday.

"What are you doing here?" Standing in the doorway of Dr. Cooper's office, a mug of—more than likely—chai tea to his mouth.

"Same as you, looks like."

Smiling, I walked deeper into his office. The smell of eucalyptus permeated my senses. "You've been here all day, I haven't." Helping myself to the seat in front of his huge desk.

"Because you've been avoiding me."

"A little. I was nervous about the results."

"Why?"

"I just got in my head," I admitted. "I thought I failed."

He put his hand over his heart like I'd stabbed him there, "ouch! So, you thought my teaching was going to fail you?"

"It wasn't that. I had faith in all you've trained and taught me. Like I said, I got in my own head."

"It happens to the best of us," Dr. Cooper took another sip of the tea before sifting through the papers on his desk. He found the one he was looking for and came around the desk to hand it over to me. "Congratulations," his arms were wrapped around me in a congratulatory embrace.

Quickly hugging him, I smiled. I was beaming inside.

"I knew you could do it," he boasted, clearly having more confidence in me than I had in myself.

"That makes one of us," I toyed with the straps on my briefcase.

"Well, you passed the first two with flying colors. Why did you think differently?" All I could do was shrug my shoulders. "Believe in yourself, I do." He shot me one of his infamous smiles. If I wasn't so tethered to Nolan, maybe I would've given Dr. Cooper a ride. His caring spirit is unmatched, and I never received it from any boss I ever had in the past.

"I appreciate you," leaning into him again for a hug.

"Same," he returned to his seat. "Now, I can take some vacation days since I can leave you in charge."

"Go ahead, I can handle it alone."

He nodded, "I know. I got you down for some surgeries alone coming up. However, you need to hire a practitioner as soon as possible to assist you. I have a couple in mind if you would like the list. I'm on a hunt for one myself." I smiled again, knowing I no longer held the title, thanks to him pushing me to further my career. I happily took his list of only three names before going to my office to finish the tasks on my to-do list. He left thirty minutes later, reminding me not to forget to set the alarm.

Harmony came by on her lunch break to bring me food from *The Lounge.* Unfortunately, the tasks took longer than normal because the internet kept going out. I had to phone the tech department to get it corrected.

"So, do I need to find another place to stay?" Harmony asked with a mouthful of bread.

"I mean, you can stay there until my lease runs out, but I'm not renewing." It's a huge leap I'm taking moving in with Nolan, but it's one I'm willing to take. I've never lived with anyone other than my parents and Harmony. I know Nolan's ticks, though, so it will be easy to adjust. We're basically living together now because we barely spend time apart. "Then after that, we can talk to the front office about you taking over the apartment."

"Okay, I like that option. I do not want to bunk with Quentin at his parent's house," she rolled her eyes.

I smacked my lips, "their house is big as shit, though."

"I know, but still—that shit is bum. How is my little god baby?"

"Good, we had an appointment last week, and my blood pressure is down. Carmen suggested I cut back on work, so I've been really enjoying that. Have you ever thought about having kids, Harms?"

Harmony avoided the topic in college, but we're getting older now and time waits for no one. Harmony shrugged her shoulder, looking away from me, but I saw her glossy eyes.

"Did I say something wrong?"

"No," she answered quickly, she sniffled turning back to me with a smile. "Just because you and Nolan decided to procreate doesn't mean the rest of us have to," she laughed loud, even louder when I threw a piece of my bread at her.

"Whatever," was my only rebuttal. Thing is, Nolan and I didn't decide—it just happened. I don't regret the conception of our child. Everyone likes a surprise here and there.

"I was pregnant by Quentin once."

"When? You didn't tell me shit," she preaches to me about holding back but does the same.

"Five years ago."

Searching her teary eyes, I asked, "what happened? Did you lose it?"

"Something like that." She sighed, wiping her eyes free of the tears. "Oh, I forgot to tell you," she fumbled with her purse, digging deep for something. Her eyes lit up when she pulled out a small flyer, placing it in front of my face. "*The Lounge* is hosting an open mic night. We should go."

I felt like there was more to the story, but I didn't press. Although losing a child is hard, I saw the toll it took on Nolan's parents. The nights Nolan snuck to my house because they were fighting too loud, and he couldn't sleep.

"Open mic? That's different," I examined the glossy flyer in her hand.

"I know, I talked Bobby into it. I think it'll be fun. You'll come right?"

"Yes, I'll talk to Nolan about it. In the meantime, I got to finish this email, so I can go home. Nolan's getting antsy."

"Yuck!" She pretended like she was vomiting, *overdramatic ass.*

"Don't act like Q isn't waiting for you."

"He's not," she said matter of factly.

"Ya'll all right?" I asked. I was basically thrown into the backseat of their rollercoaster relationship since conception.

Her brows furrowed, and she sighed heavily, "oh yeah, he's just making runs for the family. Hurry up so I can walk you out. People crazy out here."

I laughed. Harmony wouldn't bust a grape in a fruit brawl. I would not rely on her protecting me from anything or anybody. "Ezeke is here; he just came from work."

"Ezekiel, your best friend," she was very sarcastic, but I waved her off. I don't like this shift in their relationship. She doesn't want him? Fine but they were friends first. Go back into that. "Will I see you later, or are you spending the night with Nolan?"

"Harms, it's Friday."

"Meaning?"

"Ezeke sent it in the group chat; we're having a movie night at his place."

She scrolled through her phone, "nope, I'm not in that fucking chat."

"You're welcome to come."

"Hell no, I don't go where I'm not invited."

I pushed out a breath, "I literally just invited you."

"Initially, Lani. Not spur of the moment type shit. How are you just now telling me about this anyway? You didn't notice I wasn't in the chat?"

"Nolan read the text to me. What's the big deal? Go home, change, and meet us at Ezeke's by 9:30."

"No," she folded her arms. I laughed because I wasn't going to nurse her. I finished the email that's been sitting in the draft folder, directed the appointment calls, gathered my bag, and headed out with her in tow.

Ezeke's handsome face greeted me with a smile. Harmony brushed past him, going to her car—pulling off without saying anything to him. "What's her problem?"

I raised my eyebrows, tossing my bag into the backseat of my car. "Is she not in the group chat Ezeke?"

"Why wouldn't she be?"

"She said she didn't get the invite for tonight."

"Since when do any of us need an invite to hang with each other? Harmony's on some different shit, and I'm not feeling it. She violated by putting her hands on me—I forgave that. But lately, her energy is off."

I nodded my head because I felt everything he was saying. This is the wave of Q. Harmony gets like this every time they get back together. My relationship with Harmony is the same. I wonder if her friendship with Ezeke has run its course. This is exactly why I kept my attraction to Nolan a secret for so long. When feelings are not reciprocated, the space for friendship dissipates.

I HOVERED OVER NOLAN, my thighs on either side of his head. Cradling my ass in his big hands as I rolled my hips—riding his face. My hands gripping the headboard all while struggling to steady my wobbly knees. We'd tried to go a day without indulging in each other, but I couldn't keep my hands to myself when we crossed the threshold of his place. I'm happy his appetite for me is just as strong as mine is for him. His fingers occupying my holes, I arched my back in submission to his touch. "Fuck!" I moaned breathlessly. Nolan was relentless, always building me up, taking me over the edge—surpassing my limits. He pushed me deeper on his face, grazing my sensitive bud with his teeth, holding that motion in place while I creamed again. Sliding down his body, I kissed him tasting my juices on his tongue.

Just a year ago, we wouldn't have been here—in this space. His mouth, hands, and fingers exploring my body was a dream to me. Something I would pleasure myself thinking about. Reality is way better than fantasy.

"What time is it?"

I slide down his dick, relishing in him fitting perfectly inside of me. "Shiiittt, Lani," his fingers dug into my hips. "We're gonna be late," he groaned, but he didn't stop the automatic pull of his hips meeting my movements.

"For what?" I balanced myself, putting my hands on his chest as I rode him.

Nolan flipped me to my back, kissing my lips and drilling into me at a steady pace. "We have a flight to catch."

Nolan

Lani ran into her dad's arms when we spotted him waiting for us in the airport. I gathered our bags since she abandoned them to practically run in the crowded airport. I gave Kolby dap when he met me halfway to take a few of the bags out of my hand.

"What's up, bro?"

"I can't call it. I see things haven't changed," he laughed.

"I blame ya'll," I teased.

"Nah, blame that nigga," he nodded towards their dad, who still embraced his little girl. "Congrats by the way. Can't say I didn't see that shit coming."

I shook my head, "'Preciate it, man."

"How's Kennedy?" Kolby grinned as we walked towards Lani and Michael.

My entire childhood, I was thinking we were creating lifelong friendships. We did—but looking now with adult eyes, feelings were developing, romantic feelings.

"Nigga, married. I thought you were heading down the aisle."

He blew out an exaggerated breath, "that shit, no bueno. On a scale of one to ten, what are my chances of getting Kennedy back?"

I eyed him, thinking he was about to start laughing. When that didn't happen, I knew he was dead ass serious. Kolby's been my brother, so keeping it hot with him is only right. Kennedy is not thinking about his ass—at all.

"She's in deep, man. I'm sorry. I'll tell her you asked about her, though."

As much as I liked giving Socari a hard time, I respected that nigga. He takes good care of my sister and always places her on a pedestal. If I had to choose Socari or Kolby for my big sister, hands down, it would be Socari. He's a better family guy.

"Damn, that's all right. That nigga better make her happy because it's niggas like me waiting until he fucks up."

The ride was beautiful from the airport to their home. I've only seen pictures of Hawaii from Lani and Michael and the photos didn't do this place any justice. Now I know why they moved here and continue to live here while their children are all over the United States. Because of the views, the oceans, and the calmness in the air. I'd imagine this is what heaven looks like—feels like. Lani and her dad chatted while me and Kolby fell into our own conversation. Catching up really because he moved here almost a year ago—fell on hard times and his mom urged him to come home to regroup. Last I knew, Kolby had a contract—touring the world as a food critic. Not sure what happened but it's also not my business.

"Are you all right back there?" Michael directed his question to me. Lani looked back, winking at me while biting her bottom lip. I couldn't wait to give her the business in this beautiful place.

"Yes, sir," I shifted in the seat allowing her eyes to fall to the place I intended.

"How are your parents? Last we talked ya'll were doing some rearranging."

That's one way to word packing up my deceased brother's room over twenty years after his death, but I know Michael didn't mean any harm. That was his way of making the situation—less heavy.

"They're doing good. They send their love."

"Mama Steph knew we were coming?" Lani's eyes full of shock when I nodded. "She held out on me, and that woman cannot hold a secret."

I had to pay her to hold this one. Literally had to take her shopping for a new outfit before she agreed to keep her mouth closed. She swears Lani needs to know everything.

The house was quaint, not like the house Lani grew up in. It was perfect for them. Good thing we decided to get a hotel because otherwise they would be awoken in the middle of the night hearing their daughter scream my name. Keeping my hands to myself no longer applied to Lani. My hands *needed* to be on her.

Lani's mom and Hawaiian native, Kana, stood on the front porch with her hands on her hips. Lani started to run up to her, "aye," looking back at me I told her, "save your energy."

"Shut up!" I made a mental note to make her pay for that later. Leaning down, I wrapped my arms around Kana. "Nolan, we have to go to the beach before dinner." Her face held a gleam I hadn't seen in a while. I know I make her happy, but this is where she gets the most joy—being around her family. Mine as a substitute holds her over until she's back in their presence.

We did everything she wanted to do, showing me places she and Harmony visited on her last trip.

"I understand why you wanted to stay here," I told her as we passed a restaurant she commented on wanting to visit before we leave.

"How do you know I considered it?"

"I know you, Lani, and I know this place is too beautiful for you not to have that thought. Especially since the time we were going through was so ugly. It's serene being here."

"It is, but I like my life with you."

"I'm only saying I understand." She leaned into me as we walked the warm sands of the beach. Holding onto her from behind as the sun set. "How did your parents take the baby news?"

"You're still upright, so I think pretty well."

"Fuck outta here, your parents love me. Questionable if more than they love you."

"Shut up!" She nudged my side.

I pressed her against me, letting her feel my hard dick on her back, "say that shit later."

If it didn't require sending Lani back on the plane to North Carolina alone, I would stay here for the remainder of the summer. I'd email some lie to Principal Danders informing her that I would attend meetings via video calls. But then I'll miss Lani like fucking crazy. The shift in our relationship is crazy. We were able to fall into us so fast without it feeling weird. Doing things to each other I wouldn't have even thought was possible, but now that we are— I'm indulging every chance I get. Including on this beach full of natives and tourists. I cupped her breasts under the white sheer cover up that hid the pink two-piece bathing suit. Leaning down, I pressed my lips against her skin, placing soft kisses on the nape of her neck.

"I feel like I'm on a different planet," she looked out at the water. My arms tightened around her waist allowing her to relax against my chest. "The last time I was here, I was immersed in the view. Harmony had to pull me away some nights because I would literally sit out here all day." A smile curled on her lips, but her mood was somber.

The heat of her tears warmed my chest, "how long do you need to stay?" Emotions leaking out her face from the unspoken tug at her heart. We'd only been in Hawaii for about five hours, but the fear of leaving was already on her mind.

"I don't know. I'm sorry I'm a fucking mess."

"Stop talking like that. Let me know how long you need, and I'll make it happen." Lani nodded. She kissed me as she stood, pulling me up after. "What would I do without you?"

Swiping my thumbs under her eyes, I replied, "I don't know, but we're never going to find out."

MY PHONE BUZZING on the nightstand awoke me from my slumber as Lani lay on my chest. I struggled to reach it before the caller hung up. "Hello?" My eyes could barely open. I just pressed the phone to my ear.

"Nolan, can you wake Lani up?" Harmony sobbed.

"What's wrong, Harms?" I clutched Lani closer to me. No way was I going to wake her.

"I really need to talk to her."

"Talk to me," I suggested.

I like Harmony because Lani loves her. But nine times out of ten, this call was about the nigga she's madly in love with. He'd probably found some way to disappoint her—again. After she sighed, she spilled the beans, making what I predicted to be true. This time he was caught with another woman at his parent's house. Harmony made a scene and was escorted out by his brothers.

"Answer this," I said. I didn't interrupt her as she spoke, rather sobbed, through words.

"What?"

"Why do you keep going back to him?"

"I love him."

"Besides that."

"There's nothing outside of that."

I yawned, "sure there is. I love Lani, but it comes a time in life when you have to protect your peace and yourself. He's got you too open, too vulnerable, and you're not guarding your heart. What qualities do you like in him?"

"I don't know. He's caring."

"But he doesn't care about your feelings if he's having other chicks around his family,"

I played devil's advocate, not to deter her away from him. But to make her think harder about choosing him. I didn't care about the who, what, when, and how. I cared about her feelings being hurt, and I thrived on the bigger picture—which she was neglecting to stare at.

"Hold on," I scrolled through my recent call log, clicking on Ezeke's name.

"What's up, bro?" He answered on the first ring.

"Hey, I got a favor to ask."

"Shoot."

"Me and Lani are trying to sleep. I need you to handle something for me."

"Anything."

Just what I wanted to hear. I conferenced Ezeke's call over with Harmony's.

"Harms?"

"I'm still here."

"Cool, Ezeke's taking over. Goodnight—" I hung up before either could protest. Snuggling up even closer to Lani, I drifted back to sleep.

chapter
thirty-nine

Malani

The four days originally weren't enough, hell, even the week wasn't enough. I lied, telling Nolan I needed a week with my parents because I didn't want to be selfish. I didn't want to hog his summer vacation with my inner issues. So, one week, then it's back to building our life together. Every day I spent with my family, my mind only focused on the next day, then the next, then the next, then when I had to leave. Leaving was always the hardest, saying goodbye without knowing when I would see them again. Feeling like I spent too much time with Nolan instead of them. Feeling guilty because I'm not close by. I can't call them to tell them I'm coming over—I have to plan. Plan for the days that would only feel like hours. Preparing myself for the final day because whether I wanted it to or not, it was inevitable.

I showered, wrapped the plush robe around my wet body then joined Nolan on the patio of our hotel room. He was drinking orange juice from a wine glass. He offered it to me as I got closer. "Mimosa?"

"Hell no, orange juice with a dash of pineapple juice." I took a gulp, the concoction sparing on my tongue. "Last day."

I sighed sinking back into the seat, "don't remind me."

"Baby, do you want to stay?" His worried eyes meeting mine.

"I do, but I can't. I have a lot of work to get back to."

Nodding, he asked, "how do you want to spend today?"

"With my parents."

"Alone?"

"Is that okay?"

"Yeah, I'll pack our bags." Nolan kissed my forehead then retreated inside.

I blew out a sigh of relief, thinking he was going to take that the wrong way crossed my mind several times. Dressing quickly, I called my dad to pick me up from the hotel. Nolan was showering when I left, so I sent him a text letting him know I was gone.

My parents and I sat in their living room, eating the treats my mom made, and chatting about everything. I didn't have the energy to go out anywhere. I only wanted to be surrounded by them. Feel their love around me.

I looked forward to giving my child the same love my parents have given me. The plus side of me and Nolan procreating is that we both come from loving families. There is no doubt in my mind that our parents would extend their love to our child.

I cried like a baby when Nolan came into the house letting me know it was time to go to the airport. The tears subsided as he wrapped me into his arms and whispered he will always be here for me. I didn't doubt him, ever.

***

"HAVE YOU MADE A CHOICE YET?" Was the first question Dr. Cooper asked when I walked in this morning looking sun kissed and rejuvenated.

"Have you?" I fired back at him. But, per the email I read on the flight back home, he was also still considering the candidates.

"Looks like we'll be conducting interviews."

"I'll call them."

He nodded, "you look good, welcome back. It's becoming hard to camouflage that baby bump."

"Not trying to," I sung, walking into my office. "Three o'clock in the conference room," I shut the door behind me. I only had two patients to see today for follow-ups. One was in and out. The other, I had to replace sutures because people don't know how to follow instructions. I informed her to ensure she is taking the proper care, or I will have to send her to the hospital if an infection attacks the wound. Trust the process. They be so eager to see the results when the swelling isn't down yet.

Dr. Cooper and I met in the conference room a quarter before three to discuss the candidates. I took the liberty of calling some others that met what I was looking for. The interviews took the remainder of our workday, and we still didn't have a decision. We were leaning towards the same applicant, a male, Mason. "It's your call, Dr. Dawson."

"Let's lock him in. He could assist both of us."

"Are you sure?"

Starting to second guess myself, I recanted, "maybe, this one." I pushed the application of the girl that had potential but she kept watching Dr. Cooper seductively. I didn't like that. Nothing was going to come in the way of this business, and females like her needed to be thinned out in these four walls. But if needed, I'll have a hard talk with her before signing her on.

"Professionally, no. Go with your gut. We don't have to hire two right now. Let's see how he works out. He seems to have promise."

Nodding in agreement, we bumped fists—leaving the conference room feeling like one task was complete. Before leaving for the day, we divided the patient list. Sliding most of the liposuction cases to him—since I couldn't stomach the sucking while pregnant. I snagged the labiaplasty case. "Can you sit in with me on this one?" I'd never done one before, not that I didn't have faith in completing the task. I needed to ensure I was doing it correctly. Plastic surgery is all about the look, and I do not want to botch anyone.

He looked at the paperwork with a smile, "hell yeah."

"Inappropriate!"

"Sorry, Dr. Dawson. I will be happy to assist you with the surgery."

"After I have my baby, you got me? I have to snap back."

Dr. Cooper laughed, "yeah, I got you. I'll send you my workout schedule right after the doctor clears you for full duty."

"Whatever," I rolled my eyes to the ceiling.

I picked up dinner for me and Nolan before going home. Tonight, the task was to finish packing my room and the few dishes I selected to bring to his apartment. This is really happening. I always get this feeling that one day, I'll wake up and it'll all be a dream. Like I've imagined it all and none of it is real.

"If it's a boy, we're naming him Liam," my eyes followed Nolan from the refrigerator to the oven to heat the food.

He smiled over the food, "I'd like that. After your six weeks, we can work on Nolan Jr."

"Are you crazy?"

"Yeah, for you," he was behind me now. Rubbing my stomach and kissing my neck. "I'm putting at least four babies in you. Back-to-back, too."

I laughed, turning around to face him. He leaned down, brushing his lips against mine as he picked me up. I wrapped my arms around his neck pushing my tongue into his mouth. Nolan sat me on the counter, his hands traveling up my shirt, around my back to unclasp my bra.

"Please, not on the damn counter. I still have to make sandwiches there." Harmony fussed, rummaging in the bags from *The Lounge*.

Nolan kept his hands in place, "it's not too late for you to turn your ass around and pretend like you ain't seen shit."

"Nolan!" I gave him a pointed look, then slid his hands off of me. "Help me down."

"Queen, I'm hard as fuck right now," he whispered into my ear when my feet were back on solid ground.

"I promise I'll make it up to you later," I kissed his soft lips.

"What time are we leaving?" Harmony took a bite out of the cornbread from one of the plates.

"Leaving for what?"

"Open mic night. Don't tell me you forgot."

"Uh, no," I lied—I definitely forgot. Only place I wanted to sit tonight was on Nolan's dick. But a promise is a promise.

"Ugh! You did forget, but you're coming right?"

"Yea," I looked at Nolan, who was shaking his head. "We can go, right?"

He tossed his head back, "I guess so. Let me call Ezeke."

Malani

"Welcome to the first ever open mic night at your favorite spot in Da Bern." Bobby, acting emcee, announced on the microphone. The crowd went crazy, hooting and hollering.

For the night, *The Lounge* was rearranged to fit more patrons with a stage sectioned off at the front of the room, where the grand piano normally sat. Circular tables with white tablecloths adorned the middle space. The booths alongside the walls held the same color cloths. All tables were decorated with a glass vase with pens and small cutout pieces of papers inside. Strobe lights pointed to the stage where Bobby was explaining the rules of the night, and everyone hung onto his every word. The kitchen was still open, of course. Lights were dimmed. It was a huge turnout, and we were lucky enough to be seated in our normal booth.

"Tonight," Bobby continued, "we leave the drama at home, and bring your talent to share. We have a list. Jen from *Private Place* is holding it at the side of the stage. Last minute acts are welcomed. Let's show out!"

Jen waved to the crowd, pointing to the clipboard. A few patrons practically ran over to her to sign up.

"Ooh, we should sign up!" Harmony gushed, still reeling from that wink Bobby hit her with before he left the makeshift stage. He's always flirting with somebody.

"And what the fuck are we gonna do?" Nolan replied for the table; his hand was in my lap in an attempt to finish what we tried to start in the kitchen earlier. I wasn't in the position to say shit when he started to caress me.

"Ezekiel could do poetry. He's good with words," she suggested something we all knew. "I can sing or rap," she proudly stated like she actually had the skills.

Breathing heavily, I put my hand on top of Nolan's to stop him from making me cum on his fingertips. Drawing breaths were hard with him being nasty in a room full of people, not to mention our friends directly across from us. He looked over at me, seriousness on his fine ass face as he innocently leaned into the crook of my neck, his lips kissing my spot. My hand on his slipped away as he dipped a finger in me, then another pressing as deep as the seated position allowed. I thanked God our friends weren't paying us any mind. Harmony was too busy eye fucking Bobby, and Ezeke was in his phone.

"Can't wait to taste this pussy later," Nolan whispered in my ear, bringing a fresh batch of chill bumps over my skin. When I neared my peak again, I didn't dare stop him. I craved this release, just as much as he wanted to give it to me. His fingers lingered in my messy moisture for a couple of minutes. Reaching over, I handed him a napkin, but he opted to licking his fingers clean of me instead.

Bobby was back on the stage announcing the first act when our waiter approached the table seeking our order. "Is it an open menu?" Harmony asked the beautiful brown skinned girl.

Where do Nicoyce find these beauties?

"It is—breakfast, lunch, and dinner options. Are you ready to order?"

"What ya'll want?" Harmony asked the table. "Ezekiel, put your phone away. This is family time," snatching his phone and putting it face down on the table. "I asked a question."

Ezeke rubbed his temples, "I heard you." He looked up, giving his attention to the waitress who was ready to scribble his order down on her notepad. "Emory?"

"Ezekiel, hey." She looked flustered, but her face lit up at the sight of him. "Did you move here?"

"Yeah. You, too?"

"No, I'm born and raised here. I needed to go *there* to escape for a while. It's so good seeing you." Nolan and I watched the exchange like we were on the front row to a concert. She looked way too young to know Ezeke in the way she was staring at him.

"It's good seeing you—"

"Enough of that, I'm hungry as fuck," Harmony interrupted. "Just give me a short stack of pancakes." She rolled her eyes while the rest of us gave Emory our order.

"I'll be right back with your orders," Emory said, smiling at Ezeke before leaving our table to attend to her other guests.

"You know her?" Harmony asked him with her nose up in the air.

"I do," he returned his attention back to his phone.

"Hmm, be careful with that one."

"Do you even know her Harms?" I curiously asked her.

"Yep, she used to date Quentin's little brother. He's crazy over her." She said with a major eye roll. Harmony snatched a napkin from the holder to wipe the red lipstick from her mouth.

"You good?" Nolan asked Harmony.

"Yeah, I'm going to talk to Bobby. Ezekiel, have your little friend box my food."

We roared in laughter after she stomped away from our table. It was funny how a little interaction had her pissed off, but she wore the ring of another man on her finger. That used to be me, but I knew I harbored feelings for Nolan. Harmony's trying to play hard to get, but with the way Ezeke looks and the compassion he holds in his heart—she's going to miss out on a good thing, and it will be all her fault.

Harmony had the waitress deliver her food to the table she sat at with Bobby. I guess she was really mad about pretty brown girl, Emory, knowing Ezeke.

The rest of the night was fun though and definitely an event *The Lounge* needed to put on at least once a month. Once alcoholic beverages ran through the patrons' systems, they all crowded the stage wanting to sign up. They were lit and funny as fuck. It felt good being with Nolan, his arm thrown over my shoulders pulling me in here and there for a quick kiss. He smelled amazing, and he's all mine.

This year has been a whirlwind for us, but to be here with him—I will do it all over again.

chapter
forty-one

Nolan

"If you don't tell her, I will," Ezeke said, lowly.

"You're outta your fucking mind."

"I'll sing like a canary," he teased but wasn't shit funny to me. "You're the one who peeked in the envelope."

I huffed, "nigga, I didn't know what the fuck it was."

"Since when do you get mail at my house?"

"Touché," knowing exactly what I was opening, I couldn't stop myself when I saw it just lying on Ezeke's coffee table. My promise to Lani slowly faded as I pulled the contents from the small envelope. "I didn't see shit." I lied; I saw a little, but I stuffed the paper back in before I could read the gender.

"What are ya'll whispering about?" I stood to pull the seat out for Lani to sit. My baby's belly was almost bigger than her since we were approaching the early part of the last trimester.

"I think Nolan has something to tell you," Ezeke walked away to join Harmony at the front of *The Lounge*.

Lani looked at me, beautiful as ever, dressed in a white flowy dress that accentuated her belly. The crowd in *The Lounge* for us— our baby shower.

A month back, Lani decided we would find out the gender of our baby. Ezeke was the keeper of the gender and wasn't suppose to reveal it until today. The anticipation has been killing me, like I'm dying to know.

"I peeked," waiting for her to chastise me, but it never came.

"I figured you would. Do you think Ezeke would be clumsy enough to leave the real results on his counter?"

Laughing, I thought about it. "I didn't see anything."

"Right, you wouldn't have. The words on the paper you pulled out just said, 'you have to wait, Daddy'." Lani grabbed the back of my neck, kissing me.

"All right, love birds," Harmony covered her eyes. "We have virgin eyes here." She held the microphone to her mouth, and Ezeke joined her on the stage. "After fighting hard with my best friend, *I* convinced her to do a gender reveal."

The room was filled with all of our loved ones coming from far and wide to celebrate with me and Lani. My heart was full, but so was my balls—so I couldn't wait to wrap this up.

Ezeke took the microphone from Harmony, "she really means, *I* convinced her. *I* hold the gender," he pointed to his temple. "Let's enjoy the food, and Lani and Nolan will open gifts in a few."

I grabbed Lani's hand, kissing the backside. Harmony exquisitely decorated our baby shower. She felt some type of way about Ezeke being the gender keeper that Lani put her in charge of decorations. I can't front she did a good ass job, better than I expected. It was Bohemian themed, of course, because women have to have a theme for every occasion. Everyone was sitting on large pillows except me and Lani, eating on white glass plates and drinking from wine flutes. Our moms collectively worked on the dessert table that was filled with candied fruits, chocolate-covered pretzel rods, cookies shaped in baby onesies and rattles, rustic green iced cupcakes, and mini cinnamon rolls from *The Lounge*. We had a marathon of finger foods, chicken tender sliders, meatballs, plant-based meatballs for Lani—because she couldn't stomach beef, Rotel dip, pigs in a blanket, fruit, and vegetable tray.

"Baby, this is perfect," Lani gushed, leaning over to me for another kiss.

"We might as well keep the decorations for next year," she swatted at me. Lani better get used to being pregnant.

"Shut up! And let's open these gifts."

Harmony and Ezeke surrounded us with all the gifts our family and friends purchased. Handing Lani a tissue because happy tears fell on her cheeks as we opened the gifts. A variety of clothes, shoes, socks, toys, bottles, pacifiers, and diapers. I contained my emotions when clothes read something pertaining to daddy. That shit hit me right in my gut—this was really happening.

"Now, the moment we've all been waiting for," Ezeke was back on the stage with a box and a big black balloon. Harmony set a small, white-based cake in front of us. "Baby girl—balloon, box, or cake?"

"Balloon!" Lani stood to her feet, watching in anticipation.

Our family started chanting the gender they'd guessed. Ezeke took a pin popping the balloon, and pink and blue confetti fell from the balloon onto the stage. The entire room yelled their frustration. I stayed calm because nobody was more anxious than me.

"Nolan, my boy! Box or cake?"

"I hate these fucking games," I yelled to him.

Lani covered my mouth with her hand. "Mom, Dad, excuse his potty mouth."

They laughed, nodding, Michael speaking up, "it's okay, son. I was the same way. Three times." He held up three fingers that landed him a smack to the back of the head from his wife.

"Box!" I answered, speeding up the process, because my heart was about to beat out of my chest from anticipation.

Ezeke pulled out a sword, dramatic as fuck, to open the box. Blue and pink balloons floated from the box. The crowd went crazy again.

"Only thing left is cake," Harmony said, handing me and Lani a knife.

I handed the knife to Lani, "you do it."

"No, we both do it. With our eyes closed." She smiled, sitting down next to me. "On the count of three. One," we closed our eyes, "two." Her breathing became deep, she was nervous. "Three," with her hand on top of mine, we pushed the knife down on the cake, wiggling it side to side. The room was quiet. When we opened our eyes inside the cake was blue and pink. The crowd started to laugh, but I was getting annoyed.

"Okay, okay, no more games. The next game does reveal the gender," Harmony announced.

Ezeke carried a round chess board cake to the table. Everyone clapped when he placed it in front of us. "One of the chess pieces is cake, and the inside reveals pink if it's a girl and blue for a boy."

"It's too pretty to mess up," Lani looked over at me with tears. "Can we get a hint on which piece is cake?"

"Of course, babe." Harmony smiled wide. "Nolan calls you this all the time."

"Queen!" Kennedy shouted out.

My eyes darted between the white and black Queen chess piece on the cake. "Which one do you want to try first?"

"Well, I am a *Black Queen,*" she lifted the piece from the cake. "Yes, this is cake."

"Take a bite, I want to watch."

"Close your eyes," she told me. Although I wanted to watch her, I closed my eyes. "Open your mouth."

"Baby, you're testing me," I spoke so she could only hear.

"Nolan," I opened my mouth. "Now bite," I could only imagine she was holding the chess piece to my mouth. I bit down into the pillowy soft cake. The crowd erupted but stopped abruptly. "On the count of three, we open our eyes." Not knowing she closed her, too, I agreed. "One...Two...Three."

"It's a boy!" The crowd yelled, my eyes meeting Lani's, then down to the blue cake peeking out of her mouth. We're having a baby boy!

On the car ride home, Lani fell asleep. Luckily, Ezeke rode behind us to help me take the gifts in. I then carried Lani up the steps and laid her in the bedroom. She stirred, but I kissed her fore-head, and she slipped back into her slumber.

"'Preciate it, bro. What are you about to do?"

Ezeke put the leftover food in the refrigerator, "I don't know, probably chill with Emory."

"It's like that?" I asked with a raised eyebrow.

"It's like that," he smiled, and I couldn't be happier for my boy!

"Harmony?"

"Just friends. She fell for that nigga. I respect it. I was hoping for a love story like you and Baby girl, but that wasn't in the cards for us." He shrugged like it didn't affect him, but I know better.

"What I'm hearing is you're giving up."

"Nah, I'm moving on. I can't make her want me."

"Facts," I gave him dap, respecting his decision.

After he left, I curled in the bed beside Lani. "Did I hear right?"

Snickering because I knew she wasn't asleep, "yeah, she missed her chance."

"I don't think she cares right now. Mmmm," she moaned, I kissed her neck, sliding my tongue against her skin. She took my hand, guiding it to her pussy. "I've been wet for you all day. I couldn't…mmmm."

My fingers slid into her, she was right—she was fucking drenched. "Say that shit," I urged. Hooking my fingers in and out steadily.

She fisted my shirt, "I couldn't wait, ooohhh, fuck Nolan!"

"That's not it," my fingers moved faster. "You couldn't wait for what?" I pulled her hard nipple into my mouth. "Lani, I don't hear shit."

"I couldn't wait to give you this pussy," she forced out. Seconds later, her cum coated my fingers.

"Well, give it to me," I growled, pushing the dress to her hips. She slid out of her panties and then unbuckled my belt, freeing my dick. I didn't waste time filling her, repeatedly sinking deeply into her core. I pulled out, tasting her, suckling her clit with her legs pointed towards the ceiling.

"Oh, my God!" Bounced off the wall as I dove deeper into her. Lani pulled my tie, snatching my lips, easing her tongue into my mouth. The intensity of her orgasm spilled out onto the bed. I held her legs in the crook of my arms while drilling inside of her, closing my eyes as her pussy sucked me in. The softness of her walls made me fill her up with my cum. I stayed inside of her, pulling her on top of me.

"I love you, Nolan."

"I love you, too, Queen."

chapter
forty-two

Malani

I loved seeing the delight and joy Liam brought to Nolan. It wasn't a day that went by that he didn't read or play with our baby. My heart was full watching them. Since the birth of our baby, Nolan and I have moved into a new place. Our very first home, and life was so much better. We easily slid into the role as parents. Liam tired us out the first three months, but it was all worth it. Doing life with my best friend is worth it all.

"Stop staring and come join us," Nolan smiled at me from the sofa. He held Liam in his arms while looking over meeting notes from school.

I bent down kissing both my boys before sliding against Nolan's warm body. He threw his arm around me, bringing me closer. This was our norm, enjoying and spending time with one another.

"How was work," he asked, placing the papers on the coffee table.

I couldn't help the smile that formed on my face. "It was good," I held my true emotion inside. Work was better than good. I've only been back from maternity leave for three months before Dr. Cooper took a vacation. This week was the first week I would have the practice to myself. It had been going so well, but I didn't want to jinx it. I finally got respect from female patients, and I rarely had to deal with attitude. Trust me, there are still some women who hate that Dr. Cooper and I still do consultations together, but they will have to get over it. Breast augmentation was added to our list of services, and I taught Dr. Cooper a little trick when performing them. I smile knowing that through all he has taught me, I was able to teach him something. "How was school?" I asked him. Liam was fast asleep in his daddy's arms with his mouth agape. I rubbed his little cheeks and smiled at how perfect he is.

"We had a bullshit ass meeting about new processes moving forward for the new school year. I led the discussion."

"You?" I asked with shock.

"Yeah, them motherfuckas think they're going to push back but not with me."

"Aren't you the same math teacher who refused to follow the dress code?"

"Queen, this ain't about me."

I laughed, Nolan's a great assistant principal. I think taking this role really opened his eyes to what administration really goes through. He often talks about how easier it was being a teacher. "Go lay Liam down, so we can have some quiet time." Nolan wasted no time putting Liam in the nursery and ensuring the monitor was on and pointing directly on him.

"You want to watch a movie or something?" Nolan returned to his seat next to me.

My eyes dropped to the bulge in his pants. He knew damn well I wasn't talking about watching a movie. I bit my bottom lip, eyeing him seductively "or something." For the remainder of the night, Nolan and I made love in the living room, in our bedroom, and in our master bathroom. My appetite for him grew more and more each day. Tomorrow, I will be going to the drugstore to purchase a pregnancy test.

about the author

 Brittney C. Nobles is an urban and romance author based out of her hometown of New Bern, North Carolina. She affectionately acknowledges Georgia, specifically Effingham County where she found her love for writing in high school. Brittney loves to create and share stories with family and friends. Thanks to her late mother, Mona Moore, Brittney fell in love with reading and the art of storytelling. She would watch her mother read many books until she got older and her mom allowed her to read her first urban romance. Brittney fell in love and started her journey of creating stories over the next years. She graduated from East Carolina University with a Bachelor's in English with a minor in Communications. She is happily married bearing three beautiful children. Aside from working full-time and writing, Brittney loves to travel, read and create vegan dishes for her family.

instagram.com/brittneycnobles
facebook.com/brittney.benton